Collectible Coloring Books

Dian Zillner

Photographs by Suzanne Silverthorn

Schiffer Publishing Ltd

1469 Morstein Road, West Chester, Pennsylvania 19380

Dedication

Dedicated to my first grandchild, Prather Reid Silverthorn, whose due date coincided with the date for the finished manuscript for this book.

Acknowledgements

I want to express my thanks to the many collectors and writers who answered questions and shared material in order to make this book possible. Special acknowledgement goes to Judy Lawson, Joseph Golembieski, Elaine Price, and Mary and Werner Stuecher. A special "thank you" goes to the members of my family who were so helpful during the writing of this book.

To my daughter, Suzanne Silverthorn, who took most of the photographs, and to my mother, Flossie Scofield, who did the proofreading, an extra special vote of appreciation.

Acknowledgement and extra recognition also is extended to Schiffer Publishing and its excellent staff who are so easy to work with. My editor, Kate Dooner, and my layout editor, Sue Taylor were both helpful and cooperative. Without their support and extra effort this, my second book, would not have been possible.

Notice

All the coloring books pictured in this book are from private collections. Grateful acknowledgement is made to the original publishers. The copyright holder has been identified for each item whenever possible. If any omissions or incorrect information is found, it should be given to the author and publisher and it will be amended in any future edition of the book.

Title page photo:
Pets for Coloring published by The Saalfield Publishing Co., Copyright 1927. From the collection of Lee Jackson.

Published by Schiffer Publishing, Ltd.
1469 Morstein Road
West Chester, Pennsylvania 19380
Please write for a free catalog.
This book may be purchased from the publisher.
Please include $2.00 postage.
Try your bookstore first.

Copyright © 1992 by Dian Zillner.
Library of Congress Catalog Number: 91-67780.

Printed in the United States of America.
ISBN: 0-88740-393-X

We are interested in hearing from authors with book ideas on related topics.

Contents

Introduction

The majority of coloring books produced in the last one hundred years are of little interest to today's collector, those which include general pictures of flowers, birds, children, or the alphabet. But some unique books were made. Most of today's collectors are interested in coloring books which complement another collection, whether it be Disney, television, western, paper doll, comic, movie, advertising or dolls.

Because coloring books were meant to be colored, most of the books collectors find today have been used. Of course, like all other collectibles, the best and the most expensive are those books in mint, unused condition. Most collectors accept books that have been neatly colored or those that have only a few colored pictures. Prices can vary greatly due to condition. A book in mint condition may bring three or four times as much money as one that contains poorly colored pictures or a damaged cover. When purchasing coloring books by mail, the buyer should question the seller, who usually does not specify if the book is in used or unused condition. The price should be adjusted accordingly.

A coloring book collector who is interested in the television character field has a wealth of material from which to choose. Nearly every popular program spawned a tie-in coloring book. Disney collectors also can add interest to their collections by including the many titles of coloring books produced in the images of the Disney characters. Some of the most beautiful coloring books are those made to represent movie personalities from the 1930s, 1940s and 1950s. Because of the special attention given to artwork on these books, they will bring a higher price than most coloring books.

The coloring books representing comic and cartoon characters are also in demand. The early books from the 1920s to the 1940s are the most desirable. Since the comics were such an important part of our lives in those days, many books were produced dealing with favorites like Little Orphan Annie, Dick Tracy, and Lil' Abner. These books in mint condition will rate top dollar in the collecting market.

Surprisingly enough, many advertisers have used give-away coloring books to increase business. Though these books are not as plentiful as those in other coloring book catagories, there have been enough produced to warrant a search to locate the interesting examples.

The most expensive coloring books are those that contain not only pictures to color, but also paper dolls. This type of book has been made since 1916 and these books in uncut, unused condition are very collectible. The most desirable are those containing celebrity paper dolls. Besides these special catagories, other miscellaneous coloring books have been printed as well. These include books representing real dolls, blacks, historical events (especially World War II), famous illustrators and authors, fairs, and Santa Claus.

The coloring book collector can be as discriminating in his purchases as he desires. Whatever route is chosen, a vast variety of titles is available to make the selection part of the fun of collecting.

History of Painting and Coloring Books

Children's painting and coloring books have been a part of the book publishing world for over one hundred years, and even though today's collector is mainly interested in coloring books from the United States, one English firm also produced early coloring books of equal interest.

The famous Raphael Tuck and Sons Company Ltd. opened in 1866 as a picture and frame shop. The English firm, owned by Raphael and Ernestine Tuck, soon started publishing lithographs which proved so successful that other items were added to the publishing line. Offices were later opened in New York, London, and Paris and by the 1890s, Raphael Tuck was producing fine children's books, paper dolls, and drawing and coloring books.

The Tuck company used the phrase "by appointment to her majesty the Queen" in much of their early advertising. In 1940, the Raphael House, which was headquarters for the firm, was destroyed by German bombs, and all the company records were destroyed. Therefore, it is difficult to date items that are not marked with the year.

The pictured drawing book called *The Little One's Own Drawing Book* appears to date from around 1890-1895. Other early painting books produced by the firm were part of a series called *Little Artists* which dated from around 1900. The Tuck company continued to produce fine products for many years but most collectors are especially interested in the earlier publications from around the turn of the century.

The earliest American coloring books, or painting books as they were called at that time, appear to have been produced by McLoughlin Brothers. This firm was established by John McLoughlin who came to the United States from Scotland in 1819. McLoughlin formed a company in New York in 1828 and began printing children's morality tracts. In 1840, he merged with John Eldon and the company used the Eldon name. After the retirement of the senior partners, John McLoughlin, Jr. headed the company and changed the name to McLoughlin Brothers. The firm became the largest producer of children's books in America.

By the 1870s, the company was publishing paper dolls as well as children's books and had also added games to their inventory. At this time there were no copyright laws in effect, so the McLoughlin firm copied many books that had originally been published in England. They were particularly fond of the works by the famous English illustrator, Kate Greenaway who was at her height of popularity in the late 1870s.

With the growth of competition, the McLoughlin company saw a need to produce inexpensive books for children including painting and coloring books. *The Little Folks' Painting Book* pictured here is apparently the first painting book produced by McLoughlin Brothers.

The information on the inside of the book states, "The need of a cheap, and at the same time interesting and sensible Book of Pictures for Children, to try their skill at painting, has long been felt. We have thought it best to make the book without reading matter in order to give a greater number of pictures...Anything that will keep the children still, has always been a desideratum with parents; and there is probably nothing which is so universally popular with the little ones, as painting with their own Paint-Boxes, as their Spelling-Books and Primers too often show."

The painting book began with a page of color illustrations and continued with small black and white pictures that were to be painted by a child. Each picture was only 3″ x 3″ so it was difficult for a child to paint. To complicate the task even more, Kate Greenaway illustrations were used containing many small details. Although the book is not dated, other firms were making inexpensive painting books by the early 1890s, so this example is probably from the mid to late 1880s.

The Little One's Own Drawing Book, Father Tuck's Series, No. 4540. Published by Raphael Tuck and Sons Co. Ltd., circa 1895. The small 6″ by 8″ book contains captioned pictures with tracing paper so the pictures can be traced as well as colored.

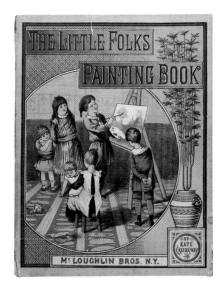

The Little Folks Painting Book by Kate Greenaway. Published by McLoughlin Brothers circa 1885. The book is 7½″ by 9½″ and contains many small pictures by Kate Greenaway to be painted by a child.

Two of the inside pages from *The Little Folks Painting Book* showing the small complicated pictures that were to be painted by a child.

McLoughlin Brothers continued to be a force in the publication of children's materials until 1920 when the firm was sold to the Milton Bradley Co. McLoughlin continued as a division of Milton Bradley until 1944 when, during World War II, it ceased to exist.

At first, all children's books to be colored were labeled as painting books. Even though the Binney and Smith Co. manufactured their first box of children's Crayolas in 1903, it was several decades before these new wax crayons replaced the child's paint box as the favorite coloring tool for children. By 1930, many of the books were labeled to be used with either paints or crayons.

Another important company in the children's publishing industry was the Saalfield Publishing Co. Founded by Arthur Saalfield in 1900 in Akron, Ohio, Saalfield published his first children's book in 1902. Mrs. Frances Trego Montgomery, one of Saalfield's writers, was author of the Billy Whiskers series of books which made the firm a profitable contender in the children's market. Within a few years, the company began to publish other paper items for children including paper dolls and painting books. These early efforts still consisted mostly of small complicated pictures for children to paint. Often, two pictures were shown, one printed in color as a demonstration, and the other in black and white for the child to color.

The Easy Painting Book. Published by McLoughlin Brothers, 1904. The small 6½" by 5½" book contains two copies of each picture, one printed in color and one in black and white.

Playtime Painting and Drawing. Published by M.A. Donohue and Co., circa 1900. Contains captioned pictures in both printed colors and black and white, as well as several drawing pages in a hard cover book.

The Delightful Paint and Crayon Coloring Book. Published by McLoughlin Brothers circa 1929. The book continues the practice of printing two copies of each picture, one in color and one in black and white. Although the pictures are larger, they are still too detailed to be colored successfully by a child.

Painting Plays for Rainy Days With Easy Drawing Lessons. Published by Thompson and Thomas in Chicago, 1908. This book has an assortment of pictures to draw and color plus printed story and verse material.

Pictured are two pages from *Painting Plays for Rainy Days* which show the still small complicated pictures children were expected to paint in the paint books of the early 1900s.

The Saalfield Company, in 1934, signed a contract to be exclusive publishers of the Shirley Temple materials. These coloring books, paper dolls, and other tie-in materials enabled the firm to survive the depression years while other companies were less fortunate. Saalfield continued to prosper in children's publishing until it was purchased by the Rand McNally Company in 1976. Three generations of the Saalfield family operated the firm during its many years of business.

Kent State University Libraries in Kent, Ohio purchased the Saalfield Company's archives, and interested researchers are still able to access this Saalfield material.

Another giant in the children's publishing business was the Whitman Publishing Company. Founded by E.H. Wadewitz as the Western Publishing Company in Racine, Wisconsin in 1907, the company's name changed to the Whitman Publishing Company in 1915. Whitman entered the paper doll and painting book market in the late 1920s. Although some of the company's books contained larger, simpler pictures for children to paint or color, most used the old format of printing small, complicated pictures. All of these early books still printed many of the pictures in both color, and black and white, to give the child a model to imitate.

Of all these early companies, the Whitman Company (now again known as the Western Publishing Company) is the only one which still produces children's books. By the 1980s, with the help of the profitable Little Golden Books, the firm became America's largest producer of children's books.

My Paint Book published by The Saalfield Publishing Co., 1915. The small book 10" by 5" contained very small pictures printed in both color and black and white.

Jumbo Paint and Drawing Book. Copyright 1911 by The Saalfield Publishing Co. Some of the pictures were printed in both black and white and color but most are only in black and white.

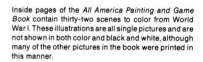

Both of these coloring books were published by the Goldsmith Publishing Co. in Cleveland, Ohio, circa 1920. The cover designs are the same, but the titles and contents of the books are quite different. One is called *My Favorite Crayon and Paint Book* and the other is *All America Painting and Game Book.*

Inside pages of the *All America Painting and Game Book* contain thirty-two scenes to color from World War I. These illustrations are all single pictures and are not shown in both color and black and white, although many of the other pictures in the book were printed in this manner.

Favorite Painting Book. Published by Saalfield Publishing Co., 1916. The book has an interesting shape, but the pictures inside continue the earlier trend of complicated small pictures for children to paint along with most pictures printed in both color and black and white.

My Big Book Painting and Drawing (#167). Published by The Saalfield Publishing Co., 1916. This book is more nearly the size of modern coloring books (10" by 15") but the company continued to print the pictures in both color and black and white.

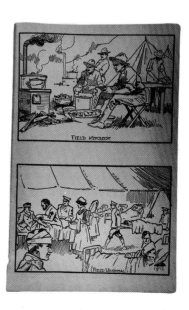

The Merrill Publishing Company, a firm that was relatively late in entering the field, published some of today's most sought after books in both the paper doll and coloring book markets. The company was established by Marion Merrill in 1934 in Chicago and contracted Regenstiner Corp. of Chicago to do the printing of the Merrill books. The company produced its first paper dolls and coloring books in 1935. The beautiful inks used by Regensteiner and the outstanding artwork on the books made this publisher's coloring books some of the nicest ever produced. Because of this quality, Merrill became the second largest publisher of children's books from the 1930s to the 1950s.

Besides the beautiful quality, the pictures were large and simple so a child could color or paint each page easily. The books no longer included a color model for the child to copy. Instead, the boy or girl was expected to use his own imagination to make the pictures suit his vision of the finished product. By 1935 the coloring book as we know it today was established, and the format has remained unchanged to the present time.

In 1944, Merrill ended its affiliation with Regenstiner, and the company became the Merrill Publishing Company. Books continued to be produced by other prints and the quality remained high throughout the 1950s. Marion Merrill died in 1978 and in 1979, Jean Woodcock purchased the artwork and archives of the firm. Merrill's best remembered publications are the many celebrity books that were produced by the company.

Although the prolific output of unique coloring books by many publishers has subsided, there are still several new publications yearly that warrant trips to the toy stores by today's collector. New Mattel Barbie books and the occasional blockbuster movie like *Dick Tracy* usually result in a collectible coloring book for a collection. For the most part however, today's celebrities no longer spawn new coloring book items, and it may be that both new and old collectors will have to concentrate mostly on what has already been published.

Mother Goose Paint and Crayon Book (#W916) was one of the first coloring books published by the Whitman Publishing Co. in 1929. The inside pictures, for the most part, continue to follow the earlier pattern of printing the pictures in both black and white and in color. The book also includes a great deal of printed material with verses and rhymes.

Patty and Her Dog Paint Book. Published by Whitman Publishing Co., 1930. Although the pictures were simple to color, they remained small in size to make room for the same picture to be shown in color.

One page from the Whitman book, *Patty and Her Dog Paint Book* from 1930 show the charming pictures already printed in color that were on each page of the book. These pictures are suitable for framing.

There were some pictures large enough and simple enough for a child to color in the Whitman book, *Mother Goose Paint and Crayon Book*, from 1929.

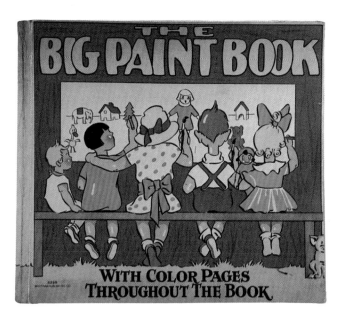

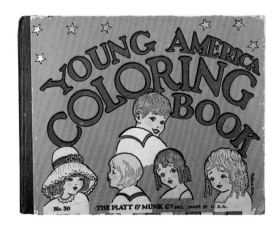

The Platt and Munk Co. was active in children's publishing beginning in 1920, but this company was an outgrowth of several earlier firms including the Platt and Peck Co. This coloring book was reprinted by the Platt and Munk Co. in 1928 but the same material had already been published earlier in both 1913 and 1923. The book called *Young America Coloring Book #50* follows the format of the earlier years by printing small pictures in both color and black and white.

The Big Paint Book With Color Pages Throughout the Book (#2038). Published by Whitman Publishing Co., 1930. Although most of the pictures were simple in this book, they remained small.

Let's Read and Paint. Verses and illustrations by Maywill M. Dudley and published by Whitman Publishing Co., 1934. This book is really more like a picture book than a paint book. There are verses on each page and each picture is shown in color, and in black and white, with the background filled in black so that no pages really look uncolored.

Animal Alphabet To Color (#M3498). Published by Merrill Publishing Co., 1935. The book was designed by Peter Mabie and is one of the first coloring books published by Merrill. This book uses large easy-to-color pictures of animals and the alphabet, and looks very much like the coloring books of today.

Personality Coloring Books

The older personality coloring books are perhaps more sought after than any of the collectible coloring books. The books from the 1930s and 1940s were so well done that the artwork alone is worth collecting. Some of the books offer illustrations that look so much like their subjects, that the collector not only acquires the cover picture of a favorite star, but also several dozen drawings inside as well.

June Allyson

June Allyson was one of Metro-Goldwyn-Mayer's (M-G-M) top stars from 1944 to 1954. Born in the Bronx in 1917, she began her career as a dancer. She received notice from M-G-M after appearing on Broadway in *Best Foot Forward* in 1941. The studio featured her in a Judy Garland—Mickey Rooney film, *Girl Crazy*, in 1943. Allyson made movie musicals throughout the rest of the decade including: *Two Girls and a Sailor; Music for Millions; Good News; and Till the Clouds Roll By*, all of which were made for M-G-M. In 1949, Allyson starred as Jo in the M-G-M remake of Louisa Mae Alcott's story, *Little Women*.

June Allyson's best remembered films are those in which she played the loving wife to James Stewart or Alan Ladd. She made *The Glenn Miller Story* in 1954, *The Stratton Story* in 1949 and *The McConnell Story* in 1955. June Allyson left M-G-M in 1954 and continued making movies until 1959 when she turned to television and stage work.

Eve Arden

Eve Arden was born in Mill Valley, California in 1912. She began her movie career at Universal Pictures in 1937 as a supporting player in *Oh Doctor!*. With this start, she continued her successful work as a character actress for many years, sometimes appearing in ten or twelve films in a single year.

In 1945, she signed a contract with Warner Brothers and made many memorable films including *Mildred Pierce* with Joan Crawford in 1945. With the end of her contract at Warners in 1951, Arden transferred her successful radio show, which was begun in 1948, to television. This 1953 hit series was called "Our Miss Brooks." It was a situation comedy about a school teacher that appeared on CBS from 1952 to 1956. Eve Arden also starred in a later television series called "The Mothers-In-Law" for NBC from 1967 to 1969.

After the end of her television series, Arden returned to movie and stage work. She had four children from her marriages in the 1940s and 1950s. The actress died in 1990.

June Allyson Coloring Book "M-G-M Star," (#1862). Published by Whitman Publishing Co., 1952. Picture and book courtesy of Joseph Golembieski.

June Allyson Coloring Book "M-G-M Star," (#1135). Published by Whitman Publishing Co., 1952. Captioned pictures of the star, mostly at home, are contained in the book.

Eve Arden Coloring Book (#2310). Copyright 1953, Saalfield Publishing Co. Contains captioned pictures of Arden at work at CBS with good likeness.

Gene Autry

Gene Autry was born in Tioga, Texas in 1907 and reached his first audience via a radio program based in Oklahoma. Later, he became a radio star on the "National Barn Dance." He moved to Hollywood in 1934 where he made his first Western, In Old Santa Fe. Autry became a versatile performer making ninety-three films in his long career. In his movies for Republic Pictures, Autry was usually featured with Smiley Burnett, his sidekick, and he also shared honors with his horse, Champion. His national radio show began in 1940 and his career expanded even more when he recorded several hit records. Autry helped write his first hit song, "That Silver-Haired Daddy of Mine." Other well-known Autry recordings include "Mexicali Rose," "Here Comes Santa Claus," and "Rudolph the Red-Nosed Reindeer," with Rudolph selling over two and a half million records.

After serving in the U.S. Air Force during World War II, Autry formed his own independent film company and made forty-six feature movies. In 1950, Autry turned to television with "The Gene Autry Show" based at Melody Ranch. Eighty-five episodes were filmed and syndicated. Popular Autry film titles include: Tumbling Tumbleweeds; In Old Monterey; and Riders in the Sky. Autry's final movie, Last of the Pony Riders, was made in 1953.

Gene Autry Cowboy Adventures to Color, (#4803). Imperial and International Copyright Secures. Published by Merrill Publishing Co., 1941. From the collection of Elaine Price.

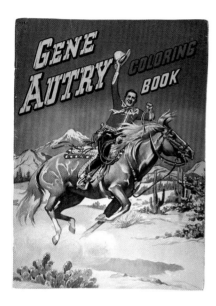

Gene Autry Coloring Book (#1157). Copyright 1949 by Gene Autry. Published by Whitman Publishing Co. Captioned pictures of Autry.

Gene Autry Coloring Book (#1153). Copyright 1951 by Gene Autry. Drawings by Toni Sgroi. Published by Whitman Publishing Co.

Gene Autry Coloring Book (#1256). Copyright 1955 by Gene Autry. Published by Whitman Publishing Co. Drawings by Tony Sgroi and Gene Wolfe.

Gene Autry Coloring Book (#1124). Copyright 1950 by Gene Autry. Drawings by Toni Sgroi. Published by Whitman Publishing Co.

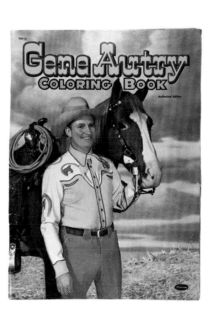

Gene Autry Coloring Book (#1860). Copyright 1951 by Gene Autry. Published by Whitman Publishing Co. Contains captioned pictures of Autry.

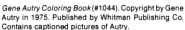

Gene Autry Coloring Book (#1044). Copyright by Gene Autry in 1975. Published by Whitman Publishing Co. Contains captioned pictures of Autry.

Gene Autry's Chuck Wagon Chatter Coloring Book (#1042). Copyright MCMLIII by Gene Autry. Contains captioned pictures to color of Gene Autry.

The Beatles

The Beatles are thought by some to be the undisputed rulers of rock and roll for the decade of the 1960s. Besides producing many hit records and several hit movies, the Beatles exerted a tremendous influence on other artists of their time.

Three of the famous four Beatles were with the group from the beginning. John Lennon (born 1940), George Harrison (born 1943), and Paul McCartney (born 1942) were all from Liverpool, England. In addition, Pete Best played drums and Stuart Sutcliffe was on guitar.

The boys began playing in local clubs during the late 1950s under the name, "Quarrymen." In 1960, Brian Epstein heard them perform, liked their potential, and became their manager. He secured a record contract for the group with EMI in 1962. In the meantime, Sutcliffe left the group and Ringo Starr (born Richard Starkey in 1940) replaced Pete Best as the group's drummer.

The first Beatle record was "Love Me Do" and in 1963, the group had a number one hit record with "Please, Please Me." By 1964, the Beatles were so popular in England that Ed Sullivan invited them to appear on his Sunday night television show. They were a bigger hit with fans in the United States than anyone had been since the early days of Frank Sinatra.

The next few years brought hit records like "She Loves You," "I Want To Hold Your Hand," and "Hey, Jude." There were also Beatles gold albums like the 1969 "Yellow Submarine" LP.

In 1964, the Liverpool boys also added film making to their other talents when they made A Hard Day's Night for United Artists. Other movies include: Help in 1965; the animated picture Yellow Submarine in 1968; and the documentary Let it Be in 1970.

As each member of the group began to expand his individual interests, it became harder to keep the whole group working together and the Beatles disbanded in 1970.

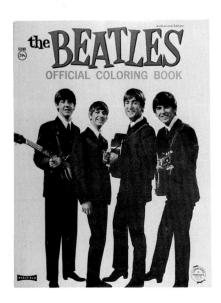

The Beatles Official Coloring Book (#5240). Copyright 1964, Nems Enterprises, Ltd. Published by Peerless Manufacturing Co. Distributed by The Saalfield Publishing Co. Captioned pictures about The Beatles' activities and travels, with good likeness.

Ann Blyth

Ann Blyth was born in Mount Kisco, New York in 1928 and made her professional debut as a singer when she was five years old. In 1941, she appeared as one of the children in the Broadway play, *Watch on the Rhine*. Universal Pictures then signed her to a movie contract and she made several musicals with Donald O'Connor including *Chip Off the Old Block* and *The Merry Monahans*.

In 1945, Warner Brothers borrowed her to play Joan Crawford's daughter in *Mildred Pierce*, a film which gave Blyth a chance to act a serious role. After a period of poor films, Miss Blyth again starred in a hit picture opposite Mario Lanza in *The Great Caruso* made for M-G-M in 1951. Other movies with M-G-M include: *All the Brothers Were Valiant*; *Rose Marie*; and *The Student Prince*. Ann Blyth's last film was *The Helen Morgan Story* made for Warner Brothers in 1957. In 1953, she married a doctor and devoted her life to being a wife and mother.

Betty Brewer

Betty Brewer was born in 1927 in Joplin, Missouri. Her parents were set back by the Depression, and when her father was out of work, Betty decided to sing outside the Hollywood Brown Derby restaurant to attract attention. Producer Sam Wood noticed her and signed her for the 1940 film, *Rangers of Fortune* starring Fred MacMurray. Brewer's short movie career as a child actress of the 1940s was begun.

Joan Carroll

Although Joan Carroll is not well remembered by most movie fans, as a child she played parts in many fine films in the early 1940s. Most of her movies were made at RKO Radio Pictures. They include: *Laddie* (1940); *Primrose Path* (1940); *Anne of Windy Poplars* (1940); *Obliging Young Lady* (1942) and *Petticoat Larceny* (1943).

In 1944, Joan got a big break when she was chosen to play Agnes, one of the young sisters in M-G-M's musical *Meet Me In St. Louis*, one of the most popular musicals ever made. Her career continued to rise with a part in the controversial movie *Tomorrow The World*, also in 1944. The film concerned the adoption of a young Nazi German boy and was made during World War II.

Joan's movie career reached its height in 1945 when she played with Bing Crosby and Ingrid Bergman in *The Bells of St. Mary's*. That film turned out to be the biggest hit RKO had ever had and the top grossing picture for the year.

Ann Blyth Coloring Book "Universal—International Star" (#2530). Published by Merrill Publishing Co., 1952. Captioned pictures look very much like the star.

Joan Carroll Coloring Book (#2423). Published by Saalfield Publishing Co., 1942. The book includes many uncaptioned pictures of the child star.

Betty Brewer Paint Book (#1043). Drawings by Ruth Wood. Published by Whitman Publishing Co., 1943. Contains captioned pictures of Betty and her friends.

Charlie Chaplin Up In the Air. Copyright 1917 by J. Keeley by arrangement with Essanay Co. M.A. Donohue and Co. (#317). Inside says copyright 1914. Contains comic strips of Charlie Chaplin in black and white for children to paint. Instructions for painting are contained in the book.

Charlie Chaplin Coloring Book (#2355). Copyright 1941 by Saalfield Publishing Co. The book contains many pictures of Chaplin's film characters.

Rosemary Clooney Color Book (#348). Star of Paramount Pictures and Columbia Records. Published by Abbott Publishing Co., 1954. Contains captioned pictures from both work and home.

Bing Crosby Coloring Book (#1295). Published by The Saalfield Publishing Co., 1954. A thin book with short captions and good pictures of Bing. Also contains pictures of Bing's sons.

Charlie Chaplin

Charles Chaplin was born in a poor district of London in 1889 where both of his parents were performers. At a young age, Charlie secured work wherever possible, eventually finding jobs in English music halls. After two tours to the United States with the Fred Karno Company, Chaplin was hired by Mack Sennett to make silent films and he moved to Los Angeles in 1913. In 1918 he set up his own studio so he could make films in his own way.

Charlie Chaplin's tramp character became known all over the world and by 1920 he was featured in *The Kid* which grossed two and a half million dollars. That same year Chaplin, Mary Pickford, Douglas Fairbanks, and D. W. Griffith formed United Artists so they could each control their own films from inception to distribution.

Chaplin continued to make important movies through the 1920s including *The Gold Rush* and *The Circus*. Even though the movie industry had introduced the new sound system in 1927, Chaplin surprised everyone by making his 1931 film, *City Lights*, as a silent picture. Another silent film followed in 1936 with Chaplin's last "Little Tramp" movie, *Modern Times*. Chaplin had one more big picture in 1940 with *The Great Dictator* (in sound) based on Adolf Hitler. Although his career continued for many more years, the film genius never again received the acclaim that had been his in the early years. Chaplin died on Christmas Day in 1977 after living in Switzerland for many years.

Rosemary Clooney

Rosemary Clooney was born in 1928 in Maysville, Kentucky and later moved to Cincinnati, Ohio where she and her sister, Betty, appeared on a local radio program on a regular basis. After leaving Cincinnati, the girls sang with Tony Pastor's band. Rosemary received a Columbia record contract in 1950 and in 1951 had her first million selling record, "Come On-'a My House."

In 1953 Rosemary Clooney began a film career when she signed with Paramount. Her most famous picture was *White Christmas* which co-starred Bing Crosby. Other films include: *The Stars Are Singing*; *Here Come the Girls*; *Red Garters*; and *Deep In My Heart*. In 1956 she had her own television program called "The Rosemary Clooney Show." She then continued her career with concerts and night club appearances.

Bing Crosby

Bing Crosby fans say the star was perhaps the greatest entertainer of the 20th century. He was a star in radio, recording, television, and of course, movies.

Crosby was born in 1903 in Tacoma, Washington. He came from a large Irish family with seven children. He and a friend from school, Alton Rinker, formed a vaudeville act and the boys were hired by bandleader, Paul Whiteman. Soon Harry Barris was added to the team and they became known as the Rhythm Boys. When the group broke up, Crosby secured work with Mack Sennett for some movie shorts. Soon Bing Crosby had his own radio show and he made his first broadcast in 1931 for CBS. After a successful singing engagement at the Paramount Theater in New York, Paramount Pictures signed him to a contract to make films for them. His first picture, *The Big Broadcast*, was released in 1932. A record contract with Decca came in 1934. He would eventually sell over 300 million records.

Although Crosby had a successful film career in the 1930s, he did not reach real stardom until the years of World War II. He teamed up with comedian Bob Hope for a series of "Road" pictures that were particularly successful. The team eventually made seven of the films, most of them box office hits. Besides these popular pictures, Crosby also made movies on his own. He had more box office movie hits during the 1940s than any other star. Some of these films include: *Holiday Inn*; *Going My Way* (he won the Oscar for best actor); *The Bells of St. Mary's*; and *Blue Skies*. Crosby continued his career in the 1950s in radio, recordings, films (*Country Girl*, *High Society*), and television.

By the 1960s Bing was no longer making pictures, but he continued his television work with a family Christmas program as the highlight of the year. Although the Crosby appearances became less frequent, he was still performing in March, 1977 when he fell from a stage during a rehearsal for a television show. In October of the same year, he died of a heart attack in Madrid, Spain shortly after finishing a round of golf.

Bette Davis

Bette Davis was a real Hollywood star during the "Golden Years of Hollywood." During the early 1940s she was the most popular female star in America.

Miss Davis was born Ruth Elizabeth Davis in Lowell, Massachusetts on April 5, 1908. She first appeared on a Broadway stage in 1928 and soon moved to Hollywood to begin her movie career. Bette's first movie role was in *Bad Sister* in 1931 for Universal Pictures. After she was dropped by Universal, her contract was picked up by Warner Brothers. Davis' career still did not take hold until she was loaned to RKO for the film, *Of Human Bondage*, in which she played Mildred, a selfish, uninhibited waitress and scored a hit.

Davis spent a total of eighteen years making films for Warner Brothers. She received Academy Awards for her roles in *Dangerous* in 1935 and *Jezebel* in 1938. She was also nominated for Oscars in the following films: *Dark Victory* (1939); *The Letter* (1940); *The Little Foxes* (1941); *Now Voyager* (1942); *Mr. Skeffington* (1944); *All About Eve* (1950); *The Star* (1952); and *What Ever Happened To Baby Jane?* (1962).

Miss Davis died in October, 1989 after several years of declining health.

Bette Davis Coloring Book "Star of Warner Brothers Pictures" (#4817). Published by Merrill Publishing Co., 1942. The pictures in the book contain scenes and costumes from her movies as well as pictures from her everyday life.

Doris Day

Doris Day was born in Cincinnati, Ohio in 1924. She began her career as a singer on radio and then became a female vocalist with several big bands including Bob Crosby and Les Brown.

Doris signed a movie contract with Warner Brothers and appeared in her first film, *Romance on the High Seas* in 1948. Other early hit pictures for Warners included: *Tea For Two*; *It's a Great Feeling*; and *The West Point Story*. By 1952, Doris Day had become the most popular female star in America.

In 1955, Doris Day played the lead in a biographical movie for M-G-M about singing star Ruth Etting. The picture, *Love Me Or Leave Me* also starred James Cagney. The Day career continued at top pace all through the 1950s and into the 1960s. She was in the list of top ten stars in Hollywood from 1957 to 1966 and was ranked number one during four different years. Some of her hit films include: *Pillow Talk*; *Lover Come Back*; *That Touch of Mink*; and *Teacher's Pet*.

After Doris Day's movie career was over, she made a successful television show called "The Doris Day Show" from 1968-1973 for CBS.

Laraine Day

Laraine Day, born in 1919, had a successful screen career beginning in 1937, but probably is equally remembered as the wife of Leo Durocher. The couple married during Durocher's term with the Brooklyn Dodgers and they did a radio show together. Laraine also wrote a sports column for awhile. They were divorced in 1960.

Day's film career was mostly involved with M-G-M pictures including: *Stella Dallas*; *Calling Dr. Kildare*; *Foreign Correspondent*; *Journey For Margaret*; *Mr. Lucky*; *The Story of Dr. Wassell*; and *The High and the Mighty*. After leaving films, Laraine Day became the official spokesperson for the "Make America Better Program" in the early 1970s.

Doris Day Coloring Book (#1138). Published by Whitman Publishing Co. Copyright 1952 by Doris Day. Photograph and book courtesy of Joseph Golembieski.

Doris Day Coloring Book, "A Warner Brothers Star." Published by Whitman Publishing Co. Copyright by Doris Day, 1955. Drawings by Kay Sampson. The captioned pictures of the star look very much like her.

Laraine Day Coloring Book (#2401). Cover signed by Avalo. Published by Saalfield Publishing Co. in 1953. Picture and book courtesy of Joseph Golembieski.

The Dionne Quints Pictures to Paint (#3490). Published by the Merrill Publishing Co., circa 1940. From the collection of Judy Fitzgibbon Lawson. The photograph is by Jean Fitzgibbon Kelley.

Dionne Quintuplets

The Dionne Quintuplets were born in Callander, Ontario, Canada on May 28, 1934 in a small farmhouse to rural parents with five other children. Two midwives and the local doctor, Dr. Allan Roy Dafoe, delivered the babies. The little girls were so small, they were not expected to survive. When the astonishing news of their birth reached the outside world, help came from many companies and individuals which helped save their lives.

The little girls (Yvonne, Cecile, Emilie, Annette, and Marie) began to thrive, and when the Canadian government took control of their upbringing, a new facility was built to house them, along with their nurses. A playground was added so that tourists could watch the children through a screen, and a new tourist industry for Canada was established. From 1934 to 1943, around three million people visited the Quints in Callander. During these years the Quints appeared in three movies for Twentieth Century-Fox (The Country Doctor, Reunion, Five Of A Kind) and several radio broadcasts. Their faces helped to sell many products and tie-in items.

The Dionne parents had been trying to regain control of the Quints since the girls were infants and finally were able to reunite their family in 1943. The large family consisted of the Quints and six other children. The Quints never seemed to "fit in" and they did not make an easy adjustment. Emilie died in 1954 of an epileptic seizure and Marie died in 1970, apparently from a clot to the brain. Although Marie, Cecile, and Annette married and had children, the marriages all ended in divorce. The three remaining sisters, Cecile, Annette, and Yvonne stay in close touch, even though they and their parents were never reconciled after a dispute over a book they helped write about their early lives.

Jimmy Durante

Jimmy Durante, "The Schnozzle," was born in 1893 and grew up in Manhattan's lower East Side. He left school in the seventh grade in order to secure work. Because he could play the piano, he began working in saloons and dance halls at the age of seventeen. Durante eventually formed a partnership with Eddie Jackson and Lou Clayton to do a nightclub act.

In 1930, Durante moved his career to Broadway when he secured a part in Cole Porter's, The New Yorker. M-G-M signed him to a contract because of this exposure and he made his first film in 1932. Although Durante appeared in pictures infrequently for several decades, probably his most well known roles occurred in the 1940s. Some of his best films include: Two Girls and a Sailor, Ziegfeld Follies; Music for Millions; and The Yellow Cab Man.

Between movie roles, Durante continued to appear on Broadway and his own radio show. He began a series of television programs in 1952 and continued to work in the medium until 1970. Jimmy Durante died in 1980 after a sixty year show business career.

Deanna Durbin

Deanna was born in Winnipeg, Canada in 1922 as Edna Mae Durbin. She and her parents soon moved to Los Angeles where it was discovered she had an unusually remarkable singing voice for a child. In 1935 she was signed by M-G-M and made a short film with another newcomer to the industry, Judy Garland.

After Miss Durbin was dropped by the studio, she began singing on the Eddie Cantor radio show and became very popular. She soon signed a contract with Universal Pictures and her first film, Three Smart Girls, was released in 1936. The film grossed $2 million, and Deanna's films were credited with making Universal Pictures a major movie studio.

Deanna Durbin continued to be a star through the years of World War II. She made a successful transition to adult roles but her popularity began to drop during those years. Miss Durbin retired from pictures after her last movie for Universal in 1949. She was only twenty-seven years old. She married the French director Charles-Henri David in 1950 and moved to France.

Some of her best films include: One Hundred Men and a Girl (1937); Mad About Music (1938); That Certain Age (1938); Christmas Holiday (1944); and Lady On A Train (1945). All of her movies were made for Universal.

Jimmy Durante Cut-Out Coloring Book (F 5035). Pictures by Rick Hackney. Published by Pocket Books, Inc., 1952. Pictures of Durante getting ready for Christmas.

Deanna Durbin and Her Trunk Full of Clothes to Color (#4805), "A Universal Pictures' Star." Published by Merrill Publishing Co., 1941. Shows her fashions and one screen costume is identified.

The Singing Star Deanna Durbin Pictures to Paint (#3479), "New Universal Pictures' Star." Published by Merrill Publishing Co., 1940. Her movies are mentioned by name and some pictures show Deanna in her costumes.

Faye Emerson

Faye Emerson was born in Elizabeth, Louisiana in 1917. She became interested in drama while she was attending a convent school in San Diego. In 1941 Faye was seen by a talent scout from Warner Brothers and was offered a screen test. She was with the studio from 1941 to 1946. Emerson played mostly "bad woman" roles in pictures like *Bad Men of Missouri; Manpower; The Hard Way;* and *The Very Thought of You.*

In 1944, Faye Emerson married Elliott Roosevelt, the son of President Franklin Roosevelt and she had an opportunity to meet world leaders and travel widely during her five year marriage. After her divorce from Roosevelt, Faye returned to acting on Broadway in, *The Play's the Thing,* and then found her most lasting fame in television. Faye Emerson began her TV career in 1951 and was one of the most famous of the early television performers. She was hostess on several shows including, "Wonderful Town," which was probably her best.

Annette Funicello

Annette Funicello received her start in show business as one of the Mouseketeers on Walt Disney's television program, "The Mickey Mouse Club." The original show aired on ABC from 1955 to 1959. Annette was one of the main children on the program and was given a lot of work in both the special segments, like "The New Adventures of Spin and Marty," and during the regular shows.

Because Annette attracted extra attention with her talent on the program, she became a Disney star in films as well. She appeared in both *The Shaggy Dog* and *Babes in Toyland.* After Annette became a teenager, she completed her film career by making "beach" movies including, *Beach Party, Pajama Party,* and *How to Stuff a Wild Bikini.*

Judy Garland

Judy Garland was born in Grand Rapids, Minnesota on June 10, 1922 as Frances Ethel Gumm. Her mother was not content to remain a small-town wife and mother, so she staged an act with her three young daughters.

Although the Gumm sisters were moderately successful in the Grand Rapids area, there was limited opportunity for growth. Mrs. Gumm talked her husband into moving to California so the girls would have a better chance for success. The sisters continued to perform in California wherever they could obtain bookings. When Judy was thirteen, their luck changed when she was called to M-G-M for an audition. She sang "Zing Went the Strings of My Heart" and was given a contract by the studio.

Judy's movie career began with a small short called *Every Sunday* which she made with another newcomer, Deanna Durbin. Her big break came when Twentieth Century-Fox wouldn't loan Shirley Temple for the role of Dorothy in *The Wizard of Oz,* and it was given to Judy instead. With the success of the Oz movie, Judy's career gained momentum and she began a series of eight films with Mickey Rooney. Some of the movies were part of the Andy Hardy series while others were Busby Berkeley extravaganzas. Some of the best were: *Babes in Arms; Strike Up the Band; Babes on Broadway;* and *Girl Crazy.*

Judy's career at M-G-M continued in high gear during the war years as she made many of the studios most successful musicals. These include: *Ziegfeld Girl; For Me and My Gal;* and *Meet Me In St. Louis.* After the war, Judy began to experience health problems and her many collapses and hospital stays interfered with her successful career. She still managed to make a number of fine films for M-G-M however. These include: *The Harvey Girls; The Pirate; Easter Parade; In the Good Old Summertime;* and *Summer Stock.*

In 1950, Judy was fired from M-G-M because of her health problems. She was only twenty-eight years old. She pulled herself together and turned to concerts. She did a smash performance at the London Palladium, and then played the Palace Theatre in New York in 1951. With the new interest in Judy as a performer, her husband Sid Luft became their producer and she starred in a successful re-make of the film, *A Star is Born.*

During the rest of her life, Judy concentrated mostly on concert and cabaret work. She did branch into television in 1963 when she did a weekly television variety show. It was not a success and was cancelled after twenty-six episodes. Judy Garland died on June 22, 1969, at the age of forty-seven from an overdose of sleeping pills.

Faye Emerson Coloring Book (#2369). Copyright MCMLII by Saalfield Publishing Co. Book from the collection of Elaine Price.

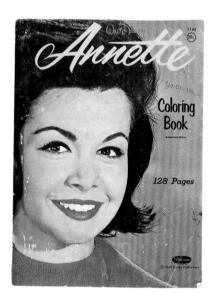

Walt Disney's Annette Coloring Book (#1145). Copyright 1964, Walt Disney Production. Drawings by Nathalee Mode with captioned pictures of her trip abroad.

Judy Garland Paint Book (#601). Metro-Goldwyn-Mayer Star. Drawings by Ruth Wood. Published by Whitman Publishing Co., 1941. Includes captioned pictures of her home and studio life and shows her sisters and mother as well.

Greer Garson Coloring Book (#3480), "Courtesy of Metro-Goldwyn-Mayer." Copyright 1944, Merrill Publishing Co. Pictures are good likeness and show both movie and home life.

Greer Garson

Greer Garson was born in County Down, Ulster, Ireland, in 1908. She became interested in amateur dramatic clubs at the London University and then moved into Birmingham theater. By 1935, she was working as a successful West End ingenue with Laurence Olivier. In 1938, she was given a contract to work for M-G-M. Greer's first Hollywood picture was filmed in London (*Goodbye Mr. Chips*) and although her part was small, she was successful.

Greer Garson's rise to the top at M-G-M began with the hit film, *Mrs. Miniver* in 1942. Garson received an Academy Award for her performance and she continued to receive parts of suffering, brave wives as she pursued her career. Although Greer's last film was not completed until 1967, nearly all of her best movies were done in the 1940s. These include: *Blossoms in the Dust*; *Random Harvest*; *Madame Curie*; *Mrs. Parkington*; *Valley of Decision*; *Adventure*; and *That Forsyte Woman*.

After divorcing the man who had played her son in *Mrs. Miniver* (Richard Ney), Greer married a wealthy Texan in 1949. She has spent most of her retirement years in Texas.

Betty Grable

Betty Grable was born in St. Louis, Missouri in 1916 as Ruth Elizabeth Grable. She and her mother moved to Hollywood in 1929 where Betty worked in the film industry for nearly ten years. It was not until 1939, however, when she went to New York and secured a part in the Broadway show, *Du Barry Was a Lady*, that she was noticed. Darryl F. Zanuck, from Twentieth Century-Fox, was so impressed with her performance that he signed her to a contract with his studio.

Her first movie for Fox was, *Down Argentine Way*, in 1940. It was such a success that the studio rushed her into another musical, *Tin Pan Alley*, the same year. Although the Fox-Grable movies did not contain great story lines, they were good escape entertainment for a nation involved in a major war. Some of the most remembered films are: *A Yank in the R.A.F.*; *Springtime in the Rockies*; *Tin Pan Alley*; *Coney Island*; *Sweet Rosie O'Grady*; *Pin Up Girl*; *Diamond Horseshoe*; and *The Dolly Sisters*.

Betty Grable was the number one pin-up girl during World War II and she was the first woman to dominate the box office since Mary Pickford. In 1943 Grable was the number one box office star in the nation and she remained among the top ten until 1951. She continued to make movies until 1955 with one of her last being the hit, *How To Marry a Millionaire*, in 1953. The success of that picture, however, was due to her co-star Marilyn Monroe. Betty Grable left a legacy of forty films. She died in 1973, of lung cancer, at the age of fifty-six.

Betty Grable Paint Book (#613). Drawings by Doris Lane Butler. Published by Whitman Publishing Co., 1941. Picture and book courtesy of Joseph Golembieski.

Betty Grable Coloring Book (#1501), "Twentieth Century-Fox Star." Merrill Publishing Co., 1951. Captioned pictures show her in screen costumes and at home with daughters.

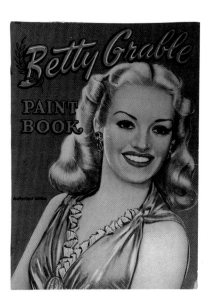

Betty Grable Paint Book (#664). Drawings by Hedwig Jo Meixner. Whitman Publishing Co., 1947. Detailed captions with pictures of her both at the studio and at home.

Betty Grable Coloring Book (#2532). Copyright 1953 by Merrill Co., Publishers. Picture and book courtesy of Elaine Price.

Rita Hayworth

Rita Hayworth was christened Margarita Carmen Cansino when she was born in 1918 in New York City. Her parents were both dancers, so Margarita began dancing lessons about as soon as she could walk. During the Depression, when Margarita was fourteen, she joined her father as his dancing partner for dancing shows in Mexico.

It was in Mexico that Margarita was seen by Winfield Sheehen from Fox studios and was given a Fox movie contract. Her first film, *Dante's Inferno*, was released in 1935. She made several more movies for Fox but received little notice. When Fox merged with Twentieth Century, Rita was out of a job.

With the guidance of Edward Judson (whom Rita later married) she secured a contract from Columbia in 1937 and her name was changed to Rita Hayworth. Although she made several minor films, Rita was not really noticed until she received a role in the picture, *Only Angels Have Wings*, in 1939. With this new interest in Rita, Columbia starred her in a musical called *Music In My Heart* in 1940 and loaned her to Warners for *Strawberry Blonde* in 1941. Twentieth Century-Fox also borrowed Rita in 1941 to make *Blood and Sand*. Rita Hayworth was suddenly a star. Some of her most famous pictures during the war years include: *You'll Never Get Rich*; *You Were Never Lovelier*, *My Gal Sal* (Twentieth Century-Fox); *Cover Girl*; and *Tonight and Every Night*.

Unlike most of the pin-up stars of the early 1940s, Rita's career did not slow down at the end of World War II. One of her most remembered pictures, *Gilda*, was not made until 1946. Rita continued her successes for Columbia with, *Down to Earth*, made in 1947; *Affair in Trinidad* in 1952; and *Salome* in 1953. Although Rita continued to make films until 1972, she was no longer the star she had been. Her best movie from this period is *Separate Tables* made for United Artists in 1958.

Rita Hayworth died, after a long illness, in May, 1987 from Alzheimer's disease.

Sonja Henie

Sonja Henie made her way to the Hollywood screen in a very unique way. She traveled the road to fame and fortune on ice skates.

Born in Oslo, Norway in 1912, Sonja began skating at the age of six and by fourteen was declared the ice skating champion of Norway. In 1927, she was awarded the world skating championship a title she held for ten years. In 1928 she won her first Olympic Gold Medal in figure skating and went on to win again in 1932, and again in 1936.

After the 1936 Olympics, Sonja and her father planned a skating tour to the United States. Darryl Zanuck from Twentieth Century-Fox saw the show and signed Sonja to a five year contract with his studio. Sonja's first film, *One In a Million*, was released in 1936 and became an immediate success. Sonja continued to make skating pictures for Fox for several years. Her best movies include: *Happy Landing*; *Thin Ice*; *My Lucky Star*, *Second Fiddle*; *Sun Valley Serenade* and *Iceland*.

Although Sonja was a successful Hollywood movie star, she still wanted to do more to promote ice skating. In 1938, she and a partner, Arthur Wirtz, began the *Hollywood Ice Revue*. The show was to become an annual touring event. Sonja, herself, skated in the revue until 1952. Several ice shows still make annual tours in different countries all over the world.

Sonja made her last film, *The Countess of Monte Carlo* for Universal in 1948. The novelty of a skating movie star had worn off so Sonja retired from films. During her career, she had invented the ice musical and made eleven films in twelve years which grossed a total of $25 million. Sonja Henie died from leukemia in 1969 at the age of fifty-seven.

Rita Hayworth Coloring Book (#3483), "Star of Columbia Pictures, Inc." Merrill Publishing Co., 1942. Several costumes are pictured but not identified.

Sonja Henie Paint Her Pictures Coloring Book (#3491). Published by Merrill Publishing Co., 1940. From the collection of Mary Stuecher. Photograph by Werner Stuecher.

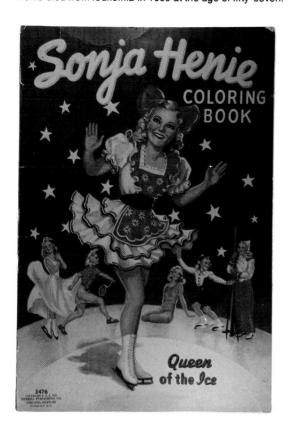

Sonja Henie Coloring Book (#3476), "Queen of the Ice." Published by Merrill Publishing Co., 1939. The captioned pictures provide good biographical information on Sonja.

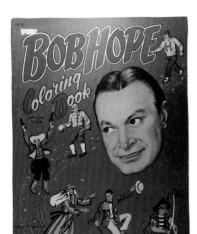

Bob Hope Coloring Book (#1257). Published by Saalfield Publishing Co., 1954. This is a soft cover book with silly captions for Hope pictures.

Betty Hutton and Her Girls A Coloring Book (#113415). Copyright 1951, Whitman Publishing Co. Contains captioned pictures of her at home with her daughters.

Bob Hope

Bob Hope has had a varied career which began in vaudeville, led to Broadway, then to radio, the movies, and television. For over half a century, Hope has used his talent to entertain Americans, but he is particularly remembered for bringing entertainment to the United States servicemen.

Bob Hope was born in London in 1904, and came to America at the age of four. As he grew older he began work in vaudeville and then became a Broadway star in *Roberta*. Hope began his radio show on the NBC Blue network in 1934. His successful program was rated number one in the country in 1944. Hope continued the weekly broadcasts until the late 1950s and also starred in television beginning in 1952. Bob Hope still continues to do television specials, sometimes using material that has been used in his shows for servicemen based all around the world.

Bob Hope made his first motion picture, *The Big Broadcast of 1938*, for Paramount. He stayed with that studio for almost twenty years through most of his film career. Many more movies followed, including the "Road" pictures he made co-starring Bing Crosby. There were a total of seven of these road pictures, and the popularity of these films helped make Hope the fifth most popular film star in history during the height of his career. The first road picture was, *The Road To Singapore*, in 1940. Other remembered Hope films include: *The Cat and the Canary (1939); Seven Little Foys (1955); The Paleface (1948); and The Facts of Life (1960).*

Bob Hope's theme song, "Thanks For the Memory," came from his first film, *The Big Broadcast of 1938*, and he has used it ever since, usually changing the lyrics to reflect current events and locations when giving a performance.

Betty Hutton

Betty Hutton (The Blonde Bombshell) was born in Battle Creek, Michigan in 1921. Her career followed several stages before she became a movie star. Betty began as a band singer with Vincent Lopez, moved to vaudeville, and then secured a part in the Broadway production of *Panama Hattie in 1940.*

Paramount then offered the young singer a contract and she made her first film, *The Fleet's In*, in 1942. Hutton became known for her exuberant, brash behavior in films, and she used this unusual characterization to become a Hollywood star during the 1940s. Her best films include: *Star Spangled Rhythm*; *And the Angels Sing*; *Here Come the Waves*; *Annie Get Your Gun*; *The Miracle of Morgan's Creek*; *Incendiary Blonde*; *Dream Girl*; *The Perils of Pauline*; and *The Greatest Show on Earth*.

After a dispute with Paramount in the early 1950s, Hutton left the studio without fulfilling her contract. After that episode, she worked in only one other picture, *Spring Reunion made for UA in 1957.*

Gloria Jean

Gloria Jean was born Gloria Jean Schoonover in Buffalo, New York in 1928. She was blessed with a natural singing voice and spent her early years singing for church groups and local functions. After receiving formal training she sang a child's part in an opera in New York.

After that experience, she received the lead role in the 1939 Universal Pictures musical, *The Underpup*. Since the picture was a success, the Schoonover family moved to California so the young star could continue her career. Although Gloria Jean worked for Universal until she was eighteen, she never became a really big star like the studio's earlier teen-age singing actress, Deanna Durbin.

After she was finished at Universal, Gloria Jean did film work at other studios and made her last picture in 1963. In 1965, she left the show business she loved and went to work as a receptionist. Gloria Jean's movies include: *If I Had My Way* (1940, Universal); *A Little Bit Of Heaven* (1940, Universal); *Never Give a Sucker an Even Break* (1941, Universal); *What's Cookin'?* (1942, Universal); *Get Hep to Love* (1942, Universal); and *Mister Big* (1943, Universal).

Gloria Jean Book To Color (#1665), "A Universal Pictures' Star." Published by Saalfield Publishing Co., 1941. Book and photograph courtesy of Joseph Golembieski.

Gloria Jean Coloring Book (#1667), Universal Pictures, Inc. Copyright 1941, Saalfield Publishing Co. Book and photograph courtesy of Elaine Price.

Gloria Jean Coloring Book (#158), "A New Universal Star." Published by Saalfield Publishing Co., 1940. The pictures have good captions and give good biographical information.

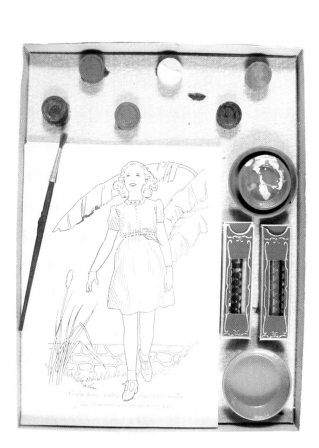

The inside of *Gloria Jean Coloring Box.* From the collection of Mary Stuecher. Photograph by Werner Stuecher.

Gloria Jean Coloring Box (#1681), "A New Universal Pictures Star." The Saalfield Publishing Co., 1940. From the collection of Mary Stuecher. Photograph by Werner Stuecher.

Grace Kelly

Grace Kelly was born into a wealthy Philadelphia family in 1929. She began her career as a model and also did television commercials. She moved into theater work in 1949 with a part in, *The Father*. Her film career began in 1951 with a part in Twentieth Century-Fox's production of *Fourteen Hours*. In 1952, she received her first recognition playing opposite Gary Cooper in United Artists' *High Noon*. Kelly became a favorite performer for Alfred Hitchcock in the pictures, *Dial M For Murder* (Warners 1954), *Rear Window* (Paramount 1954), and *To Catch a Thief* (Paramount 1955).

Other Kelly films include: *Mogambo* (1953 M-G-M); *The Bridges at Toko-Ri* (1954 Paramount); *Green Fire* (1954 M-G-M); *The Swan* (1956 M-G-M); and *High Society* (1956 M-G-M). Miss Kelly was given an Academy Award for Best Actress for her performance in Paramount's, *The Country Girl* in 1954.

Kelly made only eleven films in her career as an actress before giving it up to become a real life Princess when she married Prince Rainier of Monaco in 1955. After living in Monaco for nearly thirty years and raising three children, Princess Grace was killed in an automobile accident in September, 1982.

Piper Laurie

Piper Laurie was a popular young film actress for Universal during the 1950s. Born in 1932, she made her first film in 1950. Some of her pictures include: *Louisa*; *The Milkman*; *Francis Goes to the Races*; *Son of Ali Baba*; *Mississippi Gambler*; and *Dawn at Socorro*. Perhaps Piper Laurie received even more fame in her middle years when she played the important role of Catherine in David Lynch's television production, "Twin Peaks" during the television seasons of 1990-1991.

Lennon Sisters

The Lennon Sisters, Dianne, Kathy, Peggy and Janet were first featured on the Lawrence Welk show when the youngest, Janet, was only nine years old. The program ran on ABC from 1955 until 1971. Although the sisters weren't members of the cast from the beginning to the end, they did sing on the program for many years.

The Lennons were also featured on another television show on ABC during the 1969-1970 season. The program was called "Jimmy Durante Presents the Lennon Sisters Hour."

Grace Kelly Coloring Book (#1752), "MGM Star." Whitman Publishing Co., 1956. Drawings by Louis Liets. Contains captioned pictures to color.

Piper Laurie Coloring Book (#2531). Universal International Star. Copyright 1953 by Merrill Publishing Company. Contains captioned pictures of the star in her personal life.

The Lennon Sisters Coloring Book (#158). Copyright 1958 by Teleklew Productions, Inc. Published by Whitman Publishing Co. Drawings by Joan Gravelle. Captioned pictures really look like the girls.

Janet Lennon Coloring Book (#1209). Copyright 1961 by Teleklew Productions, Inc. Published by Whitman Publishing Co. Drawings by Nathalee Mode.

Diana Lynn

Dolly Loehr (Diana Lynn) was born in 1926, and even though her life was short, she had a varied professional career. Diana was signed to a Paramount contract at the age of thirteen as a result of her ability to play the piano. She received her high school education on the Paramount movie lot. During these years she played the "kid sister" in many of the studio's films. The best include *The Major and the Minor* (1942) and *The Miracle of Morgan's Creek* (1944).

In 1944 Diana starred as Emily Kimbrough in, *Our Hearts Were Young and Gay*. Gail Russell played Cornelia Otis Skinner. Other movies of note are: *And the Angels Sing; Ruthless; Paid in Full; Bedtime for Bonzo;* and *Plunder in the Sun*.

Besides appearing in films, the young star worked in radio, recorded classical and popular songs, and made her concert debut in Los Angeles in 1943. With the end of her film career in the mid 1950s, Diana began acting in television dramas where she added another interesting aspect to her career.

Diana Lynn died in 1971 at the age of forty-five from a brain hemorrhage.

Jeanette MacDonald

Jeanette MacDonald's screen biography lists her birth date as 1907 but her early school records, in Philadelphia, record 1903 as her birth year. Jeanette took singing and dancing lessons as a young girl and made her first professional appearance in Philadelphia at the age of nine.

Jeanette joined her sister in the chorus at the Capitol Theater in New York City around 1920, and by 1923 had a leading role in the stage musical *The Magic Ring*. For the next four years she played major roles in Broadway musicals.

While in Chicago, starring in *Boom*, Jeanette was seen by Hollywood director Ernst Lubitsch and he cast her in her first film, *The Love Parade*, opposite Maurice Chevalier in 1929. Jeanette continued her film career at Paramount, making several pictures, two of which were with Chevalier—*One Hour With You* and *Love Me Tonight*.

In 1933, Jeanette signed with M-G-M and made several more operetta movies with them, including her last picture with Chevalier, *The Merry Widow*, in 1934.

In 1935 the studio teamed its famous soprano with a newcomer to produce a Victor Herbert operetta, called *Naughty Marietta*. The newcomer's name was Nelson Eddy, and the pair clicked. The success of Jeanette and Nelson continued to grow as they made several hit movies in the 1930s. The films include: *Rose Marie* (1936); *Maytime* (1937); *Girl of the Golden West* (1938); and *Sweethearts* (1938). MacDonald also filmed the hit movie *San Francisco* with the "King of Hollywood," Clark Gable in 1936.

The stardom Jeanette experienced earlier began to wane in the 1940s. She and Eddy made *New Moon* and *Bitter Sweet* in 1940, but the public seemed to be tired of operettas and the pictures were not very successful. The last starring movies Jeanette made for M-G-M were *Smilin' Through* (co-starring with her real life husband, Gene Raymond), *I Married an Angel*, and *Cairo*.

After MacDonald left film making in 1942, she concentrated on radio, concerts, and recordings. She returned to pictures in the late 1940s in mature supporting roles in several M-G-M films.

Jeanette MacDonald died of a heart attack in 1965 with her husband of thirty years, Gene Raymond, at her side.

Carmen Miranda

Carmen Miranda was born in Marco de Canavezes, Portugal in 1909. Her real name was Maria do Carmo Miranda da Cunha. She and her parents soon moved from Portugal and settled in Brazil where she became both a movie and a singing star.

After her success in Brazil, Miranda came to the United States to do a Broadway musical. She was signed for movies by Twentieth Century-Fox and in 1940 made her first film, *Down Argentine Way*. Miranda became known for her trademark turban hats which were piled high with fruit. Her costumes also included lots of jewelry and high heeled platform shoes.

Carman Miranda made ten films for Fox and then did four more movies for other studios before her film career ended. She died of a heart attack in 1955. Some of her best films were: *Weekend in Havana; Springtime in the Rockies; The Gang's All Here;* and *Four Jills in a Jeep*.

Diana Lynn Coloring Book (#1278). Published by Saalfield Publishing Co., 1954. This is a thin, soft cover book. Photograph and book courtesy of Joseph Golembieski.

Jeanette MacDonald Costume Parade Paint Book (#3461), "By Courtesy of Metro-Goldwyn-Mayer." Published by Merrill Publishing Co., 1941. Movie costumes are shown but not all are identified. Book also contains a paper doll and clothing to be colored and cut out.

Carmen Miranda Paint Book (#669). Published by Whitman Publishing Co., 1942. Photograph and book courtesy of Joseph Golembieski.

Carmen Miranda Coloring Book (#2370). Copyright by Saalfield Publishing Co. From the collection of Elaine Price.

Draw and Paint Tom Mix. Copyright 1935 by Whitman Publishing Co. Contains captioned pictures of the star as a cowboy.

Margaret O'Brien A Metro-Goldwyn-Mayer Star Paint Book (#1155). Drawings by Hedwig Jo Meixner. Whitman Publishing Co., 1947. Good likeness in captioned pictures.

Tom Mix

Tom Mix was the "King of the Cowboys" during the 1920s as the highest paid cowboy star ever. In 1925, he earned $17,000 per week for his film work.

Mix was born in Mix Run, Pennsylvania in 1881. He was well prepared for his film career as he had been a rodeo performer, a cowboy, and a marshall before he made his first western in 1910.

Mix's screen persona showed a character that did not drink or smoke and who rarely killed his enemies. Mix did many of his own stunts and was usually dressed in fancy white western type costumes, starting the tradition that the hero wears a white hat.

Mix joined the Fox Studios in 1917 where most of his pictures were filmed. During the late 1920s, he moved to FBO and then on to Universal to make his movies. Tom Mix's last screen appearance was in 1935 for a Mascot serial called *The Miracle Rider*.

At the end of his film career, Tom Mix toured the country with his famous horse, Tony, in "The Tom Mix Circus." Tom Mix died in 1940 as the result of a car crash in Arizona.

Margaret O'Brien

Margaret was born in Los Angeles in 1937 as Angela Maxine O'Brien. She started her career as a model and then worked her way into the movies. Margaret O'Brien came on the movie scene with a remarkable role in the M-G-M film, *Journey For Margaret*, in 1942 which gave her the name Margaret. The movie was the story of an English child war refugee who was adopted by an American couple. Margaret had been selected for this role after only one other film appearance— a bit part in the M-G-M film *Babes on Broadway* (1941) where she also played an English war refugee.

With the success of the 1942 movie, Margaret's career skyrocketed. Although her film career spanned a period of nearly nineteen years and included a total of twenty-one pictures, over one third of her movie output occurred during 1943 and 1944.

Some of her most successful films from this period include: *Thousands Cheer*; *Lost Angel*; *The Canterville Ghost*; *Music For Millions*; *Meet Me In St. Louis*; and *Our Vines Have Tender Grapes*.

Margaret continued to make films for M-G-M during the late 1940s with only one big hit, *Little Women*, released in 1949. Her last picture was *Heller in Pink Tights* made in 1960.

After the O'Brien film career was finished, the young actress kept busy in television and stock productions. She was recently seen in the television production, "Murder She Wrote," in 1991.

Osmond Family

The Osmond children were encouraged by their parents to learn to sing and play several instruments. At first, the four boys Allen, Jay, Merril, and Wayne sang only at local Morman Church functions. As they improved, they worked professionally and received a regular spot on Andy Williams' television program from 1962-1966. Later they appeared on the Jerry Lewis show when Donny joined his brothers at the age of nine. The group had a number one single record, "One Bad Angel" in 1970.

As sister Marie grew up, she, too, joined the family entertainment business and she and Donny became so popular that they hosted their own television variety show on ABC beginning in 1976. Little brother, Jimmy, also did some feature spots on the program.

Margaret O'Brien Coloring Book (#1155), "A Metro-Goldwyn-Mayer Star." Published by Whitman Publishing Co., 1947. From the collection of Mary Stuecher. Photograph by Werner Stuecher.

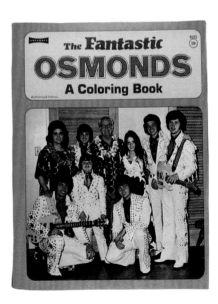

The Fantastic Osmonds A Coloring Book (#4622). Copyright 1973 by Osbro Productions. Published by The Saalfield Publishing Co. Contains captioned pictures of all the Osmonds.

Our Gang

The filming of the *Our Gang* comedies began in 1922 and continued through 1944. Two hundred and twenty-one of the shorts were made during this period. The beginning Hal Roach comedies from the series were silent films while the best *Our Gangs* were the sound films from 1934 to 1937. Some of the players from this period include: Jackie Cooper, Dickie Moore, Scotty Beckett, Stymie Beard, Spanky McFarland, Alfalfa Switzer, Darla Hood, Buckwheat Thomas, and Baby Patsy.

Hal Roach sold the whole *Our Gang* unit to M-G-M in 1938. Metro produced fifty-two films in the series but they weren't as good as the earlier Roach comedies.

The best of the series are still shown on television under the title *The Little Rascals*.

Gigi Perreau

Gigi Perreau was born in 1941 and made her film debut at the age of two in M-G-M's movie, *Madame Curie*. She had a very successful film career as a child star, making her last movie, *Hell On Wheels*, in 1967.

Some of her best films include: *Dark Waters*; *Two Girls and a Sailor*, *Mr. Skeffington*; *Yolanda and the Thief*, *Green Dolphin Street*, *Weekend With Father*, *Tammy Tell Me True*; and *My Foolish Heart*.

Jane Powell

Jane Powell became one of M-G-M's popular stars in a series of the studio's musical films during the late 1940s and into the 1950s.

Jane was born in 1928 in Portland, Oregon and began her singing career on local radio shows. With this recognition, she moved on to the Chase and Sanborn program on national radio. Jane was then signed by M-G-M, and loaned to United Artists in 1944 where she made her first film at the age of fourteen. The movie, *Song of the Open Road*, starred Edgar Bergen and Charlie McCarthy.

Jane's movie career included many M-G-M musicals including: *Holiday in Mexico* (1946); *Three Daring Daughters* (1948); *A Date With Judy* (1948); *Nancy Goes to Rio* (1950); *Royal Wedding* (1951); *Rich, Young and Pretty* (1951); and *Seven Brides For Seven Brothers* (1954). Her last picture was *Enchanted Island* made by Universal in 1958.

After the end of her movie career, Jane Powell was active in road show productions as well as night clubs. She is currently seen in television commercials.

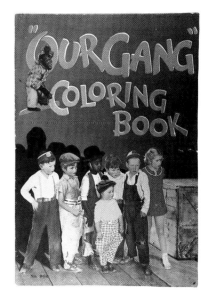

Our Gang Coloring Book (#966). Copyright 1933 by Hal Roach Studios, Inc. Published by The Saalfield Publishing Co. The whole book consists of photographs of the kids. Most are in black and white, to be painted. Others are in color to show the child what the pictures should look like when completed.

Jane Powell Coloring Book (#1861). Published by Whitman Publishing Co., 1951. Photograph and picture courtesy of Joseph Golembieski.

Jane Powell Coloring Book (#1133). Published by Whitman Publishing Co., 1951. Copyright Loew's Inc. Most of the captioned pictures deal with the actress "at home."

Gigi Perreau Coloring Book, "Motion Picture Artist Under Contract to Samuel Goldwyn Productions, Inc." Published by Saalfield Publishing Co., 1951. Contains large captioned pictures of the child actress at the studio and at home.

The Elvis Coloring Book. Copyright 1983, Tennessee Manufacturing and Distribution Co., Inc. Contains pictures with long captions which tell the story of his life.

Elvis Presley

Elvis Presley, the undisputed "King of Rock and Roll" was born in 1935 in Tupelo, Mississippi. Presley's music career started after he made a demo record as a surprise for his mother. From this recording, he received a contract with the Sun record company. His first commercial record, "That's All Right Mama," was made in 1954.

Colonel Tom Parker heard Elvis sing, knew he had talent, and became his life-long agent. Parker negotiated a contract for Presley with RCA Victor and his first number one hit song was "Heartbreak Hotel" in 1956.

Elvis was the first rock star to also become a movie star, and his film career began that same year with, *Love Me Tender*. Although the Elvis movies were not great films, they did please Elvis fans and most of them were financially quite successful. Some of the best were: *Loving You*; *Jailhouse Rock*; *King Creole*; *G.I. Blues*; *Blue Hawaii*; *Kid Galahad*; and *Frankie and Johnny*.

Elvis interrupted his show business career in 1958 when he was drafted into the army. While stationed in Germany he met Priscilla Beaulieu who he later married. After Elvis was discharged from the service in 1960, his career became even more successful. His movies continued to do good business and he was listed among the top ten box office stars from 1961 to 1966. His singing engagements included televison appearances, concerts, and night club shows. His recording career also continued on high. It wasn't until after 1967 that Elvis did not have a top 20 single hit record.

After six years of marriage, Priscilla divorced Elvis in 1973. She retained custody of their daughter, Lisa Marie. Elvis kept working, but the old spirit seemed to be gone. The superstar died on August 16, 1977 apparently from a drug overdose.

Debbie Reynolds

Debbie Reynolds has had a long and varied show business career as a performer for more than forty years. She was chosen to be Miss Burbank in 1948, and, since Warners' studio was located in Burbank, she secured a few bit parts in their pictures. In 1950, M-G-M hired Debbie to mouth Helen Kane's voice in the hit film, *Three Little Words*. Debbie's movie career was launched, and she was elevated to star status very quickly.

In 1952 she co-starred with Gene Kelly and Donald O'Connor in one of the best M-G-M musicals ever—*Singin' in the Rain*. In 1955 Debbie pleased her fans when she made what seemed to be the perfect marriage to Eddie Fisher. Two children were born to the couple before scandal erupted when Eddie left Debbie for his new love, Elizabeth Taylor.

Debbie's film career continued to soar and in both 1959 and 1960 she was one of the top ten box office stars in Hollywood. In 1960 she married Harry Karl, a shoe manufacturer. That marriage, too, caused Debbie many heartaches plus financial difficulties.

Some of the successful Debbie Reynolds' movies include: *Susan Slept Here* (1954, R.K.O.); *Hit the Deck* (1955, M-G-M); *The Tender Trap* (1955 M-G-M); *Bundle of Joy* (1956); *Tammy and the Bachelor* (1957, Universal); and *The Unsinkable Molly Brown* (1964, M-G-M).

In 1969, Debbie starred in a short lived television series called "The Debbie Reynolds Show" for NBC. In later years she continued work in both clubs and on stage.

Debbie Reynolds Coloring Book (#1133). Copyright 1953 by Whitman Publishing Co. Artist Betty Anderson. Book and photograph courtesy of Elaine Price.

Debbie Reynolds Coloring Book (#1868), "M-G-M Star." Published by Whitman Publishing Co., 1956 and 1953. Captioned pictures deal mostly with her daily life.

Roy Rogers

Roy Rogers took over the number one cowboy role from Gene Autry in 1943. He was born in Cincinnati, Ohio in 1912 and Rogers began his movie career in 1935 with the singing group, Sons of the Pioneers. In 1938 he made *Under Western Stars*, the first of his starring Westerns for Republic Pictures. Rogers made forty-two pictures for Republic, and remained the number one star of "B" Westerns until 1951. He married Dale Evans in 1948 making twenty of his Western films with her. Some of his best pictures include: *In Old Caliente* (1939); *King of the Cowboys* (1943); *Yellow Rose of Texas* (1944); *San Fernando Valley* (1944); *Man from Oklahoma* (1945); and *Springtime in the Sierras* (1947).

In 1951, Rogers turned to television where he and Dale did a program for CBS until 1964. In the show, the action took place on the Double R Ranch in Mineral City. Rogers' horse, Trigger, and the dog, Bullet, shared in the adventures. From September, 1962 until December, 1962 Rogers and Evans hosted a musical variety show on ABC.

Roy Rogers' Double-R-Bar Ranch (#1034). Coloring and Many Things To Do. Copyright 1955 by Frontiers, Inc. Drawings by John Vshler. Published by Whitman Publishing Co. Photograph and book courtesy of Joseph Golembieski.

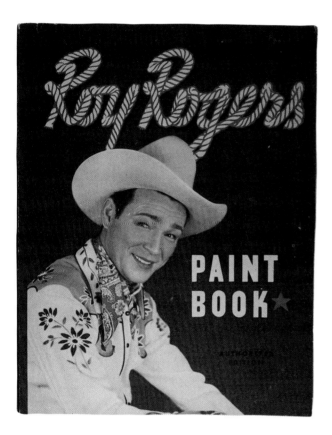

Roy Rogers Paint Book (#668). Copyright 1944 by Whitman Publishing Co. Drawings by Betty Goodan. Contains captioned pictures to color.

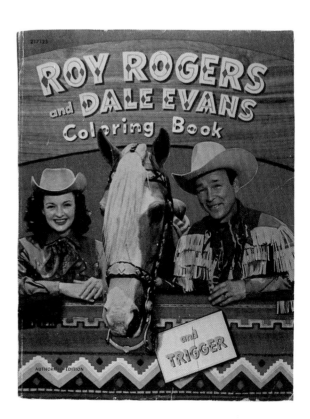

Roy Rogers and Dale Evans Coloring Book (#2171). Copyright 1951 by Roy Rogers Enterprises, Inc. Drawings by Peter Alvarado. Published by Whitman Publishing Co.

Roy Rogers and Dale Evans' Big Book To Color
(#1184). Published by Whitman Publishing Co.
Photograph and book courtesy of Joseph Golembieski.

Roy Rogers Coloring Book (#1006). Copyright
MCMXLVI, Whitman Publishing Co.

Dale Evans Coloring Book (#1755). Copyright 1957 by
Dale Evans Enterprises, Inc. Drawings by Nat Edson.
Published by Whitman Publishing Co. Photograph
and book courtesy of Elaine Price.

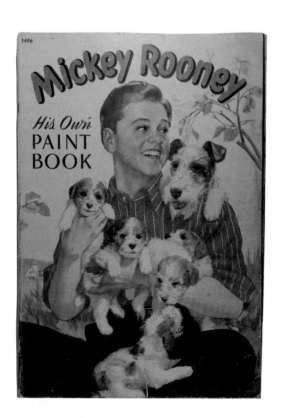

Mickey Rooney His Own Paint Book (#3496). Published
by Merrill Publishing Co., 1940. Some of the captioned
pictures are from movie roles but approximately one
third are of assorted children.

Mickey Rooney

Mickey Rooney was the number one box office movie star in the nation from
1939-1941. As a child he first caught the public's eye in, *A Midsummer Night's
Dream*, when he played Puck in 1935. In 1937 his career caught fire as he made
the first of the popular Andy Hardy series of films for M-G-M, and in 1938 he added
to his popularity when he co-starred with Judy Garland in the first of many
musicals they did together. This same year, he received a special Academy Award
for a youthful performance in *Boys' Town*.

After a successful film career in which he was nominated for an Oscar three
times, Rooney turned to television, club, and stage work. He received three Emmy
nominations for his television dramas through the years. Mickey also had a
Broadway hit co-starring with Ann Miller in, *Sugar Babes*.

Mickey Rooney's most well known films include: *Boys' Town* (1938, M-G-M);
Babes In Arms (1939, M-G-M); *Strike Up the Band* (1940, M-G-M); *The Human
Comedy* (1943, M-G-M); *Girl Crazy* (1943, M-G-M); *National Velvet* (1944, M-G-
M); and *Baby Face Nelson* (1957).

Evelyn Rudie

Evelyn Rudie, the child actress, was born in 1947 and began her screen career in 1955. She had parts in *The View of Pompey's Head (1955), The Wings of Eagles (1957), The Restless Breed (1957), and The Gift of Love (1958).* Perhaps Evelyn's most popular role was the character of *Eloise* in the television adaptation of Kay Thompson's *Eloise* books.

As an adult, Rudie operated a theater workshop in Los Angeles for a time.

Ann Sheridan

The "Oomph Girl," as movie star Ann Sheridan was called, was born in Denton, Texas in 1915. She came to Hollywood after winning a beauty contest and made her first film, *Search For Beauty,* in 1934. Although her first movies were made for Paramount, Ann Sheridan spent most of her career working for Warner Brothers. Some of her best films are: *King's Row* (1941); *Dodge City* (1939); *Torrid Zone* (1940); *They Drive By Night* (1940); *Shine On Harvest Moon* (1944); *The Man Who Came To Dinner* (1941); *George Washington Slept Here* (1942); *I Was a Male War Bride* (Twentieth Century-Fox 1944); and *Good Sam* (RKO 1948).

Sheridan left the screen in 1957 and spent some time touring with a stage play called, *Kind Sir.* Her co-star was Scott McKay who later became her third husband in 1966. She was married earlier to S. Edward Norris from 1936-1937 and George Brent from 1942-1943. Ann Sheridan died at the age of fifty-one in 1967 after a career that had spanned more than thirty years.

Bobby Sherman

Bobby Sherman was born in Santa Monica, California in 1943. He attended high school in Van Nuys, California and later went to Pierce College. After learning to play the piano and guitar, Bobby got a spot on the ABC television show, "Shindig," in the mid 1960s. When the show folded, Sherman received the part of Jeremy Bolt on the ABC television series "Here Come the Brides." Because of the interest Bobby received from his television role, he was given a record contract by Metromedia records in 1969. His first song, "Hey Little Woman" was a hit and earned him a gold record.

Bobby Sherman became very popular with the preteenage girls and he did many concerts in the late 1960s and early 1970s. At the height of his popularity, Sherman sold ten million records and three million albums. Other hits were "Easy Come, Easy Go" and "Julie, Do Ya Love Me?" In more recent years, Sherman had his own situation comedy, "Getting Together," in 1971-1972 and was a regular on the show, "Sanchez of Beverly Hills," in 1986.

Evelyn Rudie Coloring Book (#4512). Copyright by Evelyn Rudie. Published by Saalfield Publishing Co., 1958.

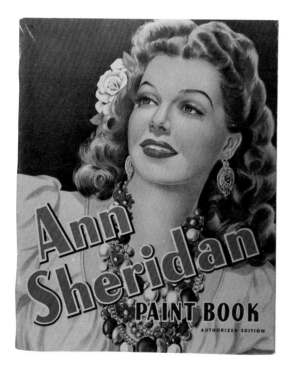

Ann Sheridan Paint Book (#678). Drawings by Lee Lunzer. Published by Whitman Publishing Co., 1944. The pictures and captions tell about her war-time activities, including a bond tour.

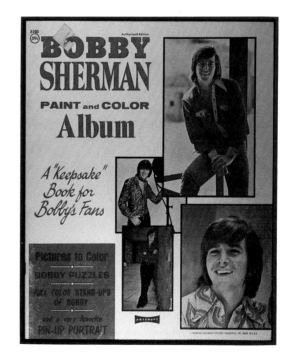

Bobby Sherman Paint and Color Album. Copyright 1971, Columbia Pictures (#5160). Contains long captions on pictures and extra pictures and cut-outs, as the book was meant for pre-teens.

Dinah Shore Paint Book (#651). Drawings by Doris L. Butler. Published by Whitman Publishing Co., 1943. Book and photograph courtesy of Joseph Golembieski.

Elizabeth Taylor Coloring Book (#1119). Drawings by Hedwig Wylie. Published by Whitman Publishing Co., 1950. Photograph and book courtesy of Joseph Golembieski.

Elizabeth Taylor Coloring Book (#2145). Published by Whitman Publishing Co., 1952. Book and photograph courtesy of Elaine Price.

Dinah Shore

Dinah Shore was born in 1917 in Winchester, Tennessee. She contracted infantile paralysis at the age of two, yet made a total recovery. Unlike most of the performers from her era, Miss Shore earned a college degree from Vanderbilt University before she began her entertainment career. Dinah began her professional career on radio and by 1940 she was appearing on the "Eddie Cantor Show." She soon secured a recording contract and then branched out into film.

Although Dinah Shore made several movies during the 1940s, her movie career never seemed to showcase her winning style. Some of her most successful pictures include: *Thank Your Lucky Stars*; *Up in Arms*; *Belle of the Yukon*; *Follow the Boys*; *Till the Clouds Roll By*; and *Fun and Fancy Free*.

It wasn't until Dinah Shore turned to television that she became a real star. She began her own program "The Dinah Shore Show" in 1956 for NBC and it ran until 1961. Miss Shore has continued to do television work since the end of her first series.

Elizabeth Taylor

Elizabeth Taylor has been a show business celebrity since the age of ten. She began her movie career during the old "Hollywood Star" system and is sometimes called "The Last Star" because of her background.

Elizabeth was born in London, England in 1932 but moved to California with her family at the beginning of World War II. After doing several bit parts in films at Universal Pictures, Elizabeth had a good role in the M-G-M movie, *Lassie Come Home*, in 1943. She then had her first starring role in *National Velvet in 1944*.

Elizabeth Taylor has been awarded two Academy Awards during her successful film career for both Butterfield 8, in 1960 and Who's Afraid of Virginia Woolf?, in 1966. Elizabeth has also generated lots of news coverage because of her personal life. Her many marriages, particularly to Eddie Fisher and Richard Burton (who already had wives at the beginning of their involvements with Elizabeth), made headlines around the world.

Elizabeth's other most memorable films include: *Father of the Bride* (1951, M-G-M); *A Place in the Sun* (1951, M-G-M); *Giant* (1956, M-G-M); *Cat On a Hot Tin Roof* (1958, M-G-M); *Suddenly Last Summer* (1959, M-G-M); *Cleopatra* (1963, Twentieth Century-Fox); and *The Taming of the Shrew* (1967, Columbia).

Elizabeth Taylor Coloring Book (#1144), "M-G-M-Star." Published by Whitman Publishing Co., 1954. The captioned pictures all deal with Elizabeth.

Shirley Temple

In 1934, in the midst of the Depression, America fell in love with a tiny, golden haired moppet Shirley Temple. Shirley was born on April 23, 1928 in Santa Monica, California. Because she loved to dance to the radio music, her mother enrolled her in a dancing school. While she was there, Shirley was seen by a movie scout and was signed to make short films for the Educational Studios.

Shirley's charm in these films caught the attention of Leo Houch, assitant director for Fox Film Corp., and he gave her a starring role in *Stand Up and Cheer*, in 1934. Shirley's golden curls and her pleasing personality made her an instant hit with the public, so she was signed to a seven year contract with Fox.

In 1934 Shirley made twelve pictures, many of them still rated as some of her best. These include: *Little Miss Marker* (Paramount); *Baby Take a Bow; The Little Colonel;* and *Bright Eyes*.

There has never been a child movie star as popular as Shirley Temple. Her good looks and talent made her a perfect role model for little girls all over the world. Mothers began shaping their own little girls' hair into ringlets in an attempt to copy Shirley's curls. Dresses, toys, dolls, and many other products were manufactured to take advantage of the Shirley name.

By 1935 Shirley Temple was in the number one position among the top ten box office stars of the country. She retained that spot through 1938.

Popular Shirley films from the 1930s include *Our Little Girl; The Littlest Rebel; Curly Top; Captain January; Poor Little Rich Girl; Stowaway; Dimples; Wee Willie Winkie; Heidi; Rebecca of Sunnybrook Farm; Just Around the Corner; Little Miss Broadway; The Little Princess;* and *Susannah of the Mounties*.

By 1940, Shirley had lost some of her little girl cuteness and her last two movies for Fox were not very successful. She continued through the 1940s making films for various companies but never again received the stardom she had known as a youngster. Perhaps the most successful film she made during this period was *Fort Apache* in 1948, which starred John Wayne and Shirley's husband John Agar.

Shirley retired from pictures in 1950. After divorcing Agar, she married Charles Black and changed her life to become a full time wife and mother.

In 1957 Shirley Temple agreed to do the "Shirley Temple Storybook" series on television. With the publicity generated by the series, the child Shirley Temple was again captured in the spotlight. Many products were produced to take advantage of this publicity.

Shirley Temple A Great Big Book To Color (#1717). Published by Saalfield Publishing Co., 1936. No pictures of Shirley are included inside the book.

Shirley Temple Coloring Book (#1772). Published by Saalfield Publishing Co., 1937. This book also does not include Shirley pictures inside.

This is My Crayon Book Shirley Temple (#1711). Published by Saalfield Publishing Co., 1935. The back of the book shows the back of the Shirley Temple figure. The inside pages do not include pictures of Shirley.

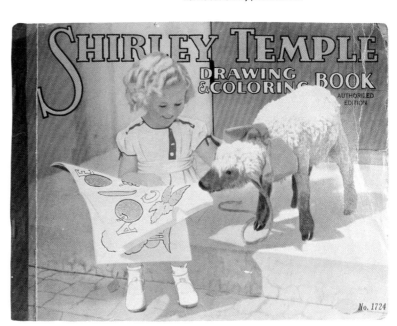

Shirley Temple Drawing and Coloring Book (#1724). Published by Saalfield Publishing Co. Copyright MCMXXXVI. The book contains no pictures of Shirley on the inside.

Shirley Temple Coloring Book (From Drawing Set Box)
#1738. Published by the Saalfield Publishing Co.,
1935. Book from the collection of Mary Stuecher.
Photograph by Werner Stuecher.

Shirley Temple My Book To Color (#1768). Published
by Saalfield Publishing Co., 1937. Captioned pictures
are of Shirley and items pertaining to her life.

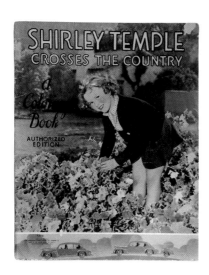

Shirley Temple Crosses the Country (#1779). Saalfield
published this book in 1939 to take advantage of the
publicity given to the Temple's real trip across the
country.

Shirley Temple's Bluebird Coloring Book. Published
by Saalfield Publishing Co., 1940. Book from the
collection of Mary Stuecher. Photograph by Werner
Stuecher.

Shirley Temple Coloring Book (#5353). Published by The Saalfield Publishing Co., 1958. Book from the collection of Mary Stuecher. Photograph by Werner Stuecher.

Shirley Temple's Busy Book (#5326). Published by The Saalfield Publishing Co., 1959. Book from the collection of Mary Stuecher. Photograph by Werner Stuecher.

Shirley Temple Coloring Book (#4624). Published by Saalfield Publishing Co., circa 1958. Many pictures of Shirley are included inside the book.

Shirley Temple Play Kit (#9859). Published by Saalfield Publishing Co., 1958. The $1.00 item included two paper dolls, lace on dresses, as well as a coloring book and crayons.

Shirley Temple Coloring Book (#4584). Published by Saalfield Publishing Co., 1958. Many pictures of Shirley are included inside the book.

Three Stooges

Columbia Pictures made 190 short subjects featuring "The Three Stooges" from 1934 to 1958. There were really five Stooges featured in the series but only three of the players participated at any one time. In the early 1920s, Shemp Howard and his brother Moe joined Ted Healy's vaudeville act. Larry Fine joined the group in 1925. The act was mostly slapstick and it was called "Ted Healy and His Stooges."

The first film was made in 1930. Shemp left the team in the early 1930s and was replaced by his brother Curly. In 1946, Shemp returned to the series when Curly became ill. Shemp was later replaced by Joe De Rita. Although the series was popular on the screen, it has probably been made even more famous by its many television showings which began in 1959.

Lana Turner

Lana Turner was born in Wallace, Idaho in 1920. According to myth, she was discovered while sipping a soda in Schwab's Drug Store in Hollywood. She soon became one of M-G-M's most glamorous stars making her first film, *They Won't Forget*, in 1937.

The best of the Turner films include: *Ziegfeld Girl* (1941, M-G-M); *Honky Tonk* (1941, M-G-M); *Somewhere I'll Find You* (1942, M-G-M); *Weekend at the Waldorf* (1945, M-G-M); *The Postman Always Rings Twice* (1946, M-G-M); *The Bad and the Beautiful* (1953, M-G-M); *Peyton Place* (1957, Twentieth Century-Fox); and *Imitation of Life* (1959, Universal).

Miss Turner was nominated in 1957 for an Academy Award for her performance in the Twentieth Century-Fox picture *Peyton Place*. Even though she didn't win the award, it was a plus for the "Sweater Girl" that she was recognized for having acting talent as well as glamour.

John Wayne

John Wayne, the personification of American masculinity, was born with the rather feminine name of Marion Michael Morrison in Winterset, Iowa in 1907. When Marion was only seven, the family left Iowa for California.

The 3 Stooges Funny Coloring Book (2855). Copyright by Norman Maurer Productions, Inc., 1960. Contains many well-drawn pictures of the Stooges. Published by Samuel Lowe Co.

John Wayne Coloring Book (#1238). Published by Saalfield Publishing Co., copyright MCMLI.

Lana Turner Paint Book, "A Metro-Goldwyn Mayer Star." Published by Whitman Publishing Co., 1947. Drawings by Doris Lane Butler. Captioned pictures deal with both her professional and her personal life.

Although his parents called Marion by his given name, he secured the nickname "Duke" because of a dog he owned named Duke. Marion was a good student and athlete in high school and after graduation he received a football scholarship to attend the University of Southern California. He didn't complete college, however, because a football injury made it impossible for him to return to active sports and he couldn't afford to attend school without the scholarship.

Wayne started his film career as a prop man for Fox. He also was able to get bit parts in several of the Fox movies, including *Hangman's House*, in 1928. He received his big break in 1930 when Raoul Walsh gave him the lead in *The Big Trail*. Marion's name was changed to John when he made this film.

Beginning in 1932 Wayne worked for Monogram, Republic, and Universal, performing in lots of cheap Western films. In 1939 he received his first really good role, as Ringo Kid, in the hit film *Stagecoach*, for United Artists. With the coming of World War II, Wayne's career gained momentum as he starred in various films, including *The Flying Tigers* (Republic); *The Long Voyage Home* (United Artists); *A Lady Takes a Chance* (RKO); *The Fighting Seabees* (Republic); *Back To Bataan* (RKO); and *They Were Expendable* (M-G-M).

By the late 1940s, Wayne had become a superstar with films such as *Fort Apache* (United Artists); *She Wore a Yellow Ribbon* (RKO); and *Red River* (United Artists).

In 1950 and 1951 Wayne became the number one box office star in the country. All through the 1950s Wayne continued to make good pictures. One of his best was *The Quiet Man*, made for Republic in 1952.

In 1956 John Wayne signed with Warner Brothers and became the highest paid actor in the world when he made $666,666 a year. For Warners he did two especially good pictures, *The Searchers* and *Rio Bravo*.

John continued his astonishing movie career in the 1960s with more hit films, including *Hatari* (Paramount); *The Longest Day* (Paramount); and *The Green Berets*. Wayne received his only Academy Award for a film he made in 1968 called *True Grit*.

Even after a battle with cancer, Wayne continued to make movies into the 1970s. His last film, *The Shootist* (Dino De Laurentis), was appropriately about a gunfighter who was dying of cancer.

John Wayne lost this battle with cancer on June 11, 1979. He made over 150 films during his fifty year career, and because of his high ranking among the top box office stars, he remains the most popular movie star ever.

Virginia Weidler

Virginia Weidler was a well-known child star during the 1930s and continued her movie career until she retired from films for marriage in 1943. Her first picture, *Mrs. Wiggs of the Cabbage Patch* appeared in 1934. In the early 1940s, Virginia had several good parts in big M-G-M productions, including *The Philadelphia Story*; *Out West With the Hardys*; *Babes on Broadway*; and *Best Foot Forward*. Her only starring role was in *The Youngest Profession*, in 1943.

Virginia Weidler died from cancer in 1968 at the age of forty-one.

Virginia Weidler Paint Book (#1043). Drawings by Ruth Wood. Copyright 1943 by Whitman Publishing Co. Book and photograph courtesy of Elaine Price.

Esther Williams

Esther Williams is the only female movie personality to become a star based on swimming ability. She was born in 1921 in Los Angeles and became a champion swimmer. She probably could have made the 1940 Olympic team, but she chose to go to work for Billy Rose in his 1939 Acquacade instead. Because of this exposure, M-G-M signed her to a contract. She started her career in a Mickey Rooney-Andy Hardy film in 1942, and then starred in *Bathing Beauty* in 1944. Most of her movies were similar with the plots designed to show off Esther doing swimming sequences with camera shots both above and below the water.

Esther remained a star in films for over ten years. In 1949 and 1950 she was rated the second biggest money making female star (Betty Grable was first). Some of her best films include: *Thrill of a Romance*; *Easy to Wed*; *Take Me Out to the Ball Game*; *Neptune's Daughter*; *Million Dollar Mermaid*; and *Dangerous When Wet*. After her film career was finished, Esther Williams became active in the business world with lines of both swim suits and swimming pools.

Esther Williams Coloring Book (#1591), "Metro-Goldwyn-Mayer Star." Published by Merrill Company, 1950. Contains captioned pictures from both work and home.

Jane Withers' Paint Book (#607). Published by Whitman Publishing Co., 1941. Styled by Hedwig Jo Meixner. Captioned pictures show Jane both at home and at work.

Jane Withers

Jane Withers was born in Atlanta, Georgia in 1926 and was already an experienced radio performer when she reached Hollywood five years later. Her Atlanta weekly radio program was called "Aunt Sally's Kiddy Club" and the children sang, did imitations and acted in skits to entertain the radio audience.

Once in Hollywood, Jane received a small part in a film called *Handle With Care*, in 1933 and, outside of a few extra calls, Jane's career was soon stalled. Jane turned to radio again where she became successful on a children's radio show in Los Angeles. When Fox was looking for a child to play opposite their darling Shirley Temple in *Bright Eyes*, someone remembered the little girl from the radio program and Jane was picked for the part. The public loved Jane's performance in the film and wanted to see more of her.

Jane began making films as fast as she could, developing her tomboy character in movie after movie. She starred in *Ginger*; *This is the Life*; *Paddy O'Day*; *Gentle Julie*; *Little Miss Nobody*; *Pepper*; *The Farmer Takes a Wife*; and *Can this Be Dixie?*, and she was still only nine years old.

By the 1940s, most of the Withers' films had deteriorated to "B" type pictures like *A Very Young Lady* (Twentieth Century-Fox); *The North Star* (RKO); *Golden Hoofs* (Fox); and *Faces in the Fog* (Republic).

In 1947 Withers gave up movies for marriage, but she did return to Hollywood in 1956 when she played a very good character role in the blockbuster film, *Giant* made by Warner Brothers.

Jane Withers then turned to television commercials for her most lasting fame when she played the plumber Josephine. In this role she promoted Comet Cleanser for seventeen years.

Loretta Young

Loretta Young was born Gretchen Michaela Young in Salt Lake City on January 6, 1913. She made her first movie, *Naughty But Nice* in 1927, and her last picture, *It Happens Every Thursday*, in 1953.

Although she starred in nearly 100 films, few of them are very memorable. Miss Young did win an Oscar in 1947 for *The Farmer's Daughter* made for RKO. Other films of note from her career include: *Laugh, Clown, Laugh*; *Taxi*; *Four Men and a Prayer*; *Come to the Stable*; *The Stranger*; and *The Accused*.

Loretta Young began a new career in 1953 when she turned to television. She starred in her own program, "The Loretta Young Show" until 1961.

Loretta Young Coloring Book (#1108). Published by Saalfield Publishing Co., 1956. The captioned pictures show the actress on her television show and at home.

Comic and Cartoon Coloring Books

Most of the "classic" comic and cartoon characters have been featured in coloring books besides the ones pictured in this chapter. The most valuable are the books with the oldest copyright dates that are in mint, unused condition. Other comic figures that have been featured in coloring books include Buck Rogers, Dennis the Menace, Little Iodine, and Winnie Winkle.

Andy Panda

Andy Panda was a character from Walter Lantz Productions made for Universal Studios. The character was also used in comic book material by 1942. Many of the stuffed toy panda bears look like Andy but they are not licensed as such.

Archie

Archie (Archie Andrews) was originated in December, 1941 for Pep Comics. By July of 1946 it was the top selling comic book in America. In 1947, Archie was transferred to a newspaper comic strip drawn by Bob Montana for King Features. Archie comics were being sold at a million copies a month by 1969. Archie was expanded even further to include a television cartoon program in 1968.

The three longest lived comic book heroes are Superman, Batman and Archie Andrews. Even though the world has changed a lot in the last fifty years, Archie and his pals Judhead, Betty, and Veronica remain much the same as they were in the 1940s. They are still teen-agers mainly concerned with dating and cars.

Little Scouts Coloring Book (#680). Copyright 1953 by Roland Coe. Published by Whitman Publishing Co. with captioned pictures.

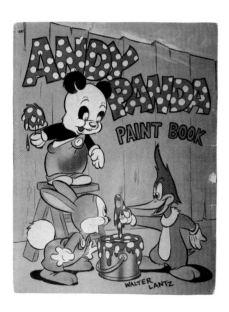

Andy Panda Paint Book (#681). Copyright 1946 by Walter Lantz Productions. Published by Whitman Publishing Co.

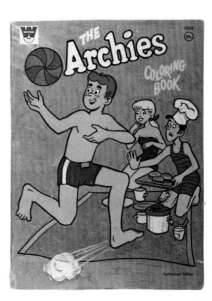

The Archies Coloring Book (#1045). Copyright 1970 by Archie Comics Publications, Inc. Published by Western Publishing Co. Contains captioned sequenced pictures to color.

Jughead Coloring Book (#1045). Copyright Archie Comic Publications, Inc., 1972. Published by Western Publishing Co. with captioned pictures.

Baby Huey

Baby Huey was a cartoon character developed by Harvey Films for cartoons distributed by Paramount. From 1959 to 1962, some of these cartoons were shown on television as part of the program "Matty's Funday Funnies." The show aired on ABC and was hosted by cartoon characters Matty and Sisterbelle.

Beetle Bailey

Mort Walker created "Beetle Bailey" for King Features in 1950. Bailey was a draftee stationed at Camp Swampy. He always wore a helmet or a hat so his eyes were never seen in the strip. Other characters in the unusual comic included Sergeant Orville Snorkel, the dog Otto, Killer Diller, Zero, Plato, Chaplain Staneglass, and Lt. Flap. The Beetle Bailey characters were later featured in animated cartoons.

Blondie

The "Blondie" comic strip began on September 15, 1930 by Murat (Chic) Young for King Features Syndicate. In the beginning, Blondie was a flapper and Dagwood Bumstead was the son of a railroad millionaire. When Dagwood and Blondie were married on February 17, 1933, the millionaire disinherited his son. Then Dagwood began work for Mr. Dithers to earn a living. Two children were born to the Bumsteads; Alexander in 1934 and Cookie in 1941. Daisy, the dog, completed the household.

For many years, "Blondie" was the most widely circulated comic strip in the world. The strip was also the basis for twenty-eight movies and a television show. In the films, Penny Singleton played Blondie and Arthur Lake was Dagwood.

Chic Young died in 1973 but his son and his assistants continue the strip.

Baby Huey the Baby Giant Coloring Book (#4536). Saalfield Publishing Co., copyright 1959. Harvey Famous Cartoons. Contains assorted pictures of characters.

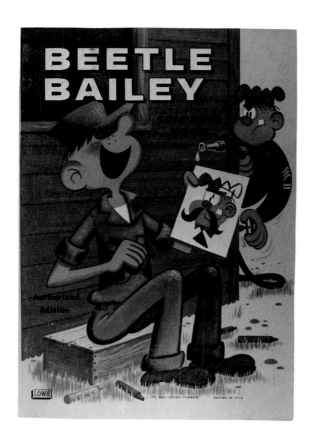

Beetle Bailey coloring Book (#2860). Copyright 1961, King Features Syndicate. Published by Samuel Lowe Co.

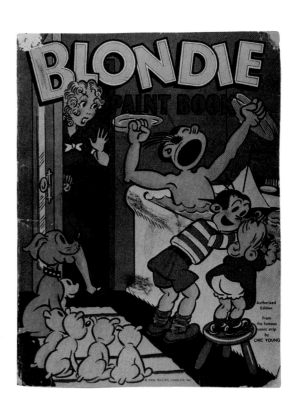

Blondie Paint Book by Chic Young. Copyright King Features, 1945. Published by Whitman Publishing Co. Contains captioned pictures to color in sequence.

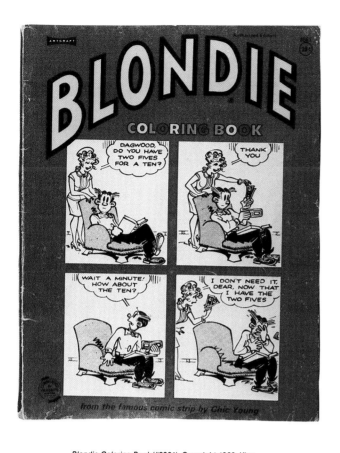

Blondie Coloring Book (#9961). Copyright 1968, King Features Syndicate. Published by Saalfield Publishing Co. Contains actual large comic strip panels to color from the famous comic strip by Chic Young.

Blondie Coloring Book (#4541). Copyright 1968, King Features Syndicate. Published by Saalfield Publishing Co. Contains large comic strip panels to color with the CBS television show cast pictured on front of the book. From the famous comic strip by Chic Young.

Boots and Her Buddies

Edgar Martin began the "Boots and Her Buddies" strip on February 18, 1924 for the NEA Service. Boots was one of several "glamour girl" comic strips that were popular through the 1940s. Boots changed from a coed, to a married woman, to a mother during several decades of adventures. The comic strip was most popular in the 1930s and 1940s. After Boots settled down to married life, she was no longer as appealing as she had been as a young beautiful blonde.

Boots and Her Buddies Coloring Book (#1182). Published by Saalfield Publishing Co., 1952. Contains large pictures to color with captions of characters.

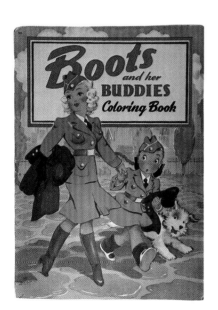

Boots and Her Buddies Coloring Book (#331). Copyright by Stephen Slesinger Inc. N.Y. Copyright 1941. 1942 NEA Service. Published by Saalfield Publishing Co. Nice big book with small parts of original strips shown with each picture to color.

Brenda Starr Coloring Book (#9675). Copyright MCMLXIV, Chicago Tribune—News Syndicate, Inc. Artist Dale Messick. Published by Saalfield Publishing Co. Photograph and book courtesy of Elaine Price.

Brenda Starr

"Brenda Starr" began as a Sunday comic strip on June 30, 1940. Dalia (Dale) Messick originated Brenda for the Chicago Tribune—New York News Syndicate. "Brenda Starr" also became a daily strip in 1945.

Brenda was a career girl who worked as a newspaper reporter for "The Flash." Brenda's adventures involved lots of romance and travel. One of her more interesting boyfriends was Basil St. John.

Bringing Up Father

"Bringing Up Father" was created by George McManus in 1913 but it did not become a regular Hearst daily strip until 1916. On April 14, 1918 it also begin to appear as a Sunday strip.

The story line involved its two main characters, Jiggs and Maggie, who moved from the lower class to the upper class by winning the Irish Sweepstakes. Maggie enjoyed her new place in society while Jiggs still wanted to spend time with his old friends at Dinty Moore's Tavern. This led to many conflicts between the couple.

"Bringing Up Father" has been used as the basis for several movies as well as animated cartoons. It was also made into a stage play called *Father* in the 1920s.

After McManus died in 1954, "Bringing Up Father" continued to be published with others in charge.

Bugs Bunny

The character of Bugs Bunny developed over several years from a movie cartoon, "Hare-um Scare-um," and another called, "A Wild Hare," in 1940. Leon Schlesinger, Fred Avery, and Ben Hardaway all helped make Bugs Bunny the star he became in the Looney Tunes and Merrie Melodies cartoons made for Warner Brothers.

Bugs first appeared in comic book form in 1941 in *Looney Tunes and Merrie Melodie*. The Sunday newspaper strip began in 1942, and the daily in 1948.

Bugs recently celebrated his fiftieth birthday and his most famous phrase, "What's up doc?" remains a part of America's pop culture.

Buster Brown

The cartoonist R.F. Outcault (who also originated Yellow Kid) first drew Buster Brown on May 4, 1902. The new character was used as a Sunday comic strip for the *New York Herald*.

Buster was supposed to be a ten-year-old boy who lived with his well-to-do family and his dog named Tige.

In 1906 Outcault began drawing for the *New York American* but was taken to court for leaving the Herald. When the case was resolved, the Herald retained the name of the strip but Outcault was allowed to use the characters. The cartoonist continued to draw Buster Brown until 1920. After that time, the character was used mostly in ads for children's clothing and Buster Brown Shoes.

Bringing Up Father Paint Book With Jiggs and Maggie (#663). From the famous comic strip by George McManus. MCMXLII, Whitman Publishing Co. Contains large uncaptioned pictures to color with small comic strip pictures at the bottom of each page.

Buster Brown's Painting Book. Copyright by Cupples and Leon Co., 1916. Most of the pictures consist of toys and other objects with only a few pictures of Buster Brown. Some of the pages show the pictures in both color and black and white.

Bugs Bunny Porky Pig Paint Book (#1152). Copyright 1946 by Warner Brothers Cartoons, Inc. Published by Whitman Publishing Co. Contains captioned pictures of Bugs, Porky Pig, Elmer Fudd and other Warner cartoon characters.

Captain and the Kids

Rudolph Dirks based the comic strip "Captain and the Kids" on his first strip called "Katzenjammer Kids." Since he could no longer use the earlier name because it belonged to another syndicate, he began drawing his new strip under the title "Hans and Fritz" in 1914. Because of World War I and the involvement of Germany as our enemy, Dirks renamed the comic "Captain and the Kids" in 1918.

The strip featured the mischievous kids and the frustration of the Captain and Mama as they tried to cope with the resulting situations. In 1930 the strip was taken over by United Features Syndicate.

Dick Tracy

The comic strip called "Dick Tracy" was developed and drawn by Chester Gould for the Chicago Tribune—New York News Syndicate beginning in 1931. The comic was so successful that it appeared as a radio show, a television program (ABC—1950-51), and several motion pictures. In 1937, Republic did a fifteen episode Dick Tracy serial, and in 1945 RKO produced four full length movies. Dick Tracy was revived again as a film character in 1990 when Warren Beatty produced the first big budget Dick Tracy film.

The comic strip has undergone many changes through the years. After a long courtship, Tracy married girlfriend Tess Trueheart in 1949 and their daughter Bonny Braids was soon added as a character. The Chester Gould villains are very unusual and include such interesting types as Flattop, Shakey, Mumbles, and Pruneface.

Feature Funnies Comic Coloring Book (#2554). Copyright, United Features Syndicate. Published by Samuel Lowe Co. Contains captioned pictures from the comics "Captain and the Kids," "Willie," "Casey Ruggles," and "Buffalo Bill."

Dick Tracy Coloring Book (#399). Copyright, Famous Artists Syndicate. Contains captioned pictures of characters used in various stories from the famous strip by Chester Gould. Published by Saalfield Publishing Co. Whitman Publishing Co. also produced a *Dick Tracy Paint Book* (#665) in 1935.

Dick Tracy Coloring Book (#2536). Copyright 1946 by Famous Artists Syndicate. Published by Saalfield Publishing Co. by permission of Famous Artists Syndicate. Book from the collection of Elaine Price.

Bonnie Braids Coloring Book (#2366). Copyright 1951, Chicago Tribune. Famous Artists Syndicate. Doll designed by the Ideal Novelty and Toy Co. Published by Saalfield Co.

Felix the Cat

Pat Sullivan began Felix as an animated cartoon in 1917 and continued to produce the cartoon until his death in 1933. There were over 100 of these cartoons including the first sound cartoon. In 1923 King Features Syndicate began a "Felix the Cat" comic strip on Sundays and then added a daily strip in 1927.

Felix has had an active life including animated cartoons made for television by Joe Orlolo Productions.

Flash Gordon

"Flash Gordon" was created by Alex Raymond in 1934 for King Features Syndicate. Flash Gordon, Dale Arden, and scientist Dr. Hans Zarkov were on a space ship to the planet Mongo during the strip's early action. The trio spent many years trying to liberate Mongo.

During World War II, Raymond joined the Marines and the strip was drawn by Austin Briggs. At the height of its popularity, "Flash Gordon" was the number one science fiction comic strip.

It was also made into a radio program in the 1930s and 1940s, and a movie serial in 1936 (starring Buster Crabbe). From 1953-1954 "Flash Gordon" also appeared as a television series.

Flash Gordon Mission of Peril Coloring Book (#06538). Copyright 1979, King Features Syndicate. Published by Rand McNally and Co. with captioned pictures that tell a story.

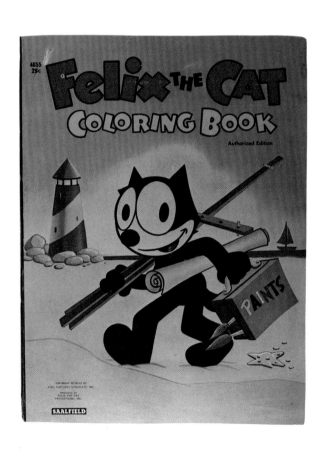

Felix the Cat Coloring Book (#4655). Copyright 1959 by King Features Syndicate. Produced by Felix the Cat Productions, Inc. Published by Saalfield Publishing Co. with captioned pictures.

The Flintstones

"The Flintstones" has been a very successful animated cartoon for all three major television networks. It began on ABC in 1960 and continued until 1966. In 1967 the cartoon switched to NBC and remained there until 1970. In 1971, the characters ran on CBS until 1974.

The cartoon takes place in the Stone Age in the town of Bedrock. Fred and Wilma and their neighbors Barney and Betty Rubble are involved in most of the adventures, assisted by the children Pebbles and Bamm Bamm. William Hanna and Joseph Barbera were responsible for the shows.

Fritzi Ritz

"Fritzi Ritz" was developed by Ernest Bushmiller in the early 1920s. Bushmiller had started working at the *New York World* as a copy boy when he was only fourteen. He became interested in art and studied at the National Academy of Drawing after work. Later he helped draw other comics until he sold Fritzi to United Features.

Fritzi was a working girl with a niece named Nancy. Nancy became more and more important in the strip, and in 1940 Fritzi was replaced as a strip by "Nancy" (also drawn by Bushmiller).

The Flintstones Coloring Book (#537). Copyright 1971, Charlton Publications Inc. Copyright 1971, Hanna-Barbera Productions, Inc. Contains large uncaptioned pictures.

Pebbles and Bamm-Bamm Play's the Thing. Copyright 1978, Hanna-Barbera Productions, Inc. Story content by Art Scott, art direction by Iraj Paran and finished art by Tom Coppola. Published by Modern Promotions. Coloring/Activity Book.

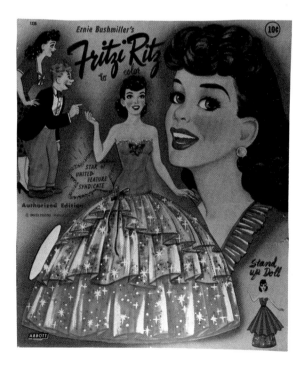

Fritzi Ritz To Color (#3335). Star of United Features Syndicate by Ernie Bushmiller. Published by Abbott Publishing. Soft cover book that contains captioned pictures, circa late 1940s.

Skeezix Color Book (#2023). Published by McLoughlin Brothers, Inc., 1929. Contains captioned pictures of characters from the "Gasoline Alley" comic strip. Most of the pictures are shown in both color and black and white. Licensed by Famous Artist Syndicate.

Skeezix Drawing and Tracing Book (#525). Licensed by Famous Artists Syndicate, copyright 1932. Published by McLoughlin Brothers Inc. Pictures are partly captioned and partly uncaptioned. Includes tissue paper to trace pictures of the cartoon characters.

Gasoline Alley

"Gasoline Alley" was first introduced as a comic strip on November 24, 1918. Frank King developed the strip for the Chicago Tribune—New York News Syndicate.

The strip began with the bachelor Walt Wallet as the main character. On February 14, 1921 he found a baby boy abandoned on his door step and decided to adopt the child and name him Skeezix. In 1926, Walt married Blossom and they had two more children, Corky and Judy.

Skeezix grew up and did his part in World War II when he was in the army. He married his girlfriend, Nina, in 1944 and began his adult life.

Although King died in 1969, the strip was continued by others. Perhaps the success of "Gasoline Alley" for so many years was due to the concept of aging the characters which no other cartoonist had done before. Walt, Skeezix, and the others seemed like real people instead of inhabitants of a comic strip.

Heart of Juliet Jones

Artist Stan Drake and writer Eliot Caplin combined their talents to begin the comic strip, "Heart of Juliet Jones," in 1953. This was a romantic comic which began with Juliet living in a small town with her sister, Eve, and her father "Pop." Juliet later married a criminal lawyer named Owen Cantrell and they moved to the city.

At the strip's peak, it was carried in 600 newspapers and received the NCS Best Story Strip award in 1969, 1970, and 1972.

Henry

"Henry" was created by Carl Anderson as a weekly cartoon for the magazine, *Saturday Evening Post,* on March 19, 1932. As a pantomime-only character, Henry did not speak. On December 17, 1934, Henry became a comic strip for King Features.

In 1942, Carl Anderson's poor health caused him to give up drawing the strip, and it was turned over to others.

Carl Anderson's Henry Paint Book (#696). Copyright 1951 by King Features Syndicate Inc. Published by Whitman Publishing Co. with captioned pictures of cartoon characters.

Juliet Jones Coloring Book (#953). Juliet and Eve from Daily Feature "The Heart of Juliet Jones" by Stan Drake. Copyright 1954 by King Features Syndicate. Published by Saalfield Publishing Co. with captioned pictures of characters.

Jane Arden

"Jane Arden" made her debut as a comic strip on November 26, 1922 in the *Des Moines Register and Tribune*. Arden was the idea of Henry Martin, but the author was Monte Barrett. Frank Ellis was the artist. Jane Arden had lots of exciting adventures as a journalist, a detective, and a war correspondent. As a reporter on a big city newspaper, she worked with another important character, Tubby, the office boy.

The "Jane Arden" comic was one of the popular strips that, for many years, printed a paper doll and clothes with the Sunday edition. Several other writers and artists continued the strip until it ended in the late 1950s.

Li'l Abner

"Li'l Abner" was one of the most popular comic strips in America during the 1940s and 1950s. It started as a daily strip in 1934 for United Features. In 1935, a Sunday strip was added. Al Capp (Alfred Gerald Caplin) was the originator of the comic and the famous characters which included: Li'l Abner, Daisy Mae, Pansy Yokum and her husband Lucifer Ornamental Yokum, Marryin' Sam, Hairless Joe, and Lonesome Polecat.

In order to take advantage of the popularity of the comic, two films were made. The 1940 movie was produced by RKO, and the 1959 picture by Paramount. Dogpatch and its inhabitants were also featured in a Broadway musical in 1957.

Jane Arden Coloring Book (#265). Published by Saalfield Publishing Co., 1942. Photograph and book courtesy of Joseph Golembieski.

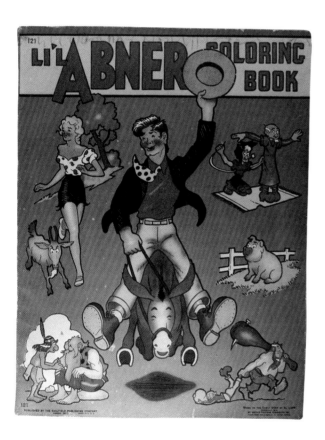

Li'l Abner Coloring Book (#121). Based on the comic strip by Al Capp. Copyright 1941, United Features Syndicate. Published by Saalfield Publishing Co. The book contains captioned pictures of the comic characters.

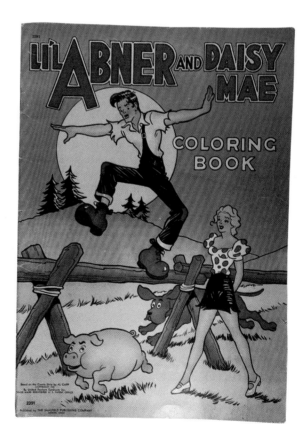

Li'l Abner and Daisy Mae Coloring Book (#2391). Based on comic strip by Al Capp. Copyright 1942, United Features Syndicate. Published by Saalfield Publishing Co. Oversized book of captioned pictures of characters.

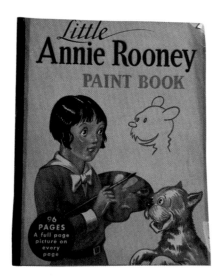

Little Annie Rooney Paint Book (#666). Copyright 1935 by King Features Syndicate Inc. Published by Whitman Publishing Co. Book and photograph courtesy of Joseph Golembieski.

Little Annie Rooney

"Little Annie Rooney" was a comic strip by Brandon Walsh that featured a twelve-year-old girl. It began as a daily strip in 1929 for King Features. The Hearst Syndicate developed "Little Annie Rooney" to combat the popularity of "Little Orphan Annie." Several artists drew the character until it was taken over by Darrell McClure in 1930. A Sunday strip was also added at that time.

"Little Annie Rooney" was an orphan with a dog called Zero. The child, Annie, was eventually adopted by the Robins family. One of her favorite sayings, "Gloryosky," became a part of the language for a while. The strip ended in the mid-1960s.

Little Audrey

Little Audrey was a little girl comic character used by Harvey Films for cartoons distributed by Paramount. Many of these cartoons were shown on the television show, "Matty's Funday Funnies" on ABC from 1959 to 1962.

Little Folks

Benjamin Thackston, known as "Tack" Knight, began "Little Folks" as a comic strip in 1931 for the *Chicago Tribune*. He had been an assistant for Gene Byrnes on the "Reg'lar Fellers" comic earlier, and the new strip which "Tack" developed in 1929 was very much like Byrnes' earlier strip which also featured "kids doings." The "Little Folks" included Kitty Carr (based on Thackston's real daughter), Baxter, Horace, and Mary Bright.

Little Lulu

"Little Lulu" had her beginning in June, 1935 as a single panel cartoon in the *Saturday Evening Post*. The comic was drawn by Marge (Marjorie Henderson Buell).

In 1945, the character was featured in a comic book by Western Publishing Co. These Lulu comics were drawn by John Stanley.

"Little Lulu" became a newspaper strip for the New York News Syndicate from 1955 to 1967. Lulu, and her boyfriend Tubby, continue to be popular even today. Western Publishing Co. gained full ownership of the feature beginning in 1972.

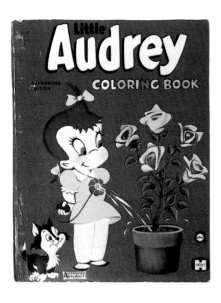

Little Audrey Coloring Book (#9535). Copyright MCMLIX, Harvey Famous Cartoons. Published by Saalfield Publishing Co.

Little Folks Painting Book by "Tack" Knight. Copyright 1931, The National Art Co. Large size book that features two captioned pictures on each page—one already in color and one uncolored, drawn in strip form.

Marge's Little Lulu Coloring Book (#1186). Copyright Marjorie Henderson Buell. Published by Whitman Publishing Co., circa 1950s.

Little Orphan Annie

Harold Gray began the "Little Orphan Annie" comic strip on August 5, 1924 for the Chicago Tribune—New York News Syndicate. Annie was so popular, she was one of the five top strips for several decades. Because the characters are so well known, (Daddy Warbucks, Punjab, and Annie's dog Sandy), producers have used them in other mediums to insure successful projects.

The radio show based on Annie was popular with children during the 1930s and 1940s. The premiums that were given away by the program are highly collectible today. Although two early movies were made featuring Annie, the best tie-in production was the Broadway musical, *Annie*, produced in 1977. The movie, based on the show, was also a success.

Harold Gray died in 1968. Perhaps it was his unusual drawing of the Annie strip, with each character having blank eyes, that added to its success, or maybe it was Annie's unusual adventures, or the interest gained by Daddy Warbucks being a millionaire at the time of the Depression. At any rate, "Little Orphan Annie" collectibles rank among the most popular items from any comic strip for today's collectors.

Little Orphan Annie Crayons (#8442). Licensed by Famous Artists Syndicate 1930 (boxed set). Published by Milton Bradley Co. Contains crayolas plus small pictures to color. From the collection of Mary Stuecher. Photograph by Werner Stuecher.

The Great Big Little Orphan Annie Paint and Crayon Book (#2017). Famous Artists Syndicate. Copyright 1935 by McLoughlin Brothers Contains 200 uncaptioned pictures from the comic by Harold Gray. Annie wears a green dress on the cover instead of red.

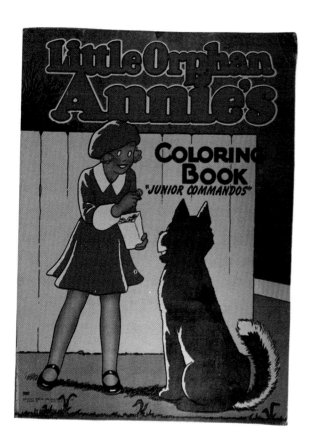

Little Orphan Annie's Coloring Book Junior Commandos (#300). Famous Artists Syndicate, copyright 1945 by Saalfield Publishing Co. Wonderful large book with captioned pictures about World War II (saving scrap etc.).

Little Orphan Annie Coloring Book (#4689). Copyright 1974, New York News, Inc. Published by Saalfield Publishing Co. Captioned pictures tell a story.

Mandrake the Magician

"Mandrake the Magician" was born as a comic in 1934 when Lee Falk wrote the story, and Phil Davis did the art work. The strip was a part of the King Features Syndicate. At first, the Magician had supernatural powers, but later his illusions and hypnotism triumphed over evil. Other prominent characters were Princess Narda and Lothar.

Davis died in 1964 and another artist took over the drawing. In 1939, a movie serial was made based on the comic strip.

Mr. Magoo

Mr. Magoo was an unusual cartoon character. The old man, Quincy Magoo, was very nearsighted and had difficulty seeing anything. His mistaken identity of people and objects added to the humor. Although the animation was good, perhaps the voice, supplied by actor Jim Backus, was an outstanding part of the cartoon's success.

Forty-three theatrical Mr. Magoo cartoons were made by UPA Pictures and two won Academy Awards in 1954 and 1956.

The animated cartoons were syndicated in 1963 and NBC aired the "Mr. Magoo" series during the 1964-1965 season. Magoo has also been used on many television commercials for General Electric.

Nancy

Ernest Bushmiller began drawing a comic strip about Fritzi Ritz, a beautiful young woman, in the 1920s. In that comic, Nancy appeared as the heroine's eight-year-old niece. In 1940, Bushmiller made Nancy the star of her own strip, and by the 1950s and 1960s the comic really took off. "Nancy" is a kid strip with a boy named Sluggo as Nancy's friend. The comic is drawn very plainly and the two main characters remain popular today.

Mandrake the Magician Coloring Book (#2942-4). Copyright King Features Syndicate, Inc. by Lee Falk Ottenheimer Pub. Inc. Captioned pictures tell a story.

Nancy and Sluggo with doll and clothes (#1053). Copyright United Features Syndicate, Inc. 1972. Published by Western Publishing Co. Contains mostly uncaptioned pictures plus a paper doll on the back cover of Nancy, and clothes to color and cut out.

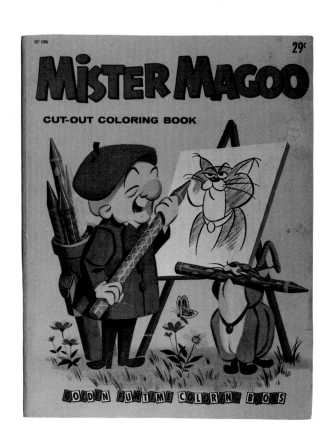

Mister Magoo Cut-out Coloring Book (#GF 186). Copyright 1961, U.P.A. Pictures, Inc. Story by Nita Jones, pictures by Richard Gonzales. Published by Golden Press. Captioned pictures to color plus character cut-outs on insides of front and back cover.

Peanuts

"Peanuts" has been called the most successful comic strip of all time. The famous characters were created by Charles Schulz as "Li'l Folks" in 1950, and the strip was accepted by United Features Syndicate and renamed "Peanuts." The daily strip was first printed on October 2, 1950 and the Sunday comic was added on January 6, 1952.

"Peanuts" was most successful during the 1960s. The characters; Charlie Brown, Lucy, Linus, Schroeder, Peppermint Patty, and Charlie's dog, Snoopy, were also used in a successful Broadway musical called, *You're a Good Man, Charlie Brown,* in 1967.

CBS has also profited from the comic by producing many well-received animated cartoons. The annual income from the many-licensed products is approximately $50,000,000 a year.

Popeye

Popeye began as part of the "Thimble Theater" comic strip which was started by Elzie Crisler Segar for the W.R. Hearst chain in 1919. Popeye became a part of the strip in 1929. Other important characters were: Olive Oyl, Jeep, Swee'pea and Wimpy. Paramount took advantage of the popularity of the characters by making animated movie cartoons beginning in 1932.

When Segar died in 1938 other artists continued to draw the strip. Popeye is still an important comic character, especially on television. A *Popeye* movie was made in 1980 which starred Robin Williams as Popeye.

Prince Valiant

"Prince Valiant" was a King Features Syndicate product which began in 1937 under the direction of Harold Foster. The story involved Prince Valiant and his adventures as a member of King Arthur's Round Table. In 1946, he married Princess Aleta and they produced four children. The comic strip appeared only on Sunday and was never a daily strip.

In 1953, a movie was made based on the Prince starring Janet Leigh and Robert Wagner.

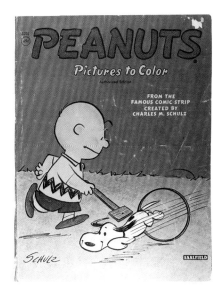

Peanuts Pictures to Color (#5331). From the famous comic strip created by Charles M. Schultz. United Features Syndicate. Published by Saalfield Publishing Co., 1960 with mostly large strip panels.

Popeye Coloring Book (#2834). Copyright 1959, King Features Syndicate. Published by Samuel Lowe Co. Captioned pictures of the characters tell a story.

Prince Valiant Coloring Book. Copyright 1954, King Features Syndicate. Published by Saalfield Publishing Co. Drawings by Harold Foster. Captioned pictures tell a story.

I'm Popeye the Sailorman! Color and Read. Copyright King Features Syndicate, 1972. Published by Western Publishing Co. Pages have balloon captions that tell a story. Pages are partly colored.

Red Ryder Coloring Book (#1155) by Fred Harman. copyright 1952 by Stephen Slesinger. Published by Whitman Publishing Co. Large captioned pictures of characters.

Red Ryder

"Red Ryder," developed by Fred Harman, began with the Sunday Newspaper Enterprise Association Service on November 6, 1938. The daily strip was added on March 27, 1939.

The action of the comic took place in the 1890s in Rimrock, Colorado. Although Ryder owned a ranch, he spent most of his time helping the sheriff catch the bad guys. Another important character in the strip was Little Beaver, a Navajo orphan who was adopted by Red Ryder.

The characters were so popular with the public that twenty-two movies were made which featured Red Ryder and Little Beaver. Harman quit the strip in 1960 but it continued under other artists for several years.

The Road Runner

The Road Runner, as a character, was first developed by Warner Brothers in 1949 in "Cartoon Fast and Furryous" by Chuck Jones. More animated cartoons were made, and Wile E. Coyote was also used. Mel Blanc provided the voices.

"The Road Runner Show" was shown on CBS television during the 1967-1968 season using both the theater cartoons as well as those made for television.

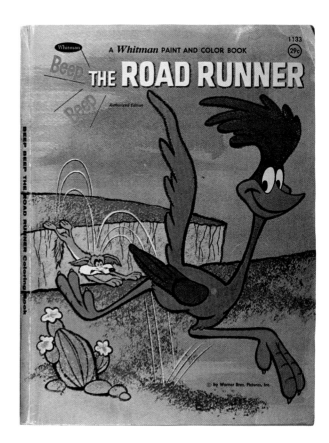

Beep Beep The Road Runner Paint and Color Book (#1133). Copyright 1967, Warner Brothers Pictures, Inc. Drawings by Phil de Lara. Published by Whitman Publishing Co.

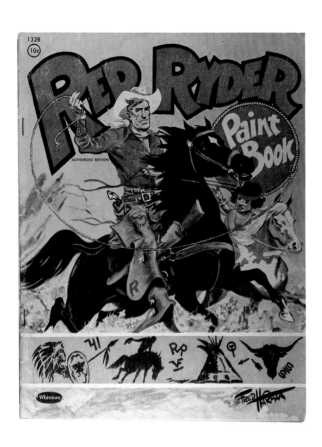

Red Ryder Paint Book (#1328) by Fred Harman. Copyright 1952, Stephen Slesinger. Published by Whitman Publishing Co. Captioned pictures of characters.

Skippy

"Skippy" was first drawn by Percy Crosby for the original *Life* magazine in 1919. Because people seemed to enjoy the character, Crosby began a "Skippy" syndication in the early 1920s. King Features took over the distribution in 1928. Both a daily strip and a Sunday strip were soon appearing in the nation's newspapers.

Skippy was a ten-year-old boy who always wore a plaid hat and short pants. He was the leader of several other children (Snooky Wayne and Sidney Saunders) who schemed against adults in a sometimes vicious manner.

Crosby became ill in 1942 and instead of having someone else draw "Skippy," he ended the strip. Jackie Cooper starred in a successful *Skippy* movie, based on the comic character, in 1931.

Smilin' Jack

"Smilin' Jack" was first drawn by cartoonist Zack Mosley in October, 1933 under the title, "On the Wing." In December of that year, the name was changed to "Smilin' Jack" and the strip was picked up by the News—Tribune Syndicate for a Sunday feature. In 1936, it became a daily comic strip.

The main character, Smilin' Jack, was a playboy Clark Gable type of man who made his living as a pilot. He had a friend called Pen feathers and a cook named Fat Stuff, plus several girl friends. At one point, Jack also had a wife who played parts in his adventures. In 1942, Universal Studios made a movie serial based on the comic strip. The strip was discontinued in 1973.

Smitty

"Smitty" was first drawn on November 27, 1922 by Walter Berndt for the Chicago Tribune— New York News Syndicate as a daily strip. The Syndicate added a Sunday strip on February 25, 1923. In the beginning, Smitty was an office boy who worked for Mr. Bailey. Although Smitty grew up during his years in Berndt's strip, it happened very slowly. He met a girl in the office in the late 1950s and they were soon married. The strip was discontinued in 1973.

Steve Canyon

Milton Caniff, the creator of "Terry and the Pirates," was also the creator of "Steve Canyon." Caniff drew Canyon for Field Enterprises beginning in 1947.

The story line dealt with Steve Canyon, a former Air Force Captain who became head of an airline company. During the Korean War he re-enlisted and was sent all over the world as part of his job. The strip was at its best during the early and mid-1950s.

A television series, based on the Steve Canyon adventures, was shown during the 1958-1959 season. Dean Fredericks starred as Canyon.

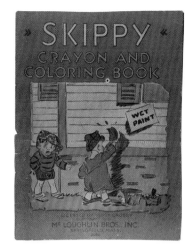

Skippy Crayon and Coloring Book (#2050). Licensed by Percy Crosby, copyright 1931 by McLoughlin Brothers, Inc. Contains captioned pictures to color, printed in both black and white and color.

Steve Canyon Coloring Book (#123410). Copyright 1952, Field Enterprises, Inc. Published by Saalfield Publishing Co. "Secret Mission." The large captioned pictures tell a story.

Smilin' Jack Coloring Book (#397). By permission of Famous Artists Syndicate. Published by Saalfield Publishing Co., 1946. Contains captioned pictures.

Smitty Color Book. Copyright 1931, Famous Artists Syndicate. Published by McLoughlin Brothers, Inc. Most pictures are done in both color and black and white.

Superman Coloring Book The Missile Base Mystery (#1031). Copyright, National Periodical Publications, Inc. Western Publishing Co., 1965. Captioned pictures of an adventure story.

Superman

"Superman" was the first costumed "super hero." He was developed by Jerry Siegel and Joe Shuster (both seventeen years old at the time) as a comic book hero in 1938.

Superman came from another planet and had a dual identity. He was Clark Kent, a newspaper reporter, in every day life and became Superman in time of trouble. Clark Kent and his fellow reporter, Lois Lane, worked for the "Daily Planet" located in Metropolis. Clark, as Superman, fought for "Truth, Justice and the American Way."

Superman appeared as a newspaper strip in 1939 and was discontinued in 1967. The character was also featured on a radio show, in the movies, and in a television series. Who could ever forget "It's a bird, it's a plane, it's Superman" as the opening segment for each Superman program? A series of three big budget films was also produced in the late 1970s and early 1980s featuring Christopher Reeve as Superman.

Terry and the Pirates

Milton Caniff developed the popular "Terry and the Pirates" for the Tribune-News Syndicate in 1934. The adventure series was located in China where during World War II, Terry became a pilot. Other characters were Pat Ryan, Dragon Lady, and Flip Corkin.

Caniff quit the strip in 1946, but it was continued by George Wunder until 1973. The strip spawned a radio show and later a television series.

Tillie the Toiler

"Tillie the Toiler" was created by Russ Westover for King Features Syndicate in 1921.

The heroine of the strip, Tillie Jones, was a career girl working as a secretary and part time fashion model for Mr. Simpkins. Clarence MacDougall (Mac) was her short boyfriend.

Because of Tillie's interest in fashion modeling, the weekly Sunday paper dolls that accompanied the strip were extra special. Each doll was outfitted in high fashion clothing which was sometimes submitted by various readers.

Tillie finally married Mac before the strip ended in 1959. Marion Davies played the part of Tillie in the *Tillie the Toiler movie made in 1927.*

Tweety

Tweety, the small yellow tongue-tied bird, was developed by Friz Freleng as a cartoon character for Warner Brothers. Tweety was first introduced in 1942 in "A Tale of Two Kittens." "Tweetie Pie," another Warner cartoon featuring the cute yellow bird, won the cartoon Oscar for 1947.

Terry and the Pirates Coloring Book (#398). Copyright 1946, Saalfield Publishing Co. Famous Artists Syndicate. Captioned pictures to color but no story line.

Tweety Coloring Book (#2953). Copyright 1955 by Warner Brothers Cartoons, Inc. Pictures by Alfred Abranz, Dave Hoffman, and Norm McGary. Published by Whitman Publishing Co. Small sized book that sold for five cents new.

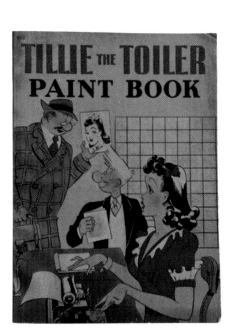

Tillie the Toiler Paint Book (#662). Copyright 1921, 1942 by King Features Syndicate Inc. Based on the Famous Comic Strip by Russ Westover. Published by Whitman Publishing Co. Photograph and book courtesy of Joseph Golembieski.

Wendy the Good Little Witch

"Wendy the Good Little Witch" began as a cartoon character in the Casper the Ghost cartoon series. The cartoons were made for Paramount Studios by Harvey Famous Cartoons and were shown in movie theaters until the 1950s. In 1953, several Casper cartoons were syndicated and shown on television. Later, a children's show called "The New Casper Cartoon Show" used the cartoons on a Saturday morning program.

The characters also became popular in comic books. When the St. John company took over the production of the Casper Comics in 1950, the studio animators worked on the comics to make them look authentic. Wendy the Good Little Witch became such a well-liked character that whole comic books were produced involving the witch character. Harvey Publishing Co. took over the production of the comics in 1953.

Wonder Woman

"Wonder Woman" was created by writer William Moulton Marston (pen name Charles Moulton) and illustrator H.G. Peter for comic books in 1941.

Wonder Woman was an Amazon Princess who lived on an island where no men were allowed. She came to the United States to help during World War II. She wore "bracelets of submission" which could be chained together by a male to make her helpless.

"Wonder Woman" was also a short-lived newspaper strip. Marston died in 1947 but others continued the Wonder Woman projects.

A popular television series, "Wonder Woman" was broadcast on ABC starting in 1976. Lynda Carter played Wonder Woman.

Woody Woodpecker

Woody Woodpecker was a character created by Walter Lantz to be used in animated theater cartoons.

Later, "The Woody Woodpecker Show" appeared on television with Woody as host of the program. Mrs. Grace Lantz was Woody's voice. The program was on ABC from 1957-1958 and on NBC from 1970 to 1972. Woody was famous for his unusual laugh.

Yogi Bear

Yogi Bear was the main character in many animated cartoons created by Hanna—Barbera Productions.

Yogi lived in Jellystone National Park. From 1973 to 1975, Yogi appeared on the television show "Yogi's Gang" for ABC along with his friends Boo Boo Bear, Huckleberry Hound, Quick Draw McGraw, and Peter Potomus. Yogi was always getting into trouble as he tried to get food from the tourists.

Wendy the Good Little Witch Coloring Book (#06416). Published by Rand McNally and Co. MCMLIX. Copyright, Harvey Famous Cartoons. Captioned pictures to color of Wendy and other cartoon characters.

Walter Lantz Flying High with Woody and his Friends—A Coloring Book (#81836). Copyright, Walter Lantz Productions. Published by Artcraft, circa 1970s.

Wonder Woman faces "The Menace of the Mole Men" (#1653-43). A book to color. Copyright 1975, D.C. Comics, Inc. Published by Western Publishing Co. Large comic sequences that tell a story.

Yogi Bear and the Great Green Giant. Copyright 1976, Hanna-Barbera Productions. Published by Modern Promotions. Includes large pictures to color.

Paper Doll and Doll Related Coloring Books

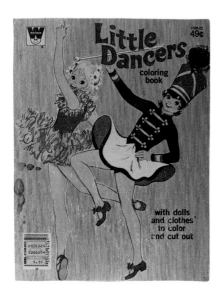

Little Dancers Coloring Book (#1105-22). Published by Whitman Publishing Co., 1972. Contains two paper dolls on the back cover, plus clothes to color and cut out inside. Other pages have pictures of dancers to color.

Because the number of doll and paper doll collectors continues to increase, the coloring books related to both are very popular. Especially desirable are the books that contain celebrity paper dolls as well as pages to color. These books are particularly in demand if they are in mint, uncut, uncolored condition.

Besides the books pictured in this chapter, other paper doll/coloring books include the following items produced by Saalfield Publishing Co.: *Raggedy Ann and Andy Paper Dolls/Coloring Book* 1944; *Indian Paper Dolls and Coloring Book* 1956; *Wedding Day Coloring Book and Paper Dolls* #3954; *Space 1999 Coloring Book with Paper Dolls* 1976; *The Addams Family Activity Book with Paper Dolls* #3731; *Paper Dolly Coloring Book* 1942; and *Story of the Ballet* #4515.

Samuel Lowe Co. also produced combination coloring and paper doll books, including *Rosemary Clooney* #2595 and *Pam and Her Pram* 1956. Merrill Publishing Co.'s contribution to the combination book field included *Rainy Day Fun* 1951; *Children of Other Lands* 1954; and *Color, Cut and Paste* 1936.

The most expensive coloring book and paper doll combination is the *Percy Reeves Movy—Dolls Painting Book #1*. The book features paper dolls of many silent stars, including May Allison, Charlie Chaplin, Geraldine Farrar, Elsie Ferguson, Mary Pickford, Norma Talmadge, Marguerite Clark, and Douglas Fairbanks. Each star's wardrobe was printed in both color and in black and white so the child could paint the clothing to match the art. The book was published around 1920.

Besides the dolls pictured in this chapter, several other dolls were honored in coloring books. These include: Ideal Toy Co.'s Tammy doll family; Mattel, Inc.'s Chatty Cathy; and numerous books produced in Mattel's Barbie doll family's images.

Baby Alive

Baby Alive was a vinyl doll made by Kenner during the late 1970s and early 1980s that could do so many things she seemed like a real baby. The doll came with plastic food which she could chew and swallow by pulling a lever on her back. The doll also was a drink and wet product with rooted hair. She came in both black and white models. A 13″ tall doll sold for $14.99 in the 1983 J.C. Penney's Christmas catalog.

Baby Tenderlove

Baby Tenderlove was a popular Mattel doll for many years, from the early 1970s. The original baby doll was 15″ tall with a one-piece vinyl body, rooted white hair, painted eyes and an open mouth. Later models were made that talked and cried. A smaller size doll was also manufactured.

Baby Alive Coloring Book (#1661). Trademark of Kenner Products. Published by Whitman Publishing Co. Copyright General Mills Fun Group, Inc., 1976. Contains captioned pictures to color.

Baby Tenderlove Coloring Book with Doll and Clothes to Cut Out and Color (#1077). Trademark of Mattel, Inc. Whitman Publishing Co., 1971. Includes one paper doll on back cover and clothes to color and cut out. Also has other uncaptioned pictures to color.

Betsy McCall

The Betsy McCall figure began as a monthly paper doll series for the *McCall* magazine during the early 1950s. With the success of these magazine paper dolls, the image of Betsy McCall was expanded to real dolls, paper dolls, and to story and coloring books.

Ideal Toy Corp. made the first doll in 1952. It was a 14″ model with a hard plastic body and a vinyl head. In the early 1960s, the American Character Corp. manufactured several different sizes of a new issue of the doll. The most popular model was the 8″ hard plastic doll with jointed knees and an extensive wardrobe. The doll sold for around $3 during its years of production. The same company also produced a 14″ doll and a 36″ model during these years.

Many different sets of Betsy McCall paper dolls were also manufactured through the years. Whitman Publishing Co. produced a set called, *Betsy McCall* (#1969) in 1971, the same year this coloring book was made.

Cheerful Tearful

Cheerful Tearful was another popular baby doll made by Mattel, Inc. in the 1960s. The doll had a plastic body with vinyl arms, legs, and head. When her arms were moved, her face changed expression from sad to glad. The doll had blonde rooted hair, blue painted eyes, and an open mouth. The 1966 Montgomery Ward catalog listed her price at $7.99.

Betsy McCall Coloring Book (#1069). Copyright The McCall Publishing Co. Whitman Publishing Co., 1971. Contains captioned pictures about Betsy's trip to Hawaii.

The Doll House Family Creative Cut-Outs. Contains five stand up plastic dolls, and clothes to cut out (some printed in color and others for the child to color). The package originally sold for 29 cents, and was #C—102. Made by the Trim Molded Products Co., circa 1950s.

Cheerful Tearful (#1851-E). Trademark of Mattel, Inc. Drawings by Nathalee Mode. Published by Western Publishing Co., 1966. Captioned pictures of the doll.

Dolls to Cut Out An Activity Coloring Book (#3750). Contains five paper dolls with clothes to color plus patterned paper to color and use to make doll clothing. Published by Treasure Books, 1957.

Dollies to Paint Cutout and Dress (#218). Copyright by Saalfield Publishing Co. This book has some dolls like #1180 and also some different. The format is the same. Circa 1920.

Doris Day Coloring Book and Cut Out Dolls and Clothes (#2107). Published by Whitman Publishing Co. Copyright 1953 by Doris Day. Contains two paper dolls on the outside of the book plus printed clothes in color as well as in black and white to be colored. Also contains other captioned Day pictures to color. See personality section for information on Doris Day.

Dollies to Paint, Cut Out, and Dress (#1180). Copyright by The Saalfield Publishing Co., 1918. Contains six different paper dolls and clothing. Each design is printed in both color and black and white.

Drowsy

Mattel, Inc. scored another hit in the toy market when the company produced the "Drowsy" doll in the mid-1960s. The 16" tall doll had a cloth body, arms and legs, and vinyl hands and head. She had rooted blonde hair, painted sleepy blue eyes, and a closed mouth. By pulling her string mechanism the doll could say eleven different phrases. The 1966 Montgomery Ward Christmas catalog listed a Drowsy doll for $4.99.

The doll was also modeled in paper doll form by Whitman Publishing Co. in 1973. The book called *Drowsy: A Cuddly Paper Doll* is #1964.

Rhonda Fleming

Rhonda Fleming appeared in movies for over a decade, but she never really became a star. The beautiful redhead began her film career in 1944 in *Since You Went Away*. She continued to play small parts in *Spellbound* and *The Spiral Staircase*. Then she received a co-starring role in *A Connecticut Yankee In King Arthur's Court* opposite Bing Crosby in 1949. Other Fleming movies include; *Those Redheads From Seattle; The Buster Keaton Story* and *Gunfight at the O.K. Corral*.

G. I. Joe

Hasbro began to make the famous G. I. Joe dolls in 1964. The dolls were unique because they were jointed at the neck, shoulders, elbows, wrists, waists, hips, knees, and ankles. The 12" tall all plastic dolls had either molded or painted features. All kinds of accessories were made for the dolls so they could carry on military activity in any branch of the service. The Sears Christmas catalog for 1964 listed the basic doll for $2.32. Currently there are many people who collect only G. I. Joe dolls and accessories.

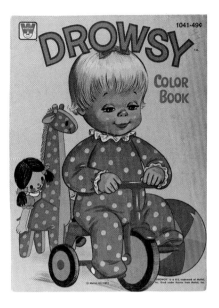

Drowsy Color Book (#1041). Copyright Mattel, Inc., 1976. Published by Whitman Publishing Co. Contains captioned pictures of the doll.

Coronation Paper Dolls and Coloring Book (#4450). Copyright, The Saalfield Publishing Co. Contains four paper dolls (Queen Elizabeth, Prince Philip, Charles and Anne). Also contains four pages of clothes in color and good captioned pictures to color. See history section for more information on the Coronation.

G. I. Joe Action Coloring Book (#1156). Licensed by Hassenfeld Brothers, Inc. Copyright, Hassenfeld Brothers, Inc., 1965. Published by Whitman Publishing Co. Contains captioned pictures of G. I. Joe and Sailors plus equipment pieces.

Rhonda Fleming Paper Dolls and Coloring Book (#4320). Published by Saalfield Publishing Co., 1954. Contains two paper dolls on the back cover and four pages of clothes printed in color. The rest of the book includes captioned pictures to color.

Judy Garland Fashion Paint Book (#674). Published by Whitman Publishing Co., 1940. Contains a paper doll that is not Judy. Photograph and book courtesy of Joseph Golembieski. See personality section for information on Judy Garland.

The Heart Family (#1054). Copyright Mattel, Inc. 1985. Published by Golden Book, Western Publishing Co. Contains uncaptioned pictures of the dolls.

Heart Family

Mattel, Inc. produced the Heart Family dolls during the 1980s. The basic family consisted of a father, mother, and two children. Because the dolls were small, they were perfect models for lots of accessories including cars, furniture, school rooms, playgrounds, etc. The Mattel firm also produced these "extras."

Mary Hartline

Mary Hartline was a favorite television personality with children during the 1950s. She was a regular on the "Super Circus" program on ABC from January 16, 1949 until June 3, 1956. The show offered a variety of circus acts with Jerry Colonna as ringmaster. She was called "TV's Golden Princess," and many children's products were produced to take advantage of her popularity. She was created in a doll image by the Ideal Novelty and Toy Co. in 1953, and Whitman Publishing Co. printed several different sets of paper dolls. Mail order premiums, which included a Mary Hartline paper doll, were offered to children by Kelloggs who sponsored the circus program.

Miss Hartline also had her own children's program called "The Mary Hartline Show" for ABC from February 12, 1951 until June 15, 1951.

Carol Heiss

Champion ice skater, Carol Heiss, was born in 1940 and grew up in Ozone Park, New York. Unlike most earlier skaters, Miss Heiss came from a family that was not well-to-do. Her parents had come from Germany and were working people. Carol received her first pair of ice skates at the age of five and did so well on them that her mother began to take her to the Brooklyn Ice Palace so she could skate.

Several people encouraged Mrs. Heiss to get lessons for the talented youngster, and the family made sacrifices so Carol could be taught by Pierre Brunet. When Carol needed costumes in order to compete in contests, they were made by her mother. Carol eventually changed schools so she could stay in New York for long hours of practice on the ice. She attended the Professional Children's School so she could have more flexible hours.

Carol began winning skating titles at the age of eleven. Her mother died of cancer, however, in 1956, and did not see her daughter win a gold medal for figure skating in the 1960 Olympics held in Squaw Valley, California.

Mary Hartline Cut-Out Dolls Coloring Book (#2104). Copyright M.H.E. Published by Whitman Publishing Co., 1952. Includes two paper dolls and clothing, as well as pictures to color.

Carol Heiss Coloring 'n Cut-Out Book (#1133). Copyright 1961 by Oakwood Enter., Inc. Contains one doll on the back cover plus clothes to color and cut out inside.

In Old New York Colonial Paper Dolls With Pictures to Color (#4411). Published by Saalfield Publishing Co., 1957. Contains two paper dolls on the back cover and printed clothing inside. Also contains captioned pictures to color dealing with colonial times.

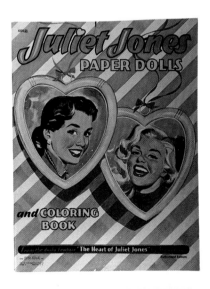

Juliet Jones Paper Dolls and Coloring Book (#4326). Copyright 1955, King Features Syndicate, Inc. Published by Saalfield Publishing Co. From the daily feature "The Heart of Juliet Jones" by Stan Drake. Contains two dolls on back cover, four pages of clothes printed in color, and the rest of the book is to be colored. See section on comics for more information on Juliet Jones.

Kewpie

Although Rose O'Neill was a famous illustrator by the age of fifteen in 1889, she is best known for her invention of the Kewpie character. The first O'Neill Kewpie drawings were published by the *Ladies Home Journal* in December of 1909. The character was so well received that it was turned into a doll in 1912.

The Kewpie doll has sold well for eighty years and it has been produced in bisque, celluloid, cloth, composition, and vinyl. Kewpie has been represented in tiny 3" models to large 36" dolls. Cameo Doll Co. has probably produced the Kewpies longer than any other firm.

Kissy

The Kissy doll was first produced by the Ideal Toy Corp. in 1962. The doll was 22" tall with plastic body and legs, vinyl arms and head, and rooted hair. The tiny Kissy doll was a 16" model and the arms could be pressed together to make her head nod and her mouth pucker with a kissing sound. In 1962, Sears listed the 22" model for $11.44.

Saalfield Publishing Co. also produced a paper doll book called *Kissy Doll*, (#1337) in 1963.

Janet Leigh

Janet Leigh's most memorable film scene is in Alfred Hitchcock's tale of suspense, *Psycho*. The scene in the shower where she is stabbed by Tony Perkins is one which movie goers never forget. Leigh received an Academy Award nomination as best supporting actress for the role.

Leigh's storybook marriage in 1951 to Tony Curtis was publicized in film magazines for many years. The couple had two daughters, Jamie and Kelly. Jamie Lee Curtis has also made a name for herself in films.

Janet Leigh made several other notable movies during her screen career including: *Words and Music; Little Women; That Forsyte Woman; Houdini; Prince Valiant; Pete Kelly's Blues; Bye Bye Birdie;* and *Harper*.

Liddle Kiddles

Mattel, Inc. produced the unique set of 3" vinyl dolls called Liddle Kiddles in the mid-1960s. They had rooted hair, rather large heads, and painted features. There were many different styles of the tiny dolls, and each doll had a different name and outfit complete with small accessories, like a fire truck for Bunson Burnie. Some of the other models included: Calamity Jiddle, Greta Griddle, and Lola Liddle.

Whitman Publishing Co. also produced a paper doll book based on the small dolls called *Liddle Kiddles: 9 Paper Dolls* (#1981) in 1967.

Christmas in Kewpieville (#9546). Copyright 1966 by Jos. L. Kallas. Licensed by Cameo Doll Products. Published by Saalfield Publishing Co. Contains two paper dolls and clothes inside to color and cut-out. Also has wonderful Kewpie illustrations.

Liddle Kiddles Coloring Book (1868-B). Trademark of Mattel, Inc. Published by Western Publishing Co., 1967. Copyright Mattel. Drawings by Frank McSavage. Contains captioned pictures of the dolls.

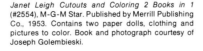

Janet Leigh Cutouts and Coloring 2 Books in 1 (#2554), M-G-M Star. Published by Merrill Publishing Co., 1953. Contains two paper dolls, clothing and pictures to color. Book and photograph courtesy of Joseph Golembieski.

Kissy Coloring and Cutout Book (#9658). Copyright 1963 by Ideal Toy Corporation. Published by Saalfield Publishing Co. Contains one paper doll on the back cover. Inside there are clothes to color and cut out, and other captioned pictures to color.

Mrs. Beasley Coloring Book With Doll and Cut-Out Clothes (1033). Copyright Family Affair Co., 1972. Published by Whitman Publishing Co. A cut-out doll of Mrs. Beasley is on the back cover with clothes to color inside. The rest of the book contains uncaptioned pictures to color.

Donny and Marie (#1641). Copyright Osbro Productions Inc., 1977. A Whitman Book published by Western Publishing Co. Contains two paper dolls (Donny and Marie) on the back cover with clothes to cut out and color inside. The other pictures to color are mostly uncaptioned. See personality section under "Osmonds" for more information about Donny and Marie.

Mrs. Beasley

The Mrs. Beasley doll was made by Mattel, Inc. during the run of the "Family Affair" television program. The show, which ran on CBS from 1966-1971, was about a bachelor father taking care of three children who had lost their parents. The small girl, Jody, (played by Anissa Jones) had a favorite doll called Mrs. Beasley, and the Mattel cloth doll was modeled after this television counterpart. The cloth doll was 22″ tall with rooted hair and a vinyl face. The doll said ten different things when a pull string activated the voice. The Sears 1972 Christmas catalog listed the doll for $10.84.

Kim Novak

Kim Novak was born in Chicago in 1933. Her first film was for RKO, in which she had a small part in *The French Line* in 1954. Kim was then signed by Columbia and appeared in the movie *Pushover* that same year.

Kim Novak became Columbia's biggest female star, taking over the position formerly held by Rita Hayworth. Kim's hit films in 1956: *Picnic*, *The Man With the Golden Arm* (United Artists), and *The Eddy Duchin Story* gave her the title of the most popular female star for the year.

Other successful pictures for Kim Novak include: Hitchcock's *Vertigo* made for Paramount in 1958, and *The Notorious Landlady* from 1962. Although Novak continued to make films into the 1970s, her best pictures are those she did in the 1950s.

Kim Novak Paper Doll s with Pictures to Color (#4409). Published by Saalfield Publishing Co. 1957. Contains two paper dolls, clothing, and pictures to color. Photograph and book courtesy of Joseph Golembieski.

Prince and Princess Paper Dolls With Pictures to Color (#4464). Published by Saalfield Publishing Co., circa 1957. Contains two paper dolls and printed clothing in color. The rest of the book contains uncaptioned pictures to color.

Patience and Prudence Coloring Book (#2532). Copyright by James and Jonathan, Inc., 1957. Drawings by George Pollard. Published by Samuel Lowe Co. The young girls had a hit record in the 1950s and became recording stars for a short while. The book contains paper dolls of the two sisters, plus clothing (all printed in black and white and made to be colored). The rest of the book has captioned pictures to color.

Raggedy Ann and Andy

The Raggedy Ann doll was patented in 1915 by John B. Gruelle (John Barton), and the first Raggedy Ann stories appeared in 1918. The earliest dolls had brown yarn hair instead of the well-known red that tops today's Raggedy Ann. They also had painted features and, of course, were made of cloth. The dolls continue to be manufactured today. Because of the popularity of the dolls, all kinds of products have been made using the Raggedy image including books, paper dolls, doll dishes, games, doll furniture, lamps, and lunch kits.

Jane Russell

The provocative star of *The Outlaw*, Jane Russell, was born in 1921 in Bemidji, Minnesota. She began her career as a model, and then enrolled in Max Reinhardt's theatrical workshop.

Howard Hughes saw her modeling pictures when he was looking for a leading lady for a new western film called *The Outlaw*. He signed Jane for the lead and filming began at RKO in 1941. The project took nine months, and when it was ready for the movie theaters, the Hays Office wouldn't give approval for it to be shown. The film was shelved until 1946 when it was finally made available for public viewing.

Although Hughes kept Jane Russell under contract until his death, she also made films for other studios. Some of her best include: *The Pale Face*; *Son of Paleface*; *Gentlemen Prefer Blondes*; *The French Line*; and *The Tall Men*.

Skipper

Although Mattel, Inc. had produced their first Barbie doll in 1959, it was not until 1963 that Skipper was included in the Barbie family. The Skipper doll was supposed to represent Barbie's little sister. She was 9″ tall with long hair and painted features. In 1965 her straight legs were replaced with knees that would bend.

Whitman Publishing Co. also produced many sets of paper dolls which included a Skipper. The 1964 book was called *Barbie and Skipper* and the 1965 paper dolls were named *Barbie, Midge and Skipper*.

Sunshine Family

Mattel, Inc. made two sets of family dolls during the mid-1970s. The group called the Sunshine Family was white, while the black set was named Happy Family. Each set included three dolls; a father (9½″ tall), a mother (9″ tall), and a baby (3″ tall). The dolls were made of vinyl with rooted hair and painted features. The Mattel Co. also produced many accessories for these dolls, including a house. The set of dolls sold for $5.94 in the Sears Christmas catalog in 1976.

Raggedy Ann and Andy Coloring Book (#2498). Copyright 1944 by The Johnny Gruelle Co. Published by Saalfield Publishing Co. Contains captioned pictures of the dolls' adventures.

Raggedy Ann and Andy Mini—Coloring Book. Copyright 1974, The Bobbs-Merrill Co., Inc. Produced for Hallmark. This is a small sized book.

The Sunshine Family Coloring Book (#1003). Copyright Mattel, Inc. 1975. Published by Whitman Publishing Co. Contains captioned pictures of the dolls as if they were people.

Skipper Barbie's Little Sister (#1115). Copyright MCMLXV Mattel, Inc. Authorized Edition about Barbie's Little Sister. Drawings by Nathalee Mode. Published by Whitman Publishing Co. Contains both captioned and uncaptioned pictures to color.

Jane Russell Paper Dolls and Coloring Book (#4451). Published by Saalfield Publishing Co., 1955. Contains two paper dolls, clothing, and pictures to color. Photograph and book courtesy of Joseph Golembieski.

Tiny Chatty Twins

The Tiny Chatty Twins were a part of Mattel, Inc. Chatty family dolls, which also included Chatty Cathy, Chatty Baby, Chatty Brother, and Charmin' Chatty. Each of the twins was 15" tall and made of plastic and vinyl. They both had rooted hair and sleep eyes. A pull string located in their backs activated voice boxes which said eleven different phrases. The dolls were featured in the Sears Christmas catalog for 1964, and sold for $6.99 each.

Tippy Toes

Tippy Toes, made in 1967, was another successful Mattel, Inc. "active" doll. She was 16" tall with a plastic body and legs, and a vinyl head and arms. She had rooted hair, painted eyes, and an open mouth with two molded teeth. A battery was responsible for her movements when a switch was pushed.

Tubbsy

In 1966 the Ideal Toy Corp. also produced an "active" battery-operated doll. Tubbsy was 18" tall with plastic body and legs, a vinyl head and arms, and an open mouth with two lower teeth. When the battery was activated, the doll's hands splashed in water and the head turned from side to side. The doll had holes in its feet in order for the water to drain out.

Wisnik Trolls

The Wisnik Trolls were also dolls produced in the mid-1960s. The 3" tall vinyl troll figures were dressed in costumes just like other dolls. They sold for $2.49 each in 1966. The Trolls had special names like Flash Troll, Maverik, Ughnik, Grannynik, and Grandpanik. Many people now collect these figures.

Tiny Chatty Twins Coloring Book (#1638). Copyright 1963, Mattel, Inc. Drawings by Nathalee Mode. Whitman Publishing Co. There are two cardboard paperdolls on the back cover, with clothes to color and cut-out inside. The book also contains lots of uncaptioned pictures to color.

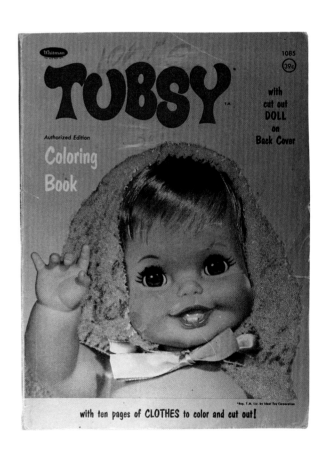

Tubbsy Coloring Book (#1085). Copyright 1968, Ideal Toy Corp. Whitman Publishing Co. Drawings by Nathalee Mode. Paper doll on back cover, with clothes to color and cut-out inside. Captioned pictures.

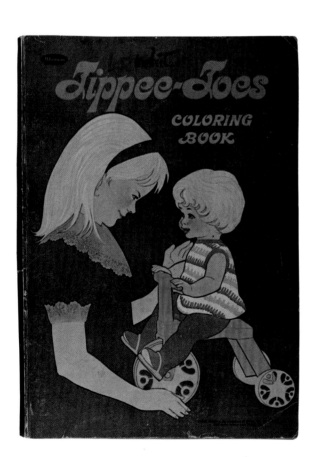

Tippee-Toes Coloring Book (#1656). Trade mark of Mattel, Inc. Copyright 1969, Mattel, Inc. Whitman Publishing Co. Drawings by Virginia Sargent. Book contains both captioned and uncaptioned drawings, a paper doll, and clothes to color and cut-out.

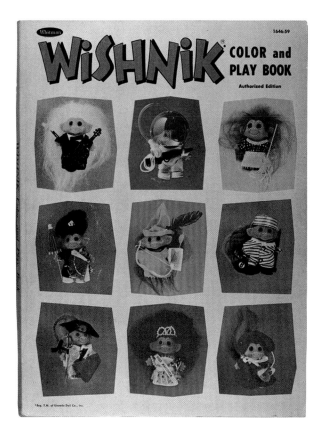

Wishnik Color and Play Book (#1646). Copyright 1966 by Uneeda Doll Co. Inc. Published by Whitman Publishing Co. Drawings by Jason Studios. Contains two paper dolls on the back cover, plus clothes to color and cut out inside. Also has uncaptioned pictures to color.

Esther Williams 2 Books in 1 Cutouts and Coloring (#2553). Published by Merrill Publishing Co., 1953. Contains two paper dolls, clothing, and pictures to color. Photograph and book courtesy of Joseph Golembieski. See personality section for information on Esther Williams.

Loretta Young Paper Dolls and Coloring Book (#4352). Loretta Young, Star of "The Loretta Young Show" NBC—TV. Miss Young's Personal Gowns by Werle'. Cover by Betty Campbell. Published by Saalfield Publishing Co. Contains two paper dolls, clothing, and pictures to color. Photograph and book courtesy of Joseph Golembieski. See personality section for more information on Loretta Young.

Walt Disney Coloring Books

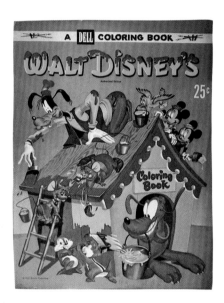

Walt Disney's Coloring Book. Copyright by Walt Disney Productions. Drawings by Walt Disney Studio—adapted by Milt Banta and Dave Hoffman. Published by Dell Publishing Co.

Walt Disney was born in Chicago in 1901. He and his family soon moved to a farm in Missouri where he grew up. Later they sold the farm and settled in Kansas City, Missouri.

After a time as a Red Cross driver in France during World War I, Disney returned to Kansas City where he experimented with animation in film. In 1923 Disney went to Los Angeles to stay with an uncle. After more experimenting, he and an associate, Ub Iwerks, designed Mickey Mouse in 1928 and made the first Mickey Mouse cartoon called "Steamboat Willie."

With this success, Disney went on to make feature animated films beginning with *Snow White and the Seven Dwarfs*, and nature films like *Living Desert*, and live action movies including *Mary Poppins*.

Besides film making, Disney also decided to use his gift of imagination in developing a Magic Kingdom called Disneyland. All of Disney's famous characters played a role in the new park which was dedicated in 1955.

Walt Disney also signed a contract with ABC for a weekly Disneyland television program which first appeared in 1954.

In 1965, land was purchased near Orlando, Florida for the even bigger theme park, Walt Disney World. Disney did not live to see the completion of the project. He died from lung cancer in 1966 and the new park opened in October, 1971.

Besides the coloring books pictured in this chapter, products were also produced for most of the other Disney films including: *Sleeping Beauty; The Three Lives of Thomasina; Pollyanna; Savage Sam; The Misadventures of Merlin Jones; The Monkey's Uncle; The Shaggy Dog; The Absent Minded Professor,* and *The Moon-Spinners.*

All of the Disney "classic" characters have been represented by many coloring books. Several rare books include: *Mickey Mouse Coloring Book* (Saalfield Publishing Co.,1931); *Donald Duck's Paint Book* (Dell Publishing, 1941); and *Dumbo Comic Paint Book* (Dell Publishing, 1941).

Alice in Wonderland

Alice in Wonderland, a 1951 Disney animated film was not as well liked by critics as some of the earlier studio productions. The movie was popular enough however, to begin its re-release life in 1974. The picture had some good songs including "I'm Late" and "The Unbirthday Song." The film, of course, was based on the story by Lewis Carroll.

Bambi

Bambi was a very popular Disney animated film dating from 1942. Although some children found the forest fire scene a bit scary, the movie enjoyed success as a re-release. Besides Bambi, other characters included Thumper the rabbit, and Flower the skunk. The story, "A Life in the Woods," by Felix Salten, provided the basis for the film.

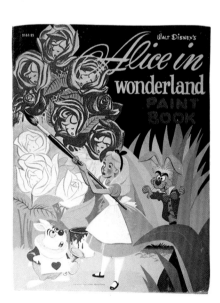

Walt Disney's Alice in Wonderland Paint Book (#2167). Copyright 1951, Walt Disney Productions. Drawings by Walt Disney Studio—adapted by Bob Grant. Published by Whitman Publishing Co. Contains captioned pictures of story.

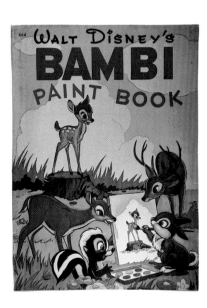

Walt Disney's Bambi Paint Book (#664). Copyright 1941, 1942 by Walt Disney Productions. Based on "Bambi, A Life in the Woods" by Felix Salten. Published by Whitman Publishing Co. Contains long captioned pictures which tell the story.

Bedknobs and Broomsticks

Bedknobs and Broomsticks was a Disney live action film produced in 1971 starring Angela Lansbury, David Tomlinson, and Roddy McDowall. The plot dealt with a witch who helped the British cause during World War II. The musical had some animated cartoon sequences, and won an Oscar for special effects.

The Black Hole

The Black Hole, a science fiction Walt Disney Studio movie from 1979, inspired the coloring book of the same name. The stars of the film included Maximilian Schell, Anthony Perkins, Ernest Borgnine, Yvette Mimieux and Robert Forster.

Blackbeard's Ghost

Blackbeard's Ghost was a live action Disney comedy from 1968. Starring in the picture were Peter Ustinov and Dean Jones. Ustinov, as Blackbeard, helped Dean Jones protect his home from racketeers who wanted to turn it into a casino.

Bon Voyage

Bon Voyage was a 1962 Disney comedy film about a typical American family and their troubles during a trip to Europe. The movie starred Fred MacMurray and Jane Wyman.

Cinderella

Cinderella, made in 1950, was Walt Disney's first animated feature film since 1942. The picture was a box office hit, and also did well as a re-release.

Walt Disney's Bambi Coloring Book (#1006). Copyright Walt Disney Productions. MCMXLI, MCMLXVI. Published by Whitman, Western Publishing Co. Contains captioned pictures.

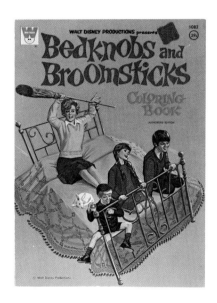

Walt Disney Productions Presents Bedknobs and Broomsticks Coloring Book (#1082). Copyright 1971, Walt Disney Productions. Published by Whitman Publishing Co. Contains captioned pictures from the movie.

Walt Disney Productions' The Black Hole Coloring Book (#1002). Copyright 1979 by Walt Disney Productions. Published by Whitman Publishing Co. Contains captioned pictures from the film.

Walt Disney Presents Blackbeard's Ghost Coloring Book (#1090). Copyright 1968 by Walt Disney Productions. Drawings by Al Anderson, Sparky Moore, and Ellis Eringer. Published by Whitman Publishing Co. Captioned pictures from the movie.

Walt Disney's Cinderella Paint Book (#2092). Copyright 1950, Walt Disney Productions. Published by Whitman Publishing Co. Contains captioned pictures from the animated film.

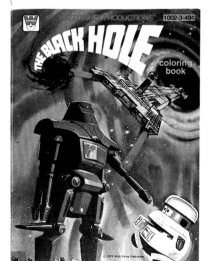

Walt Disney's Bon Voyage! Coloring Book (#1138). Copyright 1962, Walt Disney Productions. Book by Joseph and Marijane Hayes. Drawings by Al Anderson and Adam Szwejkowski. Published by Whitman Publishing Co. Contains captioned pictures from the movie.

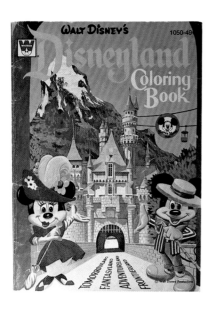

Walt Disney Edition Daniel Boone Coloring Book (#1116). Copyright 1961, Walt Disney Productions. Featuring characters from the Disney TV series based on the book *Daniel Boone* by John Bakeless. Drawings by Adam Szwejkowski. Published by Whitman Publishing Co. Contains captioned pictures.

Daniel Boone

"Daniel Boone" was a Walt Disney television production that appeared on NBC from 1964 to 1970. It then became a syndicated series of 165 episodes. The program was based on the famous pioneer frontiersman, Daniel Boone. Many of his adventures, both real and imaginary, were recounted on the show.

Disneyland

Disneyland was dedicated on July 17, 1955. It was built by W.E.D. Enterprises in Orange County, California. The original park had five themed areas: Main Street, Adventureland, Frontierland, Fantasyland, and Tomorrowland. In the mid-1960s another theme was added when New Orleans Square was opened. The original park cost $17 million.

Donald Duck

Donald Duck, as a character, was first shown in the 1934 cartoon, "The Wise Little Hen." He was developed for Disney by Dick Lundy and Fred Spencer. Donald's voice belonged to Clarence Nash. Donald Duck became the second most popular Disney character (next to Mickey Mouse).

Dumbo

Dumbo, one of the best of the Disney animated films, was made in 1941. Dumbo was a baby elephant with large ears. His friend, Timothy the Mouse, helped build his confidence and he discovered he could fly. Sterling Holloway was Dumbo's voice and Frank Churchill and Oliver Wallace received an Oscar for scoring the film.

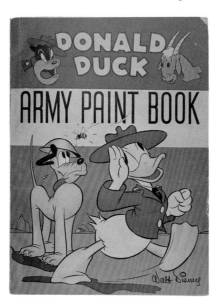

Donald Duck Army Paint Book (#668). Copyright 1942 by Walt Disney Productions. Published by Whitman Publishing Co. Captioned pictures to color.

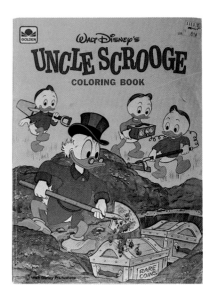

Walt Disney's Uncle Scrooge Coloring Book. Copyright 1978, Walt Disney Productions. Golden Book, published by Western Publishing Co. Contains captioned pictures.

Walt Disney's Dumbo Cut-Out Coloring Book (#F5047). Copyright 1953 by Walt Disney Productions. Pictures by Walt Disney Studio, adapted by Dick Moores. Published by Pocket Books, Inc. Cut-outs to color and cut out on backs of covers.

Walt Disney's Disneyland Coloring Book (#1050). Copyright MCMLXV, Walt Disney Productions. Published by Whitman Publishing Co. Contains captioned pictures from the park.

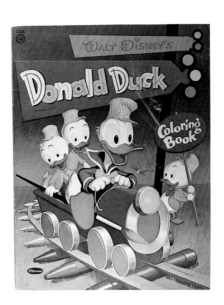

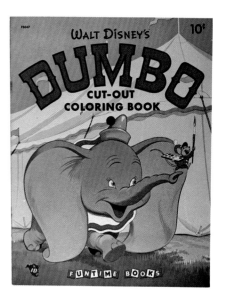

Walt Disney's Donald Duck Coloring Book (#1326). Copyright 1957, Walt Disney Productions. Drawings by Walt Disney Studio. Adapted by Milt Banta and Dave Hoffman. Published by Whitman Publishing Co. Contains captioned pictures.

Ferdinand the Bull

"Ferdinand the Bull" was a Disney Silly Symphony cartoon from 1938. The Silly Symphonies were more than just illustrated songs, they were films which combined music and animation so that they worked well together.

"Ferdinand the Bull" was based on the "Story of Ferdinand" by Munro Leaf and Robert Lawson. The story was about a bull named Ferdinand who did not want to fight in the bull fights. When some men were looking for a tough bull to use in the fights, Ferdinand happened to have just been stung by a bee and he was raging and pawing so fiercely that the men chose him for the ring. When Ferdinand was taken to the stadium, he sat and smelled the flowers thrown by the crowd and wouldn't fight. Because of his failure as a fighter, Ferdinand was taken back to his pasture where he lived happily ever after.

Fun and Fancy Free

Fun and Fancy Free was an animated cartoon feature with some live action. The film had two stories that were introduced by Jiminy Cricket. "Bongo" is the first story about a circus bear who is tired of life in the circus so he escapes to the forest.

The other story, told by Edgar Bergen, is a Disney take-off on "Jack and the Bean Stalk" with Mickey Mouse playing the part of Jack. Voices in the 1948 picture belonged to Dinah Shore, Edgar Bergen, and Charlie McCarthy.

Hardy Boys

The Hardy Boys characters, based on the stories by Franklin W. Dixon (joint pseudonym), appeared on several series of "The Mickey Mouse Club" in the mid-1950s. One adventure was "Mystery of the Applegate Treasure," and another was "Hardy Boys and the Mystery of Ghost Farm." Tim Considine and Tommy Kirk played the parts of Frank and Joe Hardy.

In Search of the Castaways

In Search of the Castaways was based on a Jules Verne adventure. The plot involves an expedition trying to locate a missing sea captain. The film, made in 1962, starred Hayley Mills, Maurice Chevalier, and George Sanders.

The Jungle Book

The Jungle Book is a Walt Disney animated film from 1967. Walt Disney died in 1966 before it was finished. The movie was based on the Mowgli Stories by Rudyard Kipling. Voices of the characters were those of Phil Harris, George Sanders, Sterling Holloway, Louis Prima, Verna Felton, Pat O'Malley, and Sebastian Cabot.

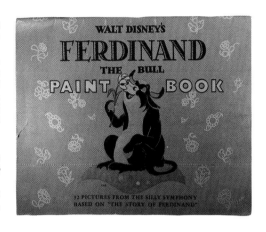

Walt Disney's Ferdinand the Bull Paint Book (#645). 32 Pictures From the Silly Symphony Based on "The Story of Ferdinand" by Muno Leaf and Robert Lawson. Copyright 1938, Walt Disney Enterprises. Published by Whitman Publishing Co. Captioned pictures tell the story of Ferdinand.

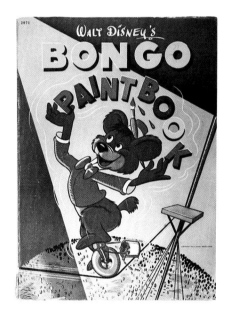

Walt Disney's Bongo Paint Book (#2071). From Motion Picture *Fun and Fancy Free*. Copyright 1948, Walt Disney Productions. Published by Whitman Publishing Co. Besides Bongo, the book also has lots of pictures of other Disney characters.

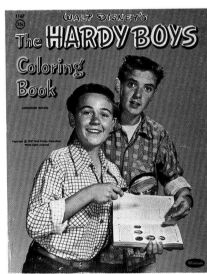

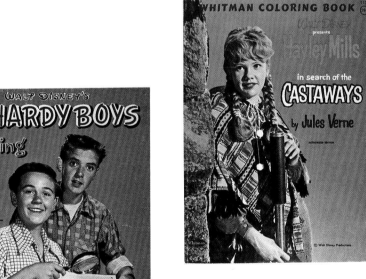

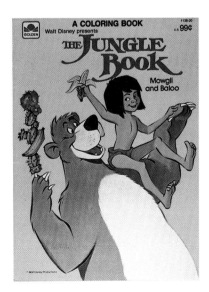

Walt Disney's The Hardy Boys Coloring Book (#1167). Copyright 1957, Walt Disney Productions. Drawings by John Usher. Published by Whitman Publishing Co. Captioned pictures tell a story from the series.

Walt Disney presents In Search of the Castaways (#1138) by Jules Verne. Hayley Mills is pictured on the cover. Copyright 1962 by Walt Disney Productions. Drawings by Adam Szwejkowski. Published by Whitman Publishing Co. Contains captioned pictures from the film.

Walt Disney Presents The Jungle Book Mowgli and Baloo (#1138). Copyright 1967, Walt Disney Productions. Adapted from the Mowgli Stories by Rudyard Kipling. A Golden Book by Western Publishing Co. Captioned pictures from the film.

Lady and the Tramp

Lady and the Tramp was a very successful animated Disney film from 1955. The movie used the cinemascope format, and was set in the modern time period. The story of the two very different dogs and their romance is enjoyable for children and adults alike.

Mary Poppins

Mary Poppins was one of the most successful films the Disney Studios had produced up to 1964. Directed by Robert Stevenson, the movie starred Julie Andrews and Dick Van Dyke. The story was about the Banks family who lived in London in 1910, and their "practically perfect nanny," Mary Poppins. The story was based on the Mary Poppins books written by P.L. Travers. Julie Andrews was given the Academy Award Best Actress award for her role, and Richard and Robert Sherman received an Oscar for the songs, including "Chim-Chim-Cheree."

Mickey Mouse

Mickey Mouse, as a cartoon character, was born in 1928. He was created by Walt Disney and Ub Iwerks. The cartoon, which starred Mickey, was originally planned as a silent film but with the advent of sound, it was changed to include the new medium. Disney developed the music and the action of his cartoons so they worked together.

Mickey Mouse became so popular that, by 1930, he was known around the world, and in 1931 *Time* magazine did a feature on the cute cartoon character. He has been the basis for television shows ("The Mickey Mouse Club"), countless cartoons, products too numerous to mention, and theme parks in California, Florida, Japan, and France.

Walt Disney's Lady and the Tramp Coloring Book (#1183). Copyright 1954, Walt Disney Productions. Drawings by Walt Disney Studio, adapted by Joe Rinald. Published by Whitman Publishing Co. Contains captioned pictures from the film.

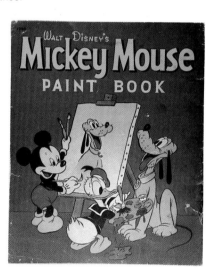

Walt Disney's Mickey Mouse Paint Book (#1069). Copyright 1937, Walt Disney Enterprises/1942 Walt Disney Productions. Published by Whitman Publishing Co. Contains uncaptioned pictures to color.

Walt Disney Presents Mary Poppins Coloring Book (1112). Copyright 1966, Walt Disney Productions. From the book by P. L. Travers. Drawings by Nathalee Mode. Published by Whitman Publishing Co. Contains pictures from the film.

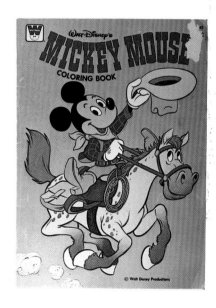

Walt Disney presents Mary Poppins Color and Read. Copyright 1973, Walt Disney Productions. Based on books by P. L. Travers. Published by Whitman Publishing Co. Pictures are already partly filled with color and the book includes a story based on the movie.

Walt Disney's Mickey Mouse Coloring Book. Copyright Walt Disney Productions MCMLXXIX, MCMLXXVI. Published by Whitman Publishing Co. Contains mostly uncaptioned pictures.

The Mickey Mouse Club

"The Mickey Mouse Club" began as an ABC television program on October 3, 1955. It ran until September, 1959. Jimmie Dodd and Roy Williams were hosts. Some of the more famous Mouseketeers were: Annette Funicello, Darlene Gillespie, "Chubby" O'Brien, Karen Pendleton, Bobby Burgess, and Cheryl Holdridge. The program had music, cartoons, children's news features, adventure serials, and guest celebrities.

"The Mickey Mouse Club" was revised twice in syndication.

Million Dollar Duck

Although the Walt Disney movie, *Million Dollar Duck* is not one of the classic films from the studio, it did provide material for tie-in products like a coloring book produced in 1971.

The plot of the movie concerned a duck that had been a reject from an experimental lab and became a pet for the son of Professor Albert Dooley. When the family discovered the duck could lay golden eggs because of a quirk from the earlier experiments, they thought they had struck it rich. Soon the family was under investigation because the U.S. Treasury Department was trying to discover the origin of the gold nuggets. At the time the duck was to be taken away, her powers disappeared, and she became just a household pet again.

Old Yeller

Old Yeller is a 1957 Disney film based on the book of the same name by Fred Gibson. The movie starred Dorothy McGuire, Fess Parker, Tommy Kirk, and Chuck Connors. The story takes place in Texas in 1859 and is about a boy and his dog.

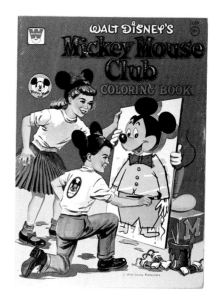

Walt Disney's Mickey Mouse Club Coloring Book (#1059). Copyright MCMLVII, Walt Disney Productions. Published by Whitman Publishing Co. Contains captioned pictures but little identification on Mouseketeers pictured.

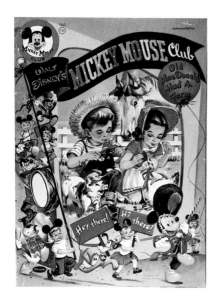

Walt Disney's Mickey Mouse Club Old MacDonald Had a Farm (#1863). Copyright 1955, Walt Disney Productions. Pictures by Walt Disney Studio. Published by Whitman Publishing Co. Contains captioned pictures, not much to do with Mickey, mostly farm related.

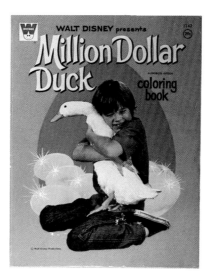

Walt Disney presents Million Dollar Duck Coloring Book (#1142). Copyright Walt Disney Productions, 1971. Published by Whitman Publishing Co. Contains captioned pictures based on the film.

Walt Disney's Old Yeller Coloring Book (#1199). Based on book by Fred Gibson. Copyright 1957 by Walt Disney Productions. Published by Whitman Publishing Co. Contains captioned pictures from the film.

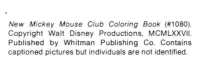

New Mickey Mouse Club Coloring Book (#1080). Copyright Walt Disney Productions, MCMLXXVII. Published by Whitman Publishing Co. Contains captioned pictures but individuals are not identified.

One Hundred and One Dalmatians

One Hundred and One Dalmatians, released in 1961, was one of Disney's best animated movies. The dogs and the villains both added much to the story. Cruella de Vil is one of the best of the Disney wicked characters. The film was based on a story by Dodie Smith.

Peter Pan

Peter Pan, the character created by Sir J. M. Barrie, was made into a feature film by the Disney studio in 1952. All the old favorites: Wendy, Tiger Lily, Tinker Bell, Captain Hook and Peter were included in this very good animated movie.

Pinocchio

Some Disney fans say *Pinocchio* is Disney's greatest animated film. It was released in 1940 to good reviews, but it was not the big box office success of the other Disney movies. The plot involves a puppet that wants to become a real boy. The Jiminy Cricket character was especially liked by the movie audience. The film won an Oscar for the song, "When You Wish Upon a Star."

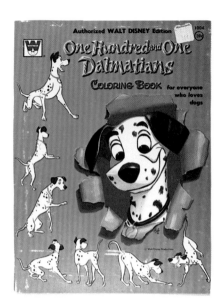

Authorized Walt Disney Edition One Hundred and One Dalmatians Coloring Book (#1004). Based on a book by Dodie Smith. Copyright Walt Disney Productions, MCMLX. Pictures by Walt Disney Studio. Published by Whitman Publishing Co. Captioned pictures.

Walt Disney's Pinocchio Paint Book. Copyright 1939 by Walt Disney Productions. Contains illustrations from the Walt Disney Motion Picture. Published by Whitman Publishing Co.

Walt Disney's Peter Pan Coloring Book (#2186). Copyright 1952 by Walt Disney Productions. Drawings by Dick Moores. Published by Whitman Publishing Co. Story (originally by Sir James Barrie) told in captioned pictures.

The Rescuers

The Rescuers was made in 1977 and was the twenty-second full length animated feature film made by the Walt Disney studio. The story concerns two brave mice who try to rescue a kidnapped girl. Voices in the movie included those of: Jim Jordon, Eva Gabor, Bob Newhart, and Geraldine Page.

Snow White and the Seven Dwarfs

Although Walt Disney had already made many movie animated cartoons, it was not until 1937 that the first Disney animated feature film was completed. RKO presented a preview of the new movie, *Snow White and the Seven Dwarfs* in December of that same year. The Disney picture was a wonderful story for children which featured many memorable characters, including the Dwarfs: Sleepy, Bashful, Sneezy, Dopey, Happy, Grumpy, and Doc. Snow White, the Prince, and the Queen also played big parts in the film. The movie was an instant success. By the mid-1950s it had grossed over eight million dollars, and was recently re-released to celebrate its fiftieth birthday. Again the film has entranced and entertained a whole new generation of youngsters. Popular songs by Larry Morey and Frank Churchill written for the picture include: "Some Day My Prince Will Come" and "Whistle While You Work."

Son of Flubber

The 1963 *Son of Flubber* movie was a sequel to the more successful film, *The Absent Minded Professor*. Fred MacMurray was again the star, with more silly inventions as part of the plot.

Walt Disney's Snow White and the Seven Dwarfs Paint Book. Copyright 1938 by Walt Disney Enterprises. Published by Whitman Publishing Co. Captioned pictures tell the story from the film.

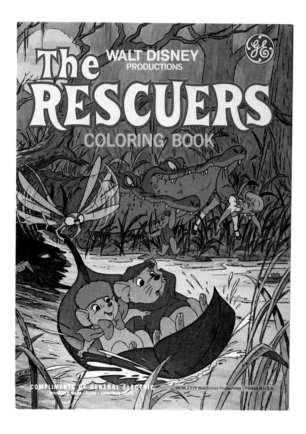

Walt Disney Productions The Rescuers Coloring Book. Compliments of General Electric. MCMLXXVIII, Walt Disney Productions. Contains captioned pictures.

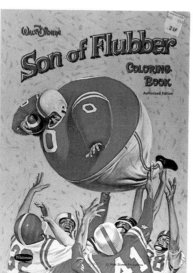

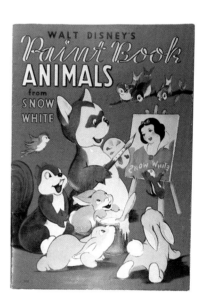

Walt Disney's Paint Book Animals from Snow White (#606). Copyright Walt Disney Enterprises, 1938. Published by Whitman Publishing Co. Pictures only the animals from the film, not Snow White or the Dwarfs.

Walt Disney's Son of Flubber Coloring Book. Copyright 1963, Walt Disney Productions. Drawings by Adam Szwejkowski and Fred Fixler. Published by Whitman Publishing Co. Captioned pictures from the movie.

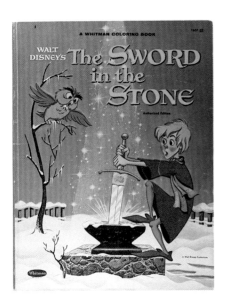

Walt Disney's The Sword in the Stone (#1637). Copyright 1963, Walt Disney Productions. Original story by T. H. White. Drawings by Tony Strobi, John Liggera, and William Lorencz. Published by Whitman Publishing Co. Contains captioned pictures.

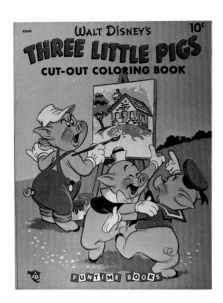

Walt Disney's Three Little Pigs Cut-Out Coloring Book (#F 5049). Copyright 1953 by Walt Disney Productions. Pictures by Walt Disney Studio adapted by Bob Grant. Published by Pocket Books, Inc. Captioned pictures tell the story. Contains cut-outs to color and cut out on backs of both covers.

The Sword in the Stone

In 1963, the Disney studios made an animated King Arthur film called *The Sword in the Stone*. The story featured Wart, a young boy who became King Arthur and Merlin the Magician. The movie was based on the book of the same name by T. H. White.

The Three Little Pigs

The Disney animation of *The Three Little Pigs*, made in 1933, was the first of the Disney films to use character and plot development. Although the cartoon was not a full length feature, it was the next step from the usual cartoon to the full length movie. The film also provided the first hit song from a Disney film with "Who's Afraid of the Big Bad Wolf?"

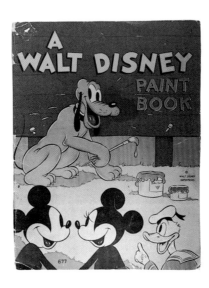

A Walt Disney Paint Book (#677). Copyright 1937 by Walt Disney Enterprises. Published by Whitman Publishing Co. Contains early pictures of Mickey, Goofy, and other Disney characters. Pluto, the Bloodhound, first made his appearance in 1930 in "The Chain Gang." Goofy played a supporting role for the first time in 1932 in "Mickey's Revue."

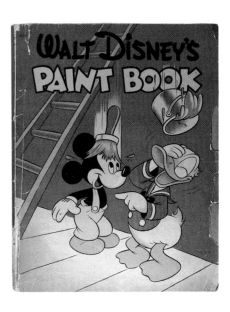

Walt Disney's Paint Book. Copyright 1944 by Walt Disney Productions. Published by Whitman Pub. Co. Contains captioned pictures of Mickey, Donald, Minnie, and many other Disney characters.

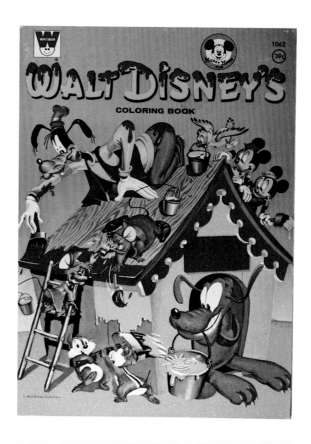

Winnie the Pooh

The Disney studios made two featurette films in the 1960s using A.A. Milne's Winnie the Pooh character for both. The first film was "Winnie the Pooh and the Hang Tree" in 1966 and the second was "Winnie the Pooh and the Blustery Day" in 1968. Both animated pictures featured Tigger, Eeyore, and Pooh Bear.

Zorro

"Zorro" was a thirty minute television series shown on ABC from 1957 to 1959. It was a Walt Disney Production starring Guy Williams. The story took place in Monterey, California around 1820. Williams played a dual role: Don Diego de la Vega, a man about town character; and the same man when he became the masked rider, Zorro. Zorro was a defender of the weak and oppressed, and he participated in many adventures while he tried to help the cause of justice.

Walt Disney presents Winnie the Pooh (#1058). Copyright MCMLXV, Walt Disney Productions. Published by Whitman Publishing Co.

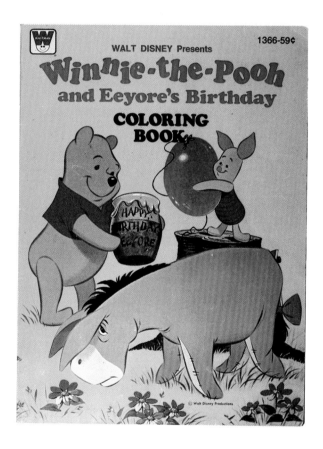

Walt Disney Presents Winnie-the-Pooh and Eeyore's Birthday Coloring Book (#1366). Copyright 1976 by Walt Disney Productions. Published by Whitman Publishing Co. Story by A. A. Milne.

Walt Disney's Zorro Coloring Book (#1158). From "Zorro" Television Series based on famous characters created by Johnston McCulley, MCMLVIII. Walt Disney Productions. Published by Whitman Publishing Co. Pictures by John Steel and Tony Pawlo.

Movie Related Coloring Books

The movie books are harder to locate when one does not include the Walt Disney category. In order to make tie-in toys profitable, the subject must appeal to children. Most movies are made for teens or adults, so coloring books are usually not designed for a film promotion unless it is a film made especially for the child trade. There have been several exceptions, and some of these books are now the most desirable and collectible of the movie coloring books. These include the *Gone With the Wind Paint Book* and *Ziegfeld Girl Paint Book*. Both of these books were successful as child products because of the publicity generated by the GWTW picture, and because of the many stars included in the Ziegfeld book. Therefore the only movie coloring books now made are the ones relating to children's films or the big budget super films like those made by Steven Spielberg.

Around the World in 80 Days

Around the World in 80 Days was a film spectacular which featured fifty stars, 68,894 extras and 74,685 costumes. It was filmed in thirteen different countries at a cost of over six million dollars. The movie was produced by Mike Todd and was based on the novel by Jules Verne. It received the Academy Award for best picture in 1956 as well as awards for writing, cinematography, film editing, and music. The stars of the film were David Niven as Phileas Fogg and Cantinflas as his man Passepartout. Many of the biggest Hollywood stars played cameo roles in the picture including: Frank Sinatra, Peter Lorre, Gilbert Roland, Charles Boyer, Marlene Dietrich, George Raft, Buster Keaton, and Shirley MacLaine. The movie was directed by Michael Anderson and released by United Artists.

Ben-Hur

The *Ben-Hur* movies were based on the book of the same name by Lew Wallace. The first film was a silent feature made in 1926 that starred Ramon Novarro and Francis X. Bushman. In the 1959 version Charlton Heston and Stephen Boyd starred. Heston won the Academy Award for Best Actor and the film was honored with an Academy Award for the best movie of the year. The picture also received nine other Oscars. The action takes place in Palestine during the time of Christ. The highlight of the film was the magnificent chariot race.

Pippi Longstocking (#1040). Copyright G.G. Communications, Inc. A Whitman Book. Copyright 1975 with permission of Astrid Lindgren and Merchandising Munich. The movie, *The New Adventures of Pippi Longstocking*, was based on the novels of Astrid Lindgren. Tami Erin and Eileen Brennan were stars of the picture. The plot involves redhaired Pippi in her adventures as she starts housekeeping in an abandoned mansion.

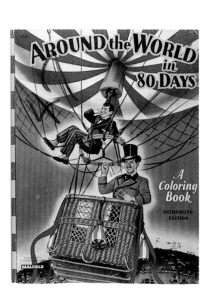

Ben-Hur Pictures to Color Based on MGM's Great New Motion Picture (#2998), directed by William Wyler. Copyright 1959, Loew's Incorp. Illustrations by George Pollar. Lowe Publishing Co. Captioned pictures tell the story.

Around the World in 80 Days (#4828). Based on the Michael Todd production of the story—*Around the World in 80 Days* by Jules Verne. Cover and Drawings by George Pollard. Published by The Saalfield Publishing Co. 1957. Contains short captions which tell the story.

Benji

Benji was a popular film in 1974 about a dog who participates in the rescue of two small children who are being kidnapped. Joe Camp originated the character "Benji." The dog was also featured in the movie *For the Love of Benji* and then starred on a television series.

Chitty Chitty Bang Bang

Chitty Chitty Bang Bang was a musical film for children released in 1968. The picture was based on a book by Ian Fleming about a flying car. Starring in the movie were Dick Van Dyke and Sally Ann Howes.

The Christmas That Almost Wasn't

The film called *The Christmas That Almost Wasn't* was an Italian—U.S. film from 1970 starring Rossano Brazzi, Paul Tripp, and Lidia Brazzi. The plot of the picture involved Santa Claus trying to earn money to pay taxes on the North Pole. He secured a job as a department store Santa, but when that didn't work out, children everywhere donated their pennies in order to save Christmas.

Doctor Doolittle

In 1967, Twentieth Century-Fox produced a children's movie based on the popular Dr. Dolittle stories written by Hugh Lofting. The movie was responsible for many toy tie-in materials including dolls and paper products. The coloring book pictured here was one of those toys. The film starred Rex Harrison, Samantha Eggar, Richard Attenborough, and Anthony Newley. The musical was nominated for best picture of the year. It was directed by Richard Fleischer.

Chitty Chitty Bang Bang Coloring Book (#1654). Copyright 1968 by Glidrose Productions Ltd. and Warfield Prod. Drawings by Jason Studios. Captioned pictures of scenes from the film.

Joe Camp's Benji (#1010-2). Published by Whitman Publishing Co. Copyright 1979, Mulberry Sq. Prod. Inc. Contains captioned and uncaptioned pictures which tell the story of one of Benji's adventures.

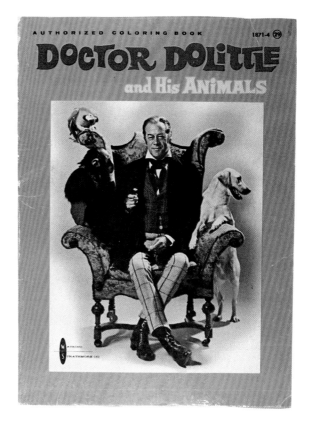

Doctor Doolittle and His Animals (#1871-4). Copyright 1967 20th Century Fox Film Corp. and Apjac Product Inc. Drawings by Jason Studios. Published by Watkins—Strathmore Co. Captioned pictures of Doolittle, animals and other characters from the film.

The Christmas That Almost Wasn't Coloring Book (#9540). Copyright MCMLXX, Childhood Productions, Inc. Published by The Saalfield Publishing Co.

Gone With the Wind Paint Book (#3403). A Selznick International Picture, M-G-M Release. Published by Merrill Publishing Co., 1940. Contains captioned pictures from the screen play.

Gone With the Wind

Gone With the Wind, one of the most popular movies ever, premiered in Atlanta, Georgia on December 14, 1939. The film was based on the best selling novel by Margaret Mitchell which had skyrocketed to success in 1936. David O. Selznick bought the film rights for $50,000 and began shooting the movie in January, 1939 with filming finishing in July. The public had insisted that Clark Gable play the part of Rhett Butler, and a nation-wide search was launched by Selznick to find a girl to play Scarlet. After Selznick had tested all the Hollywood hopefuls, he was still without a star. At last, as shooting was about to begin, Selznick's brother Myron, introduced him to Vivien Leigh, an English girl, and she won the role. Other cast members included: Leslie Howard, Olivia de Havilland, and Thomas Mitchell.

Several directors worked on the film including George Cukor, Victor Fleming, and Sam Wood. The movie lasted three hours and forty-two minutes, the longest film ever made. It won ten Academy Awards including Best Actress for Leigh, and Best Supporting actress for Hattie McDaniel. The film also captured the Best Picture award.

"Goodby, Mr. Chips"

This coloring book dates from the "Goodbye, Mr. Chips" film from 1969. It was a musical remake of the classic 1939 movie that won an Oscar for Robert Donat. The newer version starred Peter O'Toole, Petula Clark, and Michael Redgrave. O'Toole played the role of the teacher, while Clark was a showgirl.

Raiders of the Lost Ark

Raiders of the Lost Ark was one of the super hit movies made by Steven Spielberg. The film won Oscars for five technical aspects of the picture. Harrison Ford played Indiana Jones, an archeologist who was searching for the religious Ark. The cast members experienced many adventures before the end of the 1981 movie.

Return of the Jedi

Return of the Jedi was another blockbuster movie that was the third in the series of Star Wars (1977) films. The movie, released in 1983, starred Mark Hamill, Harrison Ford, Carrie Fisher, and Billy Dee Williams. The Star Wars series is in the tradition of the old Flash Gordon Saturday matinee serials, only with lots more special effects.

These science fiction films, which also included The Empire Strikes Back from 1980, offer plenty of excitement for the audience as Luke Skywalker and Princess Leia go on their many adventures.

"Goodbye, Mr. Chips" A Coloring Book Based on the MGM Motion Picture (#9569). Copyright 1969 Metro-Goldwyn-Mayer. Published by The Saalfield Publishing Co. Contains captioned pictures of scenes from the movie.

Raiders of the Lost Ark Things To Do and Color. Copyright by Lucas Film, Ltd., illustrations by Ken Barr. Random House, 1981. Contains puzzles and uncaptioned pictures of the cast to color.

Star Wars Return of the Jedi Coloring Book. Copyright Lucas Film Ltd. (LFL) 1983. TM owned by Lucas Film Ltd. Used by Kenner Products under authorization. Illustrations created and drawn by Susan Nelson. Contains very nice, mostly uncaptioned, pictures from the film.

Thief of Bagdad

The *Thief of Bagdad* was a British fantasy film made in 1940 (released by United Artists). It was an "Arabian Nights" fable directed by Lidwig Berger. The native boy was played by Sabu, while Rex Ingram and Tim Whelan were also in the picture. The special effects made the film memorable.

Valley of Gwangi

Valley of Gwangi was a film released in 1969 to take advantage of the old theme about man finding a prehistoric monster. In this movie, the adventurers locate a monster in Mexico, and decide to make money by capturing the creature and exhibiting it in the United States. More adventures follow which include some good special effects.

Ziegfeld Girl

The musical film, *Ziegfeld Girl*, was made in 1941 by Metro-Goldwyn-Mayer with an all star cast and was one of the biggest hits of the year. The story followed the careers of three Ziegfeld show girls. The parts were played by Judy Garland, Hedy Lamarr and Lana Turner. The male interest was provided by James Stewart, Tony Martin, and Philip Dorn. In the film, Judy became a star, Hedy made a wealthy marriage, and Lana became an alcoholic. It was produced by Pandro S. Berman and directed by Robert Z. Leonard. Busby Berkeley did the musical numbers.

Alexander Korda's The Thief of Bagdad Coloring Book (#1430). Copyright 1940, Alexander Korda. Adapted from the Technicolor Production published by The Saalfield Publishing Co. Contains captioned pictures of scenes from the film.

The Valley of Gwangi a Coloring Book (#9568), Charles H. Schneer Production. (#9568). Warner Brothers Seven Arts. Filmed in Dynamation, 1969. Published by The Saalfield Publishing Co. Contains captioned pictures from the film.

Ziegfeld Girl Paint Book (#3465). "An M-G-M Picture." Published by Merrill Publishing Co., 1941. The six principal cast members are featured in pictures in the book.

Advertising Coloring Books

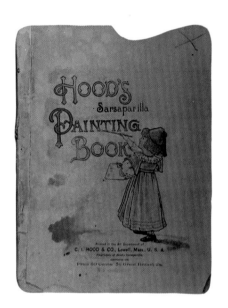

Hood's Sarsaparilla Painting Book. Copyright 1894 by C. L. Hood and Co.

Although the newer advertising coloring books aren't in too much demand, the early ones are sought after by advertising collectors as well as by people interested in coloring books.

The C.I. Hood Co. was one of the first to use the idea of advertising through coloring books. The Hood Co., located in Lowell, Massachusetts, manufactured Hood's Sarsaparilla and advertised it as a great blood purifier and building up medicine. The company also sold Hood's Pills, tooth powder, olive ointment, and other patent medicines. The Hood's Sarsaparilla Painting Book was published in 1894 to promote the company's sarsaparilla. It could only be purchased by sending three trademarks from the product plus twelve cents in stamps to the Hood Company. The paint book itself follows the trend of the day with one picture already colored and the same picture on the opposite page uncolored so the children could match the colors.

Many of the pictures advertised the company's products. Included are drawings of the Hood Laboratory, the Hood farm, several regular Hood advertisements, and ads for other advertising toys, including paper dolls and puzzles. Other early firms using advertising coloring books include Pingree, who produced The Pingree Drawing Book to help sell the company's shoes. White House Coffee also used the coloring book in 1902 when they gave Little Artists as a free premium to promote their coffee. This book had simple water color paints for coloring the pictures.

Advertising coloring books continue to be used to sell goods. Perhaps the new concept of combining both a business and a movie in a coloring book, in order to promote both products, will continue to grow and will be the wave of the future for advertising coloring books.

The Rainbow Brite "I'm a Fit Kid" Coloring Book. Copyright 1983 by Hallmark Cards in cooperation with The American Academy of Family Physicians and the President's Council on Physical Fitness and Sports. Contains a physical fitness message for children with pictures showing exercises.

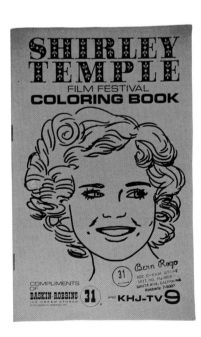

Shirley Temple Film Festival Coloring Book. Compliments of Baskin-Robbins Ice Cream Stores. Copyright Baskin-Robbins, Inc. 31 Flavors. KHJ-TV9 (California). Book printed to promote both the ice cream and the old Shirley Temple movies featured on television.

Acey Won the West. Undated. The pictures promote various products served by the Arctic Circle Drive In.

Big Boy Patriotic Coloring Book, Big Boy Restaurants 1976. Contains early U. S. History pictures which tie-in with the country's Bicentennial that year.

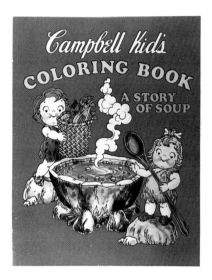

Campbell Kids' Coloring Book A Story of Soup. Copyright 1976 by Campbell Soup Co. The book contains pictures of Campbell Kids as characters from history as they eat soup. The book was a tie-in to the Bicentennial celebration for America in 1976. The Campbell Soup Co. was established in 1869. The Campbell Soup Kids were first drawn in 1904 by Grace Weiderseim Drayton and were used to promote Campbell's Soups in advertising. The Kids were such a success, they have remained a promotion device for the company all through the years.

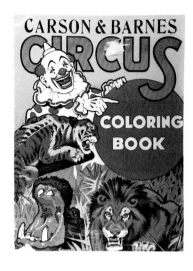

Carson and Barnes Circus Coloring Book, with circus scenes. Published by the Enquirer Printing Co. Undated.

Buster Brown Coloring Book Buster and Tige Go to the Circus. Coloring book advertising Buster Brown Shoes, circa 1950s. Brown was originally a character in a comic strip drawn by R. F. Outcault. The captioned pictures tell a story.

Chiquita Banana in a Read and Color Book (#2229). Copyright 1967 United Fruit Co. Published by Saalfield Publishing Co. Commended by Parents Magazine. Chiquita Brand Bananas, United Fruit Co. Pictures show how bananas are grown and sent to market.

The Wizard of O's Food Fun for Kids. Copyright Campbell Soup Co. 1977. From Campbell Soup Company Maker of Franco-American Products. The pictures and puzzles are about nutrition and food.

Duncan Hines Coloring Activity Book. Copyright 1984 Rand McNally and Co. Given away free with the purchase of any size of Duncan Hines Cookies, the book contains pictures to color and puzzles, mainly dealing with Duncan Hines Cookies .

Cloverbloom Mother Goose Painting Book. Armour's Cloverbloom Butter pictured on cover. These books could be secured by sending two coupons from Armour's Cloverbloom Butter Cartons and ten cents in stamps. The pictures in the book are from nursery rhymes printed in both color and black and white. A two page spread changes the original rhymes to include references to Cloverbloom Butter. Circa 1920s.

The Dutch Boy's Hobby, A paint Book for Girls and Boys. Copyright 1926 by O. C. Harn. The book advertises lead paint with lead from the National Lead Company. The small 3½" by 5" book contains many tiny pictures in both color and black and white, along with a card of watercolors to paint the pictures. The story is about lead paint lasting longer.

Cracker Jack Coloring and Activity Book. Copyright 1984, Borden, Inc. Published by Play More Inc. The captioned pictures tell a story. Although the Borden Company is more well known for its condensed milk and Elsie, the Borden cow, Cracker Jacks has been a long-lasting product. Collectors are especially interested in the original trinkets given with each box of Cracker Jacks.

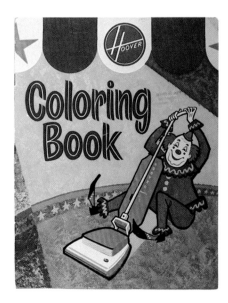

The Story of The Wizard of Oz With Pictures to Color. Illustrated by Henry E. Vallely and based on the original story by L. Frank Baum. Copyright 1939, Bobbs-Merrill Co. Published by Whitman Publishing Co. The book advertised Cocomalt, a malted food drink, with a full page ad inside the back cover. The book is mostly story with small pictures to color. Although the book has nothing to do with the M-G-M movie, it is probably no coincidence that the company chose the year the movie came out to use the Oz material.

Hoover Coloring Book. This is a nice book that shows all the Hoover products in pictures to color. Although it is undated, it appears to be circa 1960s.

Walt Disney's Classic Cinderella. Copyright 1987, The Walt Disney Co. This tie-in coloring book promoted both the re-release of the Walt Disney *Cinderella* film and the food products of McDonald's. The pictures tell the story of Cinderella.

The Good Passenger Book, by Janice Seaman and Gayle Weiner. Copyright 1983, Weiner/Seaman. The Missouri Division of Highway Safety used this book to promote safety. The pictures include instructions in fastening seat belts and other safety tips.

Presidents of the United States to Color: A History in Pictures from Washington to Johnson. Copyright MCMLXIII, MCMLXV Standard Brands Inc. Published by The Saalfield Publishing Co. Each president is featured with a picture and information. The last page pictures peanuts products, and Mr. Peanut is also featured in the book and on the cover.

Minnie Pearl's Color Book Color Me Chicken. Designed and produced by Max Harrison for Millie Pearl's Chicken System, Inc. Minnie Pearl, a veteran country music performer, is also involved in this chicken product. The pictures in the book deal with both her life and the chicken she promotes.

"Siggies" Adventures in Color. The whole book is about Siggie as he paints various items, with the back cover displaying an ad for Morris Paint. Circa 1950s.

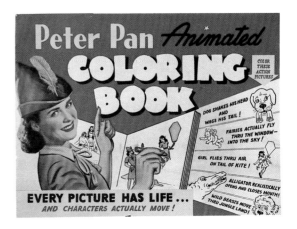

Peter Pan Animated Coloring Book. Copyright 1943 by Derby Foods. The book tells the story of Peter Pan with pictures to color. It also has extra pieces in the pictures to make parts move. The last page has the characters celebrate the ending with Peter Pan Peanut Butter. The book also contains several receipes using the product.

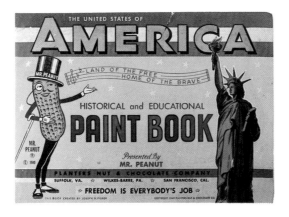

The United States of America Historical and Educational Paintbook Presented by Mr. Peanut. Copyright 1949 Planters Nut and Chocolate Co. This coloring book goes back to an earlier concept where each picture is printed in both color and black and white. The pictures depict United States historical events. The book also has a two page spread ad for Planters, and advertising on the inside and outside of the back cover.

Caring and Sharing: A Care Bear Sticker Book. Copyright 1984, Pizza Hut, Inc. by Random House. The book contains thirty-two gummed stickers to put on the pictures and the child was supposed to color the picture like the sticker. Again, this concept united two products: Care Bears and Pizza Hut in order to promote both.

Peter Pan Coloring Book. Copyright 1963, Derby Foods, Ind. The pictures tell the story of Peter Pan, and the book also includes advertising.

Western-Southern Life Safety Color Book. Book includes pictures which illustrate basic safety rules. Undated.

Treasure Island Cut-Out Coloring Book based on the story by Robert Louis Stevenson. Copyright 1968 by Western Publishing Co. Pictures by Bob Jenney. The captioned pictures tell the story. Also included were a small box of crayons. The book was used to promote Quaker Oats and an ad for the company appears on the back of the book. Characters to color and cut-out are also on the back of the cover.

Television and Radio Related Coloring Books

Toys relating to television and radio programs are among the most popular items in the current collectible field. Although coloring books from this area are just beginning to be discovered by today's collectors, they are already increasing in value because of an escalating interest by toy collectors. The most important television coloring books are the examples from the early years, the books from westerns, and the books from especially popular programs.

Besides the books pictured in this chapter, other coloring books were also manufactured to tie in with the following television series: "Have Gun Will Travel" (Lowe, 1960); "Green Acres" (Whitman, 1967); "Get Smart" (Saalfield, 1965); "Dragnet" (Jack Webb's Safety Squad Coloring Book); "The Munsters" (Whitman, 1965); and "Wagon Train" (Whitman, 1960).

The chapter on cartoon and comic characters also pictures several coloring books about television cartoon characters.

The A-Team

Mr. T became a star on the series "The A-Team" on NBC in 1983. The adventure series was about a soldier-of-fortune organization. George Peppard portrayed John "Hannibal" Smith. Mr. T (Lawrence Tureaud) was B.A. Baracus and Templeton and Murdock were played by Dirk Benedict and Dwight Schultz.

Punky Brewster (#1025). Copyright NBC, Inc. 1987, 1986. A Golden Book, Western Publishing Co. Contains captioned pictures of television show characters.

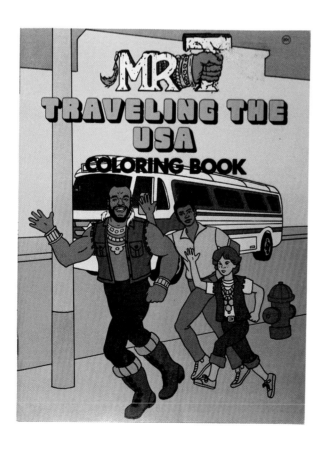

Mr. T Traveling the USA Coloring Book. Copyright 1983, Ruby—Spears Enterprises, Inc. Big T Enterprises, Inc. Published by Harbor House Publishers, Inc. Contains captioned pictures to color.

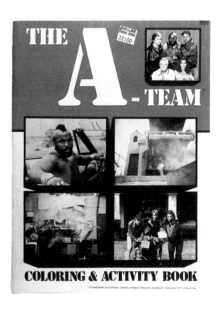

The A-Team Coloring and Activity Book. Copyright 1983 by Steven J. Cannell Productions. Universal City Studios. Published by Modern Promotions. The book contains pictures to color plus puzzles and other activities.

The Addams Family An Activity Book (#4331). Published by Saalfield Publishing Co., 1965. Includes pictures to color, puzzles, and cut outs of the Addams Family characters.

Ozzie and Harriet, David and Ricky Coloring Book (#125910). Published by The Saalfield Publishing Co. Contains captioned pictures to be colored of the cast members.

The Adventures of Rin Tin Tin Coloring Book (#1257). Published by Whitman Publishing Co., 1955. Copyright Screen Gems, Inc. The captioned pictures tell the story of the dog's adventure.

The Addams Family

"The Addams Family" was a popular ABC thirty minute weekly program that aired from 1964 to 1966. The sixty-four episodes revolved around a very unusual family based on characters created by cartoonist Charles Addams for *The New Yorker* magazine. The family lived in a Gothic house that looked like a Halloween haunted house. The head of the household was Gomez, a rich lawyer played by John Austin, and his wife Morticia, played by Carolyn Jones. Their children were Wednesday (Lisa Loring) and Pugsley (Ken Weatherwax). Another strange character was Uncle Fester, a role created by former child movie star, Jackie Coogan. Although the Addams family members wanted to be like everyone else in their community, their strangeness prevented this and the story line revolved on this premise.

The Adventures of Ozzie and Harriet

"The Adventures of Ozzie and Harriet" began as a typical family situation comedy in 1952. The television family was a real life family as well, and each member used his own name in the program. The father and mother were veteran show business personalities, Ozzie and Harriet (Hilliard) Nelson; and their sons were David and Ricky. As the boys grew up, Ricky became a teen idol singing star and the series outlasted other shows of its kind because of his popularity. The program ran on ABC from 1952 to 1966. Other cast members included Don DeFore as Mr. Thornberry, and in later years, the boy's wives, June and Kris Nelson.

The Adventures of Rin Tin Tin

Rin Tin Tin was the name of a very famous movie dog from the early days of film. The name was reactivated for a television program which began as a half hour series in 1954. In "The Adventures of Rin Tin Tin," a boy named Rusty and his dog were found by cavalry officer, Lieutenant Masters after the two survived an Indian raid. The plots of the series revolved around the 101st Cavalry stationed in California in the 1880s. The dog (owned and trained by Lee Duncan) and the boy Rusty (played by Lee Aaker) helped the Lieutenant (played by James Brown) and the other cavalry members in the action each week. The series was on ABC from 1954 to 1958, and continued another run for the same network from 1959 to 1961. Then the program moved to CBS and played from 1962 to 1964.

Alvin Show

The "Alvin Show" was an animated cartoon show that aired on CBS from 1961 to 1962. The Alvin character came from the 1958 song, "The Chipmunk Song" that sold over four million copies in records. The show was about songwriter-manager Dave Seville and the Singing Chipmunks(Alvin, Theodore and Simon). The animals' voices got their unique sound by speeding up the sound tracks.

The Andy Griffith Show

"The Andy Griffith Show" appeared on CBS television from 1960 to 1968. In its 249 episodes, Sheriff Andy Taylor (Andy Griffith) appeared as a concerned single parent raising his son Opie (Ronny Howard). Andy's Aunt Bee (Frances Bavier) provided a woman's touch to the household. The series was based in the rural commumity of Mayberry, North Carolina. Although the main characters had jobs in law enforcement, the small town had very little crime so the weekly stories usually revolved around the life of the popular Mayberry residents. Comedy highlights were provided by Don Knotts in his role as deputy Barney Fife and by Jim Nabors who played the part of Gormer Pyle.

Annie Oakley

"Annie Oakley" aired on ABC from 1953 to 1958. The story took place in the 1860s and centered around Annie Oakley (Gail Davis), who was an expert sharpshooter, and her brother Tagg (Jimmy Hawkins). The program was mainly geared to children and many toys and other products were produced to tie-in with the show.

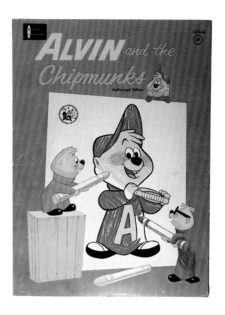

Alvin and the Chipmunks (#1878-G). Drawings by Phil DeLara. A Watkins-Strathmore Book. Copyright 1966, Ross Bagdasarian. Published by Western Publishing Co.

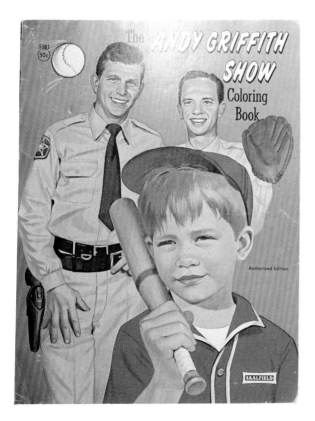

The Andy Griffith Show coloring book published by Saalfield Publishing Co. Copyright MCMLXIII by Mayberry Enterprises, Inc. The book is very thick and is filled with captioned pictures of the cast.

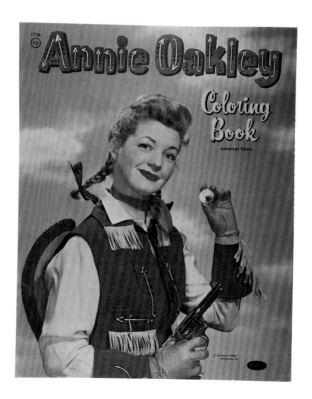

Annie Oakley Coloring Book (#1756). Copyright by Annie Oakley Enterprises, Inc., 1957. Published by Whitman Publishing Co. with captioned pictures of the cast members.

Bat Masterson

"Bat Masterson" was another popular western from the 1950s. Gene Barry starred as Masterson, a law enforcement man. Bat's trademarks, a gold tipped cane, a derby hat, and special gun were used by Barry in his characterization of the legendary law man.

Batman

"Batman" became the "camp" television show from 1966 to 1968 when it was on the ABC schedule. Many celebrities asked to do guest spots on the program in order to get in on the fun. The show was based on the comic character created by Bob Kane. Adam West played Bruce Wayne/Batman, the hero who fought for good against various evil characters. Dick Greyson/Robin was played by Burt Ward. Silent film star Neil Hamilton was Gordon and 1940s Twentieth Century-Fox star Cesar Romero was the Joker.

Ben Casey

"Ben Casey" was one of the popular medical television programs from the early 1960s. The sixty minute show aired on ABC from 1961 to 1966. The series made Vincent Edwards a star in his role as Dr. Ben Casey. His boss was portrayed by Sam Jaffe, and Betty Ackerman was Dr. Maggie Graham.

The Beverly Hillbillies

"The Beverly Hillbillies" was a highly rated television program during its most successful seasons. It was often listed among the top ten most watched TV shows in the nation. The plot involved the Clampett family who had become millionaires when oil was discovered on their home property. Now wealthy, the family packed up and moved to Beverly Hills, California where they purchased a mansion and tried to combine the two life styles, hillbilly and rich, with unexpected results. Cast members included: Jed Clampett (Buddy Ebsen); Granny (Irene Ryan); Elly May (Donna Douglas); and Jethro (Max Baer).

Bat Masterson Coloring Book (#4634). MCMLIX ZIV Television Programs, Inc. Published by Saalfield Publishing Co. California National Productions, Inc.

Pow Robin Strikes for Batman (#1833). Copyright 1966 by National Periodical Publications, Inc. Published by Watkins-Strathmore Co.

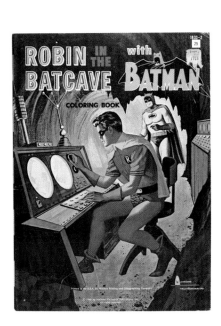

Robin in the Batman Cave with Batman (#1833-2), 1968. Copyright by National Periodical Publications, Inc. Published by the Watkins-Strathmore Co. The book contains captioned pictures of the characters.

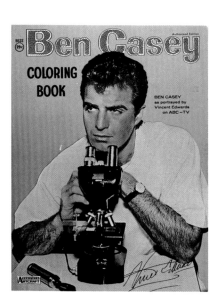

Ben Casey Coloring Book (#9532). Published by Saalfield Publishing Co., 1963. Copyright by Bing Crosby Productions, drawings by Ray Quigley. Captioned pictures tell the story of Casey, the other doctors and several of their cases.

The Beverly Hillbillies Color Book (#1883). Published by Western Publishing Co., 1964. Copyright by Filmway TV Productions, Watkins-Strathmore Book with pictures of the main cast members.

Bewitched

The comedy series "Bewitched" joined other farfetched programs that spanned the air waves in the early 1960s. The show included a witch named Samantha (Elizabeth Montgomery) who was married to Darren Stevens and her mother Endora (Agnes Moorehead). The plot concerned the use of magic tricks and the casting of spells by the women in the series. Advertising executive Stevens was played at different times by Dick York and Dick Sargent. The show ran on ABC from 1964 to 1972.

Bionic Woman

"Bionic Woman" was a spin-off program from ABC's popular "Six Million Dollar Man." The main character, Jaime Sommers (Lindsay Wagner), was injured in a sky-diving accident and Dr. Rudy Wells (Martin E. Brooks) performed a bionic operation, but she died anyway. Another doctor then performed cryogenic surgery and brought her back to life, with her bionic limbs. She then became an agent for the Office of Scientific Intelligence.

Other players included: Richard Anderson as Oscar Goldman and Martha Scott as Helen Elgin. The show aired on ABC from 1976 to 1977 and on NBC from 1977 to 1978.

Bonanza

"Bonanza," at its height, was seen in seventy-nine countries by 400 million people and it is one of the most popular television programs of all time. It became the number one rated television show during the 1964-1965 season, and it stayed in that position until the 1967-1968 season. The series only dropped after Dan Blocker's death in 1972.

The hour long western began on NBC in September, 1959 and after 440 episodes, ended in January 1973. The story took place in Virginia City, Nevada in the nineteenth century. The main characters were: Ben Cartwright, a widower—Lorne Greene; his sons Adam—Pernell Roberts; Hoss—Dan Blocker; and Little Joe—Michael Landon. The family lived on a 1,000 square mile ranch called the Ponderosa. Pernell Roberts left the show in 1965 but the program continued to be top rated even after his departure. It was the first major western to be filmed in color.

Bewitched Fun and Activity Book (#8908). Published by Treasure Books. Copyright 1965 by Screen Gems, Inc. Illustrations by Tony Tallarico. Includes pictures to color, games and puzzles.

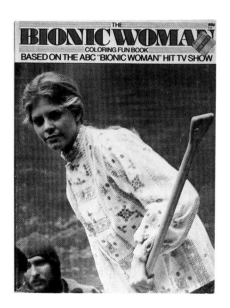

The Bionic Woman Coloring Fun Book based on the ABC "Bionic Woman" hit TV show. Copyright 1976, Universal City Studios, Inc. Published by Treasure Books by Tony Tallarico. About one half of the captioned pictures deal with the television show.

Bonanza, A Coloring Book (#1617). Published by Saalfield Publishing Co., 1960 and 1965. National Broadcasting Co., Inc. Assorted pictures of the cast and locations to color.

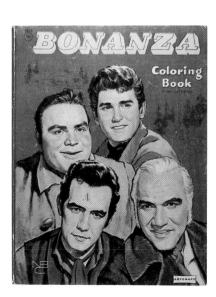

Bonanza Coloring Book (#4635). Published by Saalfield Publishing Co., 1970. National Broadcasting Co. Includes many cast pictures to color with captions.

The Brady Bunch

"The Brady Bunch" was a typical half hour family sit-com from the 1960s that began on ABC in 1969 and continued into the 1970s until 1974. The premise of the story line was that of a widower with three sons who married a widow with three daughters and then set up a joint household. The glue that seemed to hold the diversified family together was a housekeeper named Alice. The term "Brady Bunch" came to represent clean cut, privileged, well-behaved children. The term is still used in the vocabulary of many Americans, usually to explain that their own families had not followed the Brady example of child rearing. The Brady parents were played by Robert Reed and Florence Henderson. The children were: Marcia—Maureen McCormick; Janice—Eve Plumb; Cindy—Susan Olsen; Greg—Barry Williams; Peter—Christopher Knight; Bobby—Michael Lookinland. The housekeeper Alice was played by Ann B. Davis.

Buffalo Bill, Jr.

"Buffalo Bill, Jr. was a syndicated television show produced by the Gene Autry Flying A Productions in 1955. The series consisted of forty episodes geared to the young viewer. The program was a western based in Texas in the 1890s. The characters included: Buffalo Bill, Jr. (Dick Jones); Calamity (Nancy Gilbert); and Judge Ben Wiley (Harry Cheshire).

Captain Kangaroo

"Captain Kangaroo" was the longest running children's television program. It began on CBS in 1955 starring Bob Keeshan as the Captain and Lumpy Brannum as Mr. Green Jeans. The show continued into the 1980s after changing its format. The original series was a weekday show designed for preschool children. The program featured puppets, animals, and animated features along with varied guests each day. Tom Terrific and Mighty Manfred became much-loved characters for children because of their exposure on the "Captain Kangaroo" television show. The cartoons featuring these characters were shown frequently as part of the regular broadcast. Tom Terrific was created by Terrytoons. Thirty of the four minute films were made and they were syndicated in the early 1960s.

The Brady Bunch Coloring Book (#1657). Published by Whitman Books, Western Publishing Co., 1974. Copyright by Paramount Pictures Corp. The book contains good likenesses of cast members in sequenced captioned pictures. A set of paper dolls was also produced by Whitman in 1972 called *The Brady Bunch* (#4787).

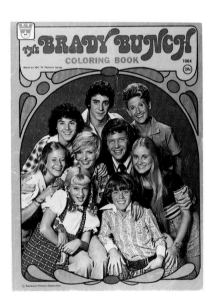

The Brady Bunch (#1004). Based on ABC TV Network Series. Copyright MCMLXXIV, MCMLXXII. Paramount Picture Corp. Published by Whitman, Western Publishing Co. Contains captioned pictures of the cast.

Buffalo Bill, Jr. Coloring Book (#1316). Published by Whitman Publishing Co., 1956. Flying A Productions. The captioned pictures carry out an adventure involving the cast members.

Captain Kangaroo Trace and Color (#1413). Published by Whitman Publishing Co., 1960. Robert Keeshan Assoc. The book contains captioned pictures of the cast and a piece of tracing paper is provided for every two pictures.

Captain Kangaroo Coloring Book (#4967). Published by Samuel Lowe Co., 1977. Robert Keeshan Associates. Assorted pictures of cast with captions.

Car 54, Where Are You?

"Car 54, Where Are You?" was a unique comedy police television show in which the two stars were reminiscent of the comic characters Mutt and Jeff. The action took place in the Bronx out of the 53rd precinct and was a take off of the Jack Webb "Dragnet" program. The two policemen, Gunther Toody and Francis Muldoon were played by Joe E. Ross and Fred Gwynne. Gunther's wife was Beatrice Pons and Capt. Martin Block was played by Paul Reed. The sixty episodes of the program aired on NBC from 1961 to 1963.

Chips

"Chips" was a not so typical crime show from the 1970s. It was unusual in that it lasted sixty minutes instead of the more usual half hour and it dealt with adventures experienced by the California Highway Patrol instead of city police officers. The series began on NBC in 1977. Leading characters were: Jon Baker played by Larry Wilcox and Francis Poncherello played by Erik Estrada. Robert Pine was the sergeant in charge of the officers.

Circus Boy

"Circus Boy" was a thirty minute children's program broadcast on NBC from 1956 to 1957 and on ABC from 1957 to 1958. The story was about a boy named Corky whose parents had been killed in a circus accident. Corky became a water boy for Bimbo the elephant who was with a traveling circus. Cast members included Mickey Braddock as Corky; Robert Lowery as Big Tim Champion; Noah Berry, Jr. as Joey the Clown; and "Big Boy" Williams as Pete.

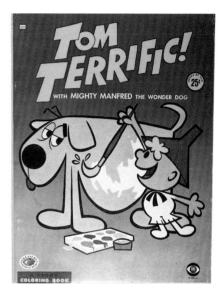

Tom Terrific with Mighty Manfred the Wonder Dog (#312). Copyright 1957, CBS Television Film Sales, Inc. Published by Treasure Books with captioned pictures to color.

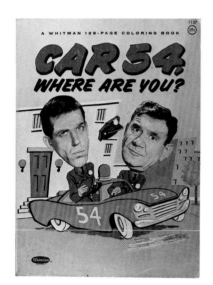

Car 54, Where Are You? (#1157) "Featuring characters seen on NBC television network." Drawings by Bob Jenney, copyright 1962, Eupollis Productions, Inc. Published by Whitman Publishing Co.

Chips Coloring and Activity Book (402-2). Published by Playmore Publishing Inc. and Waldman Publishing Corp., 1983 by MGM/UA Entertainment Co. Action pictures of the cast members with captions plus puzzles and activities.

Circus Boy Coloring Book (#1198). Published by Whitman Publishing Co., 1957. Copyright Norbert Productions, Inc. Contains captioned pictures of the characters and animals from the television series.

Cisco Kid

"Cisco Kid" was a thirty minute syndicated television show from 1951. There were 156 episodes in the series. The Cisco Kid was played by Duncan Renaldo and his companion, Pancho, was Leo Carillo. Their horses were Diablo and Loco. The action took place in New Mexico in the 1890s.

Convoy

The World War II "Convoy" television program aired on NBC from September to December in 1965. There were only thirteen, sixty minute episodes of the series which involved a convoy of 299 American ships on their way to England. Commander Dan Talbot was played by John Gavin and Captain Ben Foster was portrayed by John Larch.

Curiosity Shop

The "Curiosity Shop" was an interesting educational program which appeared on ABC from 1971-1973 in a sixty minute format. The Saturday morning program contained sketches, cartoons, puppets, and Gittel the Witch played by Barbara Minkus.

The Dick Van Dyke Show

Although "The Dick Van Dyke Show" was a 1960s situation comedy, the format seemed much like the popular shows of the 1950s. The family involved in the action included a working father, Rob Petrie (Dick Van Dyke); a stay-at-home mother, Laura (Mary Tyler Moore); and a child Richie played by Larry Matthews. The show was different in that it focused on the father's comedy writing career. In this part of the program, Morey Amsterdam and Rose Marie were Van Dyke's fellow writers. The series began on CBS in 1961 and ended in 1966.

Cisco Kid Coloring Book (#2078). Published by Saalfield Publishing Co., Doubleday and Co., 1950. Contains captioned pictures to color.

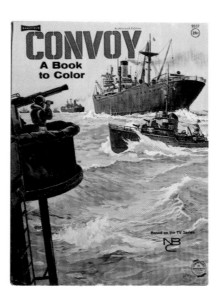

Convoy: A Book To Color (#9537). Copyright 1965, Universal Television. Published by The Saalfield Publishing Co. Contains captioned pictures from the television series.

Cisco Kid Coloring Book (#2428). Published by The Saalfield Publishing Co., Doubleday and Co., 1954. Contains captioned pictures to color.

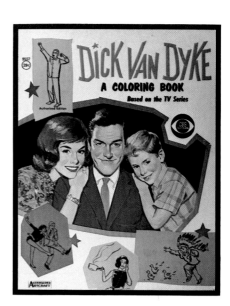

Dick Van Dyke (#9557). Based on the CBS Television Series. Copyright 1963, Calvada Prod. Published by The Saalfield Publishing Co. Contains captioned pictures of cast members.

Curiosity Shop (#5353). Copyright 1971 by American Broadcasting Co. Published by Saalfield Publishing Co. Includes captioned pictures of the television characters.

Diff'rent Strokes

"Diff'rent Strokes" was a situation comedy based in New York City. The star of the show was Gary Coleman who played Arnold Jackson. The story line involved a white millionaire, Phillip Drummone (Conrad Bain), who adopted two black boys, Arnold and Willis Jackson. Willis was played by Todd Bridges. Charlotte Rae was cast as the housekeeper. The show was a successful NBC series for several years beginning in 1978.

Dr. Kildare

The early 1960s brought many new medical shows to the television line-up. One of the best was "Dr. Kildare" based on the character made famous in a series of "B" films produced by MGM in the 1930s and 1940s. The program aired on NBC from 1961-1965 in a sixty minute format, and then was shortened to half hour segments during its last year from 1965-1966. Dr. James Kildare was played by Richard Chamberlain who was an intern and later a resident physician at Blair General Hospital. His superior, Dr. Leonard Gillespie, was played by Raymond Massey.

The Dudley Do-Right Show

"The Dudley Do-Right Show" was an animated thirty minute cartoon show on ABC from 1969 to 1970. Dudley was a naive boy who became a Canadian Mountie and the program depicted his attempts to catch bad guy Snively Whiplash.

Dukes of Hazzard

The "Dukes of Hazzard" began on the CBS network in 1979. This is one series where a car played a major role in the action. The Dodge Charger even had a name, "General Lee." The main characters were John Schneider who played Bo Duke; Catherine Bach—Daisy Duke; and Tom Wopat who was Luke Duke. The program lost some of its popularity when the two men quit the show in 1982 and were replaced by Byron Cherry and Christopher Mayer.

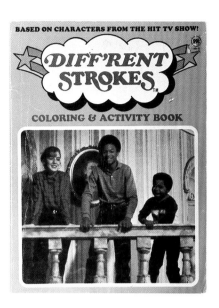

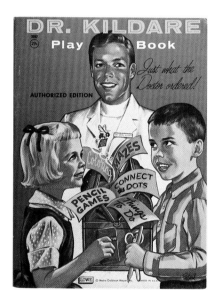

Dr. Kildare Play Book (#3092). Copyright Metro-Goldwyn-Mayer. Published by Samuel Lowe Co. Contains many pictures to color, plus games, puzzles, paper dolls, etc., but nothing inside the book pertains to the television series.

Diff'rent Strokes Color and Activity Book (#401-3). Published by Playmore Publishing, Inc. and Waldman Pub. Corp. Copyright 1983, Tandem Productions, Inc. Compiled and edited by Malvina G. Vogel. Contains captioned pictures of cast to color, plus some puzzles.

The Dukes of Hazzard Coloring and Activity Book. Copyright Warner Brothers, 1981. Published by Modern Promotions. Art by James Sherman. Contains captioned pictures of the television characters, plus puzzles.

Dudley Do-Right Comes to the Rescue (#9571). Published by Saalfield Publishing Co. in 1969. Copyright P.A.T. Ward. Filled with captioned action pictures to color.

The Dukes of Hazzard Coloring and Activity Book. Copyright Warner Brothers, 1981. Published by Modern Promotions. Art by James Sherman. Contains captioned pictures of the television characters, plus puzzles.

The Dukes of Hazzard Coloring and Activity Book. Copyright Warner Brothers, 1981. Published by Modern Promotions. Art by The Roberts Group. Contains captioned pictures of the cast to color, plus activities.

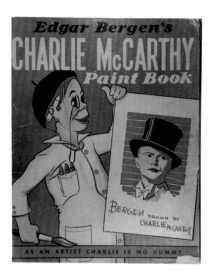

Edgar Bergen's Charlie McCarthy Paint Book (#690). Copyright 1938 by McCarthy Inc. Published by Whitman Publishing Co. Contains captioned pictures to color.

Emergency (#1840). Based on the television series created by Harold Jack Bloom and RA Cinader. Published by Saalfield, 1976. Copyright Emergency Productions. Contains captioned series of pictures that tell stories of rescues.

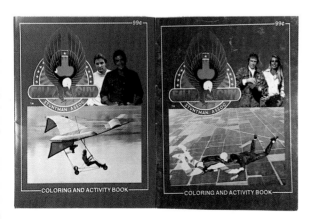

Fall Guy Coloring and Activity Book. Copyright 1982, Twentieth Century-Fox Film Corp. Published by Modern Promotions. Written and illustrated by James Sherman and Alan Weiss. Includes pictures of an adventure of Fall Guy, plus puzzles and games.

Edgar Bergen and Charlie McCarthy

In 1936, Edgar Bergen and his ventriloquist dummy, Charlie McCarthy made a guest appearance on the popular Rudy Vallee radio show. Their act was such a hit, they aired for three more months.

In 1937, Bergen started his own show sponsored by Chase and Sanborn. The program was the number one rated show in the United States for two and a half years. Even as late as 1945, the program was in fifth place after having aired for eight years. The supporting cast for the show was also excellent. Don Ameche was the master of ceremonies, the singer was Nelson Eddy, and Ray Noble led the orchestra. The comedian W.C. Fields was a frequent guest on the show and from 1937 to 1939, the "on the air" feud between Charlie and Fields provided material for many of the best programs from the series. Bergen and McCarthy were regulars on radio programs until 1956 when they moved to television.

Emergency

"Emergency" was a medical show with a difference. The action was handled by paramedics of Squad 51 of the Los Angeles County Fire Dept. The sixty minute program was broadcast on NBC from 1972 to 1977. The Doctors were played by Robert Fuller and Bobby Troup and Julie London was nurse Dixie McCall.

Fall Guy

Fall Guy made its debut as a television movie on October 28, 1981. It starred Lee Majors and Farrah Fawcett (who was then Mrs. Majors). The show was successful enough that a series began. Lee Majors was co-producer and also sang the theme song, "The Unknown Stuntman." Majors also played the part of Colt Seavers, the stuntman.

Fame

"Fame" centered on the students and teachers at New York City's High School for the Performing Arts. It was based on the movie *Fame* from 1980. Each story line gave young people a chance to showcase their talents in music and dance performance. The program began on NBC with Debbie Allen doing both the choreography and playing the role of dance teacher Lydia Grant. The show won many Emmy awards with Allen receiving two for her choreography. Although the show was a hit with critics, it did not seem to find an audience, and it was dropped by NBC after the 1982-1983 season. The program didn't die, however, as MGM/UA Television and Metromedia, Inc. continued to produce episodes to be used by independent stations until 1986.

Family Affair

CBS had a hit show with "Family Affair" for several years beginning in 1966. Brian Keith played an uncle who became guardian for his orphaned nieces and nephew, Cissy, Jody and Buffy Davis. The twins were played by Johnie Whitaker and Anissa Jones. Kathy Garver was Cissy. Sebastian Cabot played the role of the family's man servant. The series ended in 1971. See also the chapter on dolls and paper dolls for related material.

Fame Coloring and Activity Book. Copyright 1983, MGM/UA Entertainment Co. Published by Playmore Publishing Inc., and Waldman Publishing Corp. Stories by Michael J. Pellowski, art by Nick Lo Blanco, activities by Jesse Zerner, compiled and edited by Malvina G. Vogel. Captioned pictures of cast members plus puzzles and activities.

Hi! I'm Mrs. Beasley (#1364). Color and Read. Copyright Family Affair Co., 1972. A Whitman Book, Western Publishing Co. Contains pictures of the doll to color, and reading material.

Buffy and Jody Coloring Book (#1640). Copyright Family Affair Co. Drawings by Nathalee Mode. Published by Whitman Publishing Co. Mostly uncaptioned pictures of the television characters from *Family Affair*.

Fat Albert and Cosby Kids (#1066). Published by Whitman Books, Western Publishing Co., 1973. Copyright by William H. Cosby, Jr. and Filmation Associates. Captioned pictures of cast members in several sequences.

Fat Albert and the Cosby Kids Fun Book (#3203 -21). Copyright William H. Cosby and Filmation Associates. Merrigold Press. Contains uncaptioned pictures and puzzles.

Fat Albert and the Cosby Kids

"Fat Albert and the Cosby Kids" was a thirty minute animated cartoon shown on CBS beginning in 1972. Bill Cosby was the executive producer for the show and he also was the host as well as the voice for Fat Albert. Besides Albert, characters included: Rudy, Weird Harold, Edward, Mush Mouth, Donald, Becky, and Russel. The program helped children to learn to solve problems and to enhance self-worth.

Flipper

"Flipper" provided young viewers with several seasons of a pet dolphin's sea antics. NBC showed the program from 1964 until 1967. The action took place in Coral Key Park, Florida where the ranger, Porter Ricks, and his sons Sandy and Bud spent their time keeping order and protecting the park. Flipper was the family's pet dolphin. Cast members included: Ranger—Brian Kelley; Sandy—Luke Halpin; and Bud—Tommy Norden.

The Flying Nun

"The Flying Nun" was one of the most unusual of the situation comedies of the 1960s. Sally Field, as Sister Bertrille, discovered she could fly and she used this strange ability in her efforts to do good deeds in her community in San Juan, Puerto Rico. This program was aired on ABC from 1967 to 1969.

Flipper Paint With Water (#1340). Published by Whitman Publishing Co., 1964. Copyright by Ivan Tors Films and Metro-Goldwyn-Mayer Inc. About half of the pictures are paint with water and the other half are regular coloring book illustrations. The captioned pictures tell the story of a Flipper adventure.

Flying Nun (#4672). Copyright 1968, Screen Gems, Inc. Published by The Saalfield Publishing Co. Contains captioned pictures of cast members.

Foreign Legionaire From TV For You to Color (#1316). Starring Buster Crabbe and His Son Cuffy. Copyright Frantel, 1956. Published by Abbott Publishing Co. with captioned pictures.

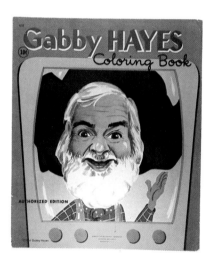

Gabby Hayes Coloring Book (#1313). Copyright 1954, Gabby Hayes. Published by Abbott Publishing Co. with captioned pictures.

Gilligan's Island (#1135). Copyright 1965 by Gladasya-UATV. Published by Whitman Publishing Co., drawings by Tom Gill. Contains captioned pictures of the cast members.

Foreign Legionaire

Early movie and Olympic star Buster Crabbe, who had achieved fame with a gold medal for swimming in the 1932 Olympics, played the lead role in this series. After his movie roles as Flash Gordon and Tarzan, the part of Captain Gallant fit Crabbe nicely. His real life son, Cullen, played Gallant's ward in this television program. The show, which aired on NBC from 1955 to 1963, took place in North Africa at the headquarters of the French Foreign Legion. It was shot on location in the Sahara, Spain, and Italy.

The Gabby Hayes Show

"The Gabby Hayes Show" was first seen on NBC in 1950 and then on ABC in 1956. The children's program was hosted by Gabby Hayes, former cowboy movie star, who also acted as story teller for tales of the American West.

Gilligan's Island

The "Gilligan's Island" show (CBS, 1964-1967) was one of those wacky situation comedies from the era that seemed to dominate the television screen. The plot followed the adventures of a group of tourists who were shipwrecked on an island in the South Pacific as they planned to be rescued. The fun came from the assortment of people marooned together. They included: The Skipper (Alan Hale, Jr.); Gilligan (Bob Denver); Ginger Grant a movie actress (Tina Louise); Millionaire Thurston Howell III (Jim Backus); his wife, Lovey (Natalie Schafer); Mary Ann Summers, a store clerk (Dawn Wells); and Professor Hinkley (Russell Johnson).

Gunsmoke

"Gunsmoke" was the longest running television western ever. It began on CBS in 1955 and ran for twenty years until 1975. The show, like "Bonanza," featured an ensemble cast of excellent characters. The story took place in Dodge City, Kansas during the 1880s. Leading players were: Matt Dillon, a United States Marshall; his deputies Chester Goode and Festus Haggen; Dr. Galen Adams; and Kitty Russell who owned the Longbranch Saloon. These parts were played by: James Arness, Dennis Weaver, Ken Curtis, Milburn Stone, and Amanda Blake.

H.R. Pufnstuf

"H.R.Pufnstuf" was a children's show broadcast by NBC from 1969 to 1971 and by ABC from 1972 to 1973. The program featured Jack Wild as Jimmy, and Billie Hayes as Miss Wichiepoo. The Sid and Marty Krofft puppets were also a part of the program. Jimmy had a talking flute which helped him when he was stranded on an island trying to find his way home.

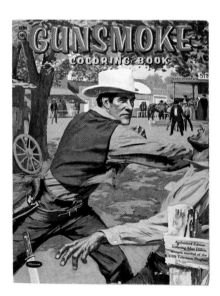

Gunsmoke Coloring Book (#1184). Published by Whitman Publishing Co., 1958. Copyright by Columbia Broadcasting System. Captioned pictures of the cast in several story lines.

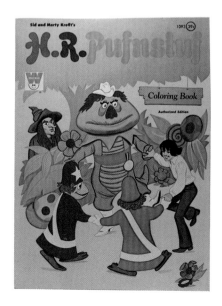

H.R. Pufnstuf (#1093). Published by Whitman Publishing Co., 1970. Sid and Marty Krofft Productions, Inc. with captioned pictures of their adventures.

Happy Days

The hit comedy series "Happy Days" premiered on ABC television in 1974. During its run it also provided a basis for several spin-off shows featuring several of its characters. These included: "Laverne and Shirley," "Mork and Mindy," and "Joanie Loves Chachi." The series was set in the 1950s and featured teenagers and their adventures at Jefferson High in Milwaukee, Wisconsin. The two main characters were Richie Cunningham played by Ron Howard and Fonzie Fonzarelli played by Henry Winkler. Winkler's portrayal of the drop out mechanic who worked at Otto's Auto Orphanage became so popular, he soon dominated the show. Ron Howard left the program after the 1979 season and turned his attention to the directing of films. The series, itself, lasted a total of eleven seasons. The Fonz's leather jacket is now in the Smithsonian.

The Harlem Globetrotters

"The Harlem Globetrotters" was an animated cartoon based on the Harlem Globetrotters basketball team. The show was a Hanna-Barbera production and made its debut on CBS in 1970 and continued until 1973.

Hee Haw

"Hee Haw," the western variety show, began on CBS TV in 1969 and remained on that network until 1971. It is still seen on many stations through syndication. The many regulars have included Buck Owens, Roy Clark, Grampa Jones, Lulu Roman, and Minnie Pearl.

Happy Days Coloring and Activity Book. Published by Playmore Publishing, Inc. and Waldman Pub. Corp., 1983. Paramount Pictures Corp. Captioned pictures, plus puzzles and games.

Happy Days Coloring and Activity Book (406-3). Published by Playmore Publishing, Inc. and Waldman Pub. Corp., 1983. Paramount Pictures Corp. Captioned pictures, plus puzzles and games.

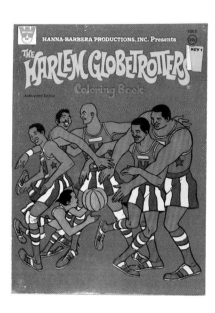

Hee Haw Coloring Book (#4538). Published by Saalfield Publishing Co. Copyright 1970, Columbia Broadcasting System, Inc. Contains mostly captioned pictures of the cast.

The Harlem Globetrotters Coloring Book (#1085). Copyright 1971, Columbia Broadcasting System Harlem Globetrotters, Inc. Hanna-Barbera Productions, Inc. Contains captioned pictures.

Hopalong Cassidy Coloring Book, "Starring William Boyd" (#1311). Published by Abbott Publishing Co.

William Boyd Coloring Book Story of Hopalong Cassidy (#1231). Copyright 1950 by Lowe Inc. Story and Pictures by Jack Crowe. Published by Samuel Lowe Co. Book from the collection of Elaine Price.

Hopalong Cassidy

William Boyd began appearing in Hopalong Cassidy films in 1935. The character was based on fiction stories by Clarence E. Mulford. The original character had a limp which accounted for the name but William Boyd changed the characterization and did away with the limp.

There were sixty-six films made in the series which were syndicated for television in 1948. A half hour television show was begun in the same year. Ninety-nine episodes were used in the series.

The part of Hopalong Cassidy was played by William Boyd and his partner, Red Connors, was played by Edgar Buchanan. Topper was the name of Cassidy's horse. The television show was so popular that numerous kid's products were made to tie-in to the program.

Howdy Doody

"Howdy Doody" was one of the first television programs made especially for children and it soon became the most popular of these children's shows. It began on NBC in 1947 and remained a favorite for many years, leaving the air in 1960. At first it was a Monday—Friday show and then in 1956 it became a Saturday morning feature. The leading character of the program was a marionette named Howdy Doody. Helping out with the show were Buffalo Bob Smith (Bob Smith); Clarabell (Bob Keeshan—later Captain Kangaroo); Story Princess (Alene Dalton); and Tim Tremble played by Don Knotts.

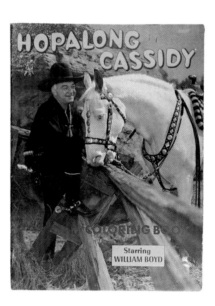

Hopalong Cassidy Coloring Book Starring William Boyd (#1200). Copyright 1950 by Doubleday and Co., illustrated by Jack Crowe. Published by Samuel Lowe Co. The captioned pictures tell a story.

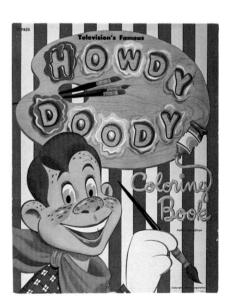

Howdy Doody Coloring Book (#217625). Copyright Kagran Corp., 1952. Published by Whitman Publishing Co. Contains captioned pictures of the cast.

Television's Famous Howdy Doody Coloring Book (#2080), with assorted Howdy Doody pictures. Published by Whitman Publishing Co. circa 1950s. Copyright Kagran Corp. Other Howdy Doody coloring books include: Whitman 2018, 2093, 2176.

I Love Lucy

The "I Love Lucy" television program is probably the most popular show that has ever been seen on any television network. Even though some of the episodes are over forty years old, they are still being shown all over the world on a daily basis.

The program began on the CBS network on October 15, 1951 and continued with a thirty minute format until September of 1956. Then "Lucy" was changed to an hour program from November 6, 1957 to September of 1958. The story line centered on Lucy and Ricky Ricardo who rented an apartment in New York City from Fred and Ethel Mertz. Ricky Ricardo was a band leader at the Tropicanna Club. Although Lucy was a housewife in her daily life, she longed to join her husband in show business. Many of the episodes were based on this thesis.

The show was so popular that forty-four million viewers watched the program the evening that Lucy's baby was born. Besides Lucille Ball and her real life husband, Desi Arnaz, the cast included William Frawley and Vivian Vance as Fred and Ethel Mertz.

The Incredible Hulk

"The Incredible Hulk" was a "Dr. Jekle and Mr. Hyde" type of show whose main character, Dr. Banner (Bill Bixby), through a scientific mistake, changed into the Green Hulk when he was angry. After an accidental fire, he left his work to try to discover how he could keep from turning into the Hulk. The Hulk was played by Lou Ferrigno. The program was first aired on CBS in 1978 and ended in 1982.

The Jackie Gleason Show

Jackie Gleason was involved with several television shows through the years including, "The Life of Riley;" "Cavalcade of Stars;" "The Honeymooners;" and several versions of "The Jackie Gleason Show." His variety shows aired on CBS from 1952 to 1955 and 1956-1961. Gleason's most popular programs were the ones which featured segments of "The Honeymooners" with Art Carney, Audrey Meadows, and Joyce Randolph playing the parts of Ed Norton, Alice Kramden, and Trixie Norton. Jackie Gleason was Ralph Kramden.

Journey to the Center of the Earth

"Journey to the Center of the Earth" was an animated cartoon appearing on ABC from 1967 to 1969. The story was based on the novel of the same name by Jules Verne. As part of the plot, Professor Lindenbrook leads a party to hunt for the center of the earth. While they are inside, an explosion seals the opening and they are trapped. The other episodes involve the various adventures they encounter as they try to find a way out.

Lucille Ball-Desi Arnaz Coloring Book (#2079). Copyright 1953 by Lucille Ball and Desi Arnaz. Drawings by Roy Schroeder. Published by Whitman Publishing Co. Pictures have short captions and contain some scenes from the "I Love Lucy" program.

I Love Lucy, Lucille Ball, Desi Arnaz, Little Ricky Coloring Book. Copyright 1955, Lucille Ball and Desi Arnaz. Drawings by Robert Bartram. Published by Dell Publishing Co. Designed, produced, and printed by Western Printing and Lithographing Co. with captioned pictures to color.

Jackie Gleason's TV Show (#2614). Copyright VIP Corp., 1956. Published by Abbott. Contains nearly all captioned Gleason pictures to color.

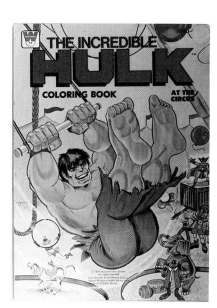

The Incredible Hulk Coloring Book At The Circus (#1040). Copyright 1977, Marvel Comics Group. Published by Whitman-Western Publishing Co. with captioned pictures to color.

Journey to the Center of the Earth (#1137). Drawings by Tony Sqroi, Ellis Eringer, and James Fletcher. Copyright 1968 by Twentieth Century-Fox Film Corp. Published by Whitman Publishing, a division of Western Publishing Co. Contains captioned pictures.

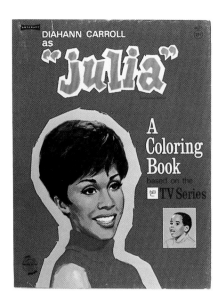

Julia. Published by Saalfield Publishing Co. Copyright by Twentieth Century Fox-Film Corp., 1968. Drawings are by Lewell Ellsworth Smith and Gary Thomas. The captioned pictures show the television characters.

Julia

"Julia" was one of the first television shows to picture a black single mother (Diahann Carroll) working as an educated professional. Julia Baker was a nurse working at the Inner Aero-Space Center for Dr. Chegley (Lloyd Nolan). Her son, Corey, was played by Marc Copage. The show was on NBC television from 1968 to 1971.

Knight Rider

"Knight Rider" began its run on television during the 1982 season. It was created by Robert Foster. David Hasselhoff starred as Michael Knight, a former policeman who becomes an investigator. A dying millionaire gives him a space age car, Knight Industries Two Thousand, which he uses in his work. The car is called KITT and can do all kinds of remarkable things.

Land of the Giants

"Land of the Giants" was a sixty minute science fiction television show that debuted on ABC in 1970. In the show, the craft, Spindthrift, gets caught in a storm and is forced to land in a forest. The three crew members and four passengers find they have landed in a world of giants.

The episodes describe the adventures of the crew and passengers as they try to repair their craft to return to earth and, at the same time, avoid being captured by the giants. Players were: Gary Conway as the captain; Don Marshall as the co-pilot; and Heather Young as the stewardess. The passengers consisted of a thief, an heiress, a tycoon, and an orphan child. The program ended in 1970 after fifty-one episodes.

Land of the Lost

"Land of the Lost" was a science fiction television program involving a forest ranger and his children who were caught in a time vortex while on the Colorado River. They were transported back to the days of prehistoric creatures and their adventures occurred as they tried to find their way back to civilization. The forest ranger and his children were played by Wesley Eure, Kathy Coleman, and Spencer Milligan.

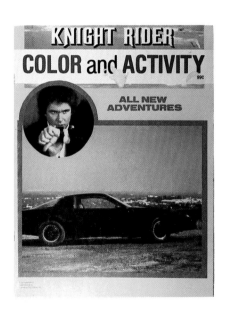

Knight Rider and Activity Book. Copyright 1984 by Universal City Studios. Published by Modern Promotions. Contains both captioned pictures to color and puzzles.

Land of the Giants Coloring Book (#1138). Copyright 1969, Kent Productions and Twentieth Century-Fox Film Corporation. Whitman Publishing, a division of Western Publishing Co. Drawings by Jason Studios. Includes captioned pictures to color.

Land of the Lost (#1045). Copyright 1975 by Sid and Marty Krofft Prod., Inc. Published by Western Publishing Co. (Whitman). Contains sequenced captioned pictures to color.

Lassie

Just as the television program featuring the dog Rin Tin Tin had its beginning in the film world, so did the television series called "Lassie." The original Lassie was the star of the film, *Lassie Come Home* made by M-G-M in 1943. The television version of "Lassie" premiered on CBS in 1951. The show featured a boy named Jeff Miller (Tommy Rettig); his mother Ellen (Jan Clayton); his Gramps (George Cleveland); and his dog Lassie. The stories were mostly based on adventures shared by Jeff and Lassie. This format lasted until 1957. Then the story line changed to feature a new boy named Timmy (Jon Provost) and his adoptive parents played by Cloris Leachman/June Lockhart and Jon Shepodd/Hugh Riley.

The plot line remained much the same until 1964 when more changes were made. At that time, and until the end of this Lassie series in 1968, a third story line was followed. In this version, Lassie was given to a forest ranger named Corey Stuart (Robert Bray) and Lassie was instrumental in helping to make rescues and in protecting the forest. The fourth Lassie format was on CBS from 1968 to 1971. In this series Lassie no longer was owned by any one person so she was free to roam the California countryside helping both animals and humans when she was needed.

Laugh-In

"Laugh-In" took the nation by storm when it appeared on television in 1968. Nothing like it had ever been seen on U.S. television. It was full of satire, political statements, and just plain silliness. Dan Rowan and Dick Martin served as co-hosts but the show was peopled with wonderful cast members and unusual guests. Cast members included: Ruth Buzzi, Judy Carne, Eileen Brennan, Goldie Hawn, Arte Johnson, and Henry Gibson. The show ended in 1973 and despite several specials during the last few years, the original wit and entertainment has not been recaptured.

Laurel and Hardy

"Laurel and Hardy" was made as an animated cartoon based on the Stan Laurel and Oliver Hardy characters from the movies. Hanna-Barbera Productions and Larry Harmon Pictures produced the five minute syndicated cartoons in 1966.

Lassie Coloring Book (#1114). Published by Whitman Publishing Co. Whitman also published a *Lassie Punch Out Book* (#1926) in 1966.

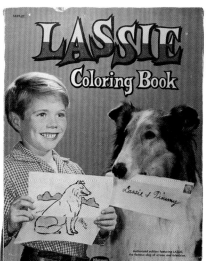

Lassie Coloring Book (#1039). Published by Whitman Publishing Co., 1958. Lassie Programs, Inc. A thick book with captioned pictures of many Lassie sequences but no real story.

Lassie Coloring Book (#1642). Copyright 1969, Wrather Corp. Published by Whitman Publishing Co.

Lassie Coloring Book (#1656). Published by Whitman Publishing Co., 1969. Lassie Television, Inc. Captioned pictures tell the story of Lassie's rescue efforts in her work with the rangers.

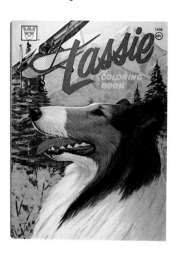

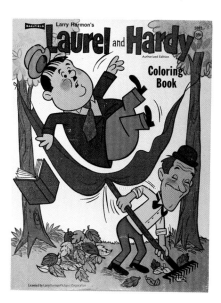

Laurel and Hardy (#3883). Copyright 1972, Larry Harmon Pictures Corp. Published by Saalfield Publishing Co. Contains captioned pictures.

Rowan and Martin's Laugh-In; A Verry Inntersting Coloring Book (#4633). Published by Saalfield Publishing Co., 1968. George Schlatter—Ed Friendly Productions and Romart, Inc. Filled with pictures and captions of the cast with punch lines similar to the television show's gags.

Laverne and Shirley

The Laverne and Shirley characters played by Penny Marshall and Cindy Williams had their beginning on the ABC "Happy Days" program. The women's series was developed from those characters and aired on ABC in 1976. In the show, the girls worked at Shotz Brewery in Milwaukee, Wisconsin in the 1950s. Boyfriends Lenny and Squiggy were played by Michael McKean and David L. Lander. After several successful seasons, the show ran into trouble when Cindy Williams quit the cast because of unresolved disagreements in 1983. The series ended the same year.

Leave It To Beaver

Although "Leave It To Beaver" was never a top rated show while it was produced, it remains a much loved nostalgic series in re-runs for present television viewers. The original program began on CBS in 1957 and then moved to ABC where it remained until 1963. The half hour situation comedy was a typical 1950s show that outlived its era. The Cleaver family had a mother who was a housewife, a father who was the breadwinner, and two average children. Perhaps it is the yearning for this comfortable family life that makes the re-runs so popular with current viewers. The program's continued success also comes from the excellent performances of the show's regulars, especially Jerry Mathers as The Beaver, and Ken Osmond as Eddie Haskell—the obnoxious friend of Beaver's brother, Wally. Other characters were: Father Ward—Hugh Beaumont; Mother June—Barbara Billingsley; and Wally—Tony Dow.

The Life and Legend of Wyatt Earp

"The Life and Legend of Wyatt Earp" was one of many popular westerns from the 1950s. During the 1959 season alone, there were thirty-two westerns on the three major networks. Wyatt Earp episodes were first based in Dodge City, Kansas and later took place in Tombstone, Arizona.

Hugh O'Brien played the sheriff, Wyatt Earp. The show premiered on ABC in 1955 and continued on the same network until 1961. The 266 episodes were eventually syndicated.

Laverne and Shirley Coloring and Activity Book (#405-2). Published by Playmore Pub. Inc. and Waldman Pub. Corp., 1983. Paramount Pictures Corp. Contains pictures to color with captions, puzzles, and activities.

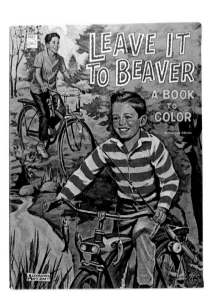

Laverne and Shirley Coloring and Activity Book (#405-4). Published by Playmore Publishing and Waldman Pub. Corp., 1983. Paramount Pictures Corp. The book contains captioned pictures describing several short sequences of cast adventures, as well as puzzles and activities.

Wyatt Earp Starring Hugh O'Brian A Book to Color (#1131). Copyright 1957, Wyatt Earp Enterprises, Inc. Published by Saalfield Publishing Co.

Leave It To Beaver; A Book to Color (#5662). Published by Saalfield Publishing, 1958, 1963. Gomalco Productions, Inc. A very thick book with about half of the pictures captioned of cast members and the other half of uncaptioned pictures of flowers, toys etc. Other coloring books from the series include those published by Whitman, 1958 and by Saalfield, 1963.

The Lone Ranger

"The Lone Ranger" continued on television after being a success on radio and in the movies. The most famous TV Lone Ranger was Clayton Moore. Tonto was played by Jay Silverheels.

The first television presentation aired on ABC from 1949 to 1957 and then periodically until 1965. There were 221 episodes by the end of the series.

The Lucy Show

In 1961, the Queen of American television comedy, Lucille Ball, began a new CBS television series without her earlier partner, husband Desi Arnaz. Although no other television comedy would ever be as popular as the original "I Love Lucy" series, the new Lucy program was very successful. Lucy chose Vivian Vance from the earlier series to work with her in the new show. The story line followed the day-to-day adventures shared by Lucy Carmichael (played by Lucille Ball) and Vivian Bagley (Vivian Vance) as they shared a home in Connecticut with their children.

In 1965, the series changed its format when Vivian left the show. In the new story, Lucy Carmichael worked as a secretary to Theodore J. Mooney (Gale Gordon) at the Westland Bank in San Francisco. This plot was the basis for the show until 1968.

Magic Land of Allakazam

The "Magic Land of Allakazam" was a children's show which aired on CBS from 1960 to 1963 and then continued on ABC in 1964. Mark Wilson was the magician in the Magical Kingdom and the show involved many magical adventures.

Hi-Yo Silver The Lone Ranger Paint Book. Copyright The Lone Ranger Inc. 1938. Drawings by Ted Horn. Whitman Publishing Co. Contains captioned pcitures.

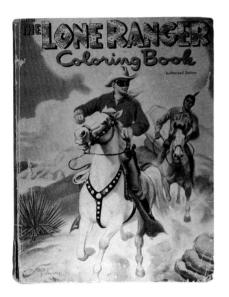

The Lone Ranger Coloring Book (#1117-15). Copyright 1951 by The Lone Ranger Inc. Published by Whitman Publishing Co. Contains captioned pictures to color.

The Lone Ranger Coloring Book (#208425). Copyright 1953 by The Lone Ranger, Inc. Created by George W. Trendle. Published by Whitman Publishing Co. Contains captioned pictures to color.

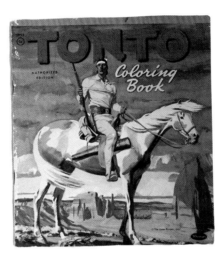

Tonto Coloring Book (#2953). Copyright 1957 The Lone Ranger, Inc. Drawings by Alexander Toth and Bob Barthram. Published by Whitman Publishing Co. Contains mostly uncaptioned pictures.

Magic Land of Allakazam (#1421). Copyright 1962 by Mark Wilson Enterprises, Inc. Drawings by Bob Jenney. Published by Whitman Publishing Co. Captioned pictures show the tricks and people from the TV show.

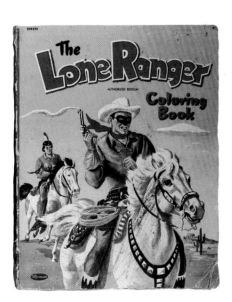

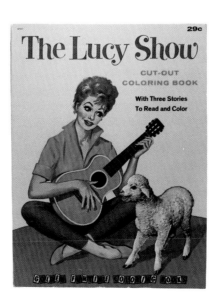

The Lucy Show Cut-Out Coloring Book. Published by Golden Press, 1963. Desily Prod. SF 227. Includes several figures to cut out and color as well as three illustrated stories to read and color.

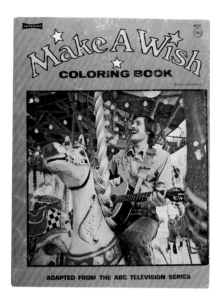

Make a Wish (#4655). Copyright 1973 by the American Broadcasting Co., Inc. Published by Saalfield Publishing Co. The pictures represent things a child could wish for.

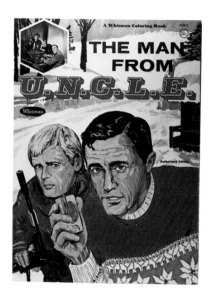

Universal City Studio A Coloring Book (#9576). "The Virginian," "Karen," "McHale's Navy," "Wagon Train." Copyright 1964 by MCA Enterprises, Inc. Published by Saalfield Publishing Co. Contains captioned pictures of studio and each of the television show characters.

Make A Wish

"Make A Wish" was an acclaimed children's program that aired on the ABC network from 1971-1976. This Sunday educational series was hosted by Tom Chaplin and the show was filled with educational animation, sketches, films, songs, and interviews. The program won a Peabody award in 1971 and an Emmy award in 1973.

The Man From U.N.C.L.E.

"The Man From U.N.C.L.E." was a popular television show in the 1960s. The program began as a sixty minute show on NBC in September, 1964. It ended its run in January, 1968 after airing 104 episodes.

The letters in the title stand for United Network Command for Law Enforcement. The plot involved the U.N.C.L.E. agents' adventures as they clashed with another international organization called THRUSH in a quest to end the crime wave being waged by that organization.

Leading characters were: Napoleon Solo (Robert Vaughn); Illya Kuryakin (David McCallum); and the head of U.N.C.L.E. Leo G. Carroll.

McHale's Navy

"McHale's Navy" was a telvision series based in the South Pacific on the island of Taratupa during World War II. It first aired in September, 1962 and ended in September, 1965. The war story starred Ernest Borgnine as Lt. Cdr. Quinton McHale. Joe Flynn and Tim Conway were also in the cast. Before the series ended, the action had moved to Southern Italy as the war neared its end.

Mister Ed

"Mister Ed" had one of the most far-fetched story lines of the silly sit-coms of the 1960s. In this thirty minute show, Wilbur and Carol Post were married and discovered that a horse, Mr. Ed, came with their house. This horse was different, however, because Mr. Ed could talk, but he would only speak to Wilbur. The plots revolved around this premise.

The program was broadcast on CBS from 1961 to 1966 and consisted of 143 episodes. Wilbur and Carol Post were played by Alan Young and Connie Hines.

The Monkees

"The Monkees," a comedy series about a rock and roll group, began on NBC in 1966 and aired until 1968. In 1966, the program won an Emmy as the year's best comedy series. When the show went off the air for NBC, the network received more letters to protest the move than had ever been received before by the network during a similar circumstance. CBS broadcast the show from 1969 to 1972 and then the series ended its life on ABC during the 1972-1973 season. The Monkees were played by Davy Jones, Mike Nesmith, Micky Dolenz and Peter Tork.

The Man From U.N.C.L.E. (#1095). Copyright 1967 by Metro-Goldwyn-Mayer Inc. Published by Whitman Publishing Co. Captioned pictures tell the story of one of their cases.

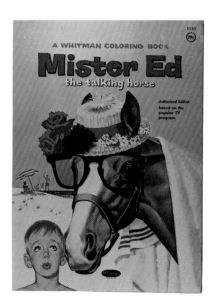

Mister Ed the Talking Horse (#1135). Copyright 1963, Mister Ed Company. Published by Whitman Publishing Co. Captioned pictures tell story of adventures.

The Monkees Big Beat Fun Book. Young World Productions LTD, London. Copyright 1986, Raybert Productions, Inc. Screen Gems, Inc. Contains pictures to color, puzzles, and two colored pictures of the popular singing group suitable for framing.

Mork and Mindy

"Mork and Mindy" was an instant hit when it aired on ABC in 1978. Mork (Robin Williams) came from the Planet of Ork. He landed in Boulder, Colorado where he became friends with Mindy McConnell (Pam Dawber). The episodes dealt with Mork's adventures as he tried to learn about the alien culture in the United States. The program's hit status was due largely to the talent of Robin Williams and the program ran until 1982.

My Favorite Martian

"My Favorite Martian" was another zany situation comedy from the 1960s. The show aired on CBS from 1963 to 1966. The story line involves a newspaper reporter named Tim O'Hara (Bill Bixby) who rescues a professor from Mars after a UFO crash. The Martian professor (Ray Walston) pretends to be Tim's uncle while he repairs his space ship so he can return to Mars.

My Little Margie

"My Little Margie" was an early successful situation comedy which aired on CBS from 1952—1953 and on NBC from 1953—1955. Altogether there were 126 episodes. The show starred silent film star Charles Farrell as father, Vern Albright, and movie star Gale Storm as his daughter, Margie. The story depicted the problems in a father and daughter relationship.

My Three Sons

"My Three Sons" was a favorite television situation comedy for over ten years. During its time on the air, new characters were added as the family was enlarged. The show aired on ABC from 1960-1965. Then it switched to CBS where it remained until 1972. The original cast included Steve Douglas, a widower raising three sons, played by Fred MacMurray. The three sons were played by Tim Considine, Don Grady, and Stanley Livingston, and their grandfather, household-helper was played by William Frawley. William Demarest replaced Frawley after several years and his character was called Uncle Charlie. The family also added another son when they adopted Ernie (Barry Livingston). The father, Steve, eventually re-married and became a stepfather to a daughter named Dodie (Dawn Lyn). The sons grew up on the series beginning college, careers, and families of their own.

Mork from ORK An Outerspace Activity Book. Published by Wonder Books by Tony Tallarico. Copyright 1979 Paramount Pictures Corp. Contains pictures of cast members to color, plus photos of cast, plus puzzles.

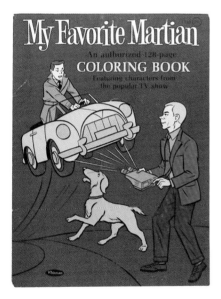

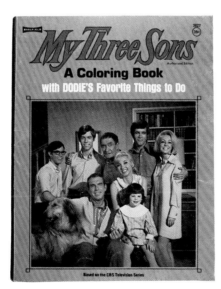

My Favorite Martian (#1148). Copyright by Jack Chertok Television, Inc. Published by Whitman Publishing Co. Drawings by Dan Gormley. Captioned pictures to color of the characters from the show.

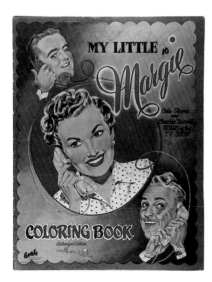

My Three Sons; A Coloring Book With Dodie's Favorite Things To Do (#3827). Copyright 1971 by Columbia Broadcasting System, Inc. Published by Saalfield Publishing Co. Contains mostly captioned pictures of the cast to color. The book also has a paper doll and clothes to color of Dodie and the triplets inside the book.

My Little Margie Coloring Book, Gale Storm and Charles Farrell Stars of the T.V. show. Copyright 1954, Rovan Films. Published by Saalfield Publishing Co. with captioned pictures to color.

My Three Sons (#1113). Copyright 1967, Columbia Broadcating System, Inc. Drawings by Bob Jenney. Published by Whitman Publishing Co. with captioned pictures to color.

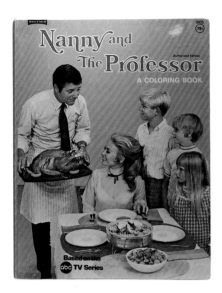

Nanny and the Professor (#3835). Copyright 1960, 1961 by Twentieth Century-Fox Film Corporation. Published by Saalfield Publishing Co.

Nanny and the Professor

"Nanny and the Professor" began on ABC on January 21, 1970. The thirty minute program ended on December 27, 1971 after sixty-five episodes. The story line involved the household of widower Professor Harold Everett (Richard Long) and his children Hal, Butch, and Prudence. Nanny was played by Juliet Mills who seemed to have the ability to spread love and joy throughout the household.

National Velvet

The "National Velvet" television series aired on NBC from 1960 to 1962. It was based on the M-G-M movie from 1944 which had starred a very young Elizabeth Taylor. The movie had been based on the book written by Enid Bagnold.

The story was about Velvet Brown (Lori Martin) who was training her horse, King, to run in the Grand National Steeple Chase. Velvet's father and mother were played by Ann Doran and Arthur Space.

Northwest Passage

The "Northwest Passage" television series began on NBC in 1958 and continued until 1959. The story took place in 1754 during the French-Indian War. Major Robert Rogers (Keith Larsen) was searching for a Northwest passage in order to link the East with the West. Buddy Ebsen was also in the cast playing the part of Sergeant Hunk Marriner.

Ozzie's Girls

"Ozzie's Girls" continued the story of the Ozzie and Harriet Nelson family. Since sons Dave and Ricky were grown, the Nelson's rented rooms to two college girls played by Susan Sennett and Brenda Sykes.

The program was a syndicated show in 1973, but without the popular Nelson boys, the show did not have much impact on viewers and only twenty-four episodes were filmed.

The Partridge Family

"The Partridge Family" was a hit show on ABC from 1970 to 1974. Much of its success was due to the cast member David Cassidy, who became a teen idol. The mother on the series, Shirley Partridge (Shirley Jones) and her children, changed from an ordinary family to a famous rock singing group on the show. Besides Cassidy, the other children were played by Susan Dey, Danny Bonaduce, and Suzanne Crough.

National Velvet Coloring Book (#2975-B). Based on M-G-M's "National Velvet" NBC television version. Copyright 1963 by Metro-Goldwyn-Mayer, Inc. Published by Whitman Western Printing. Drawings by Al Anderson and Nathalee Mode with pictures from the story to color.

MGM-TV's Northwest Passage Coloring Book (#2852). Published by Samuel Lowe Co., 1959. Full of action pictures to color.

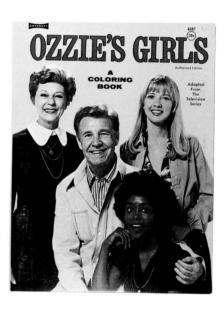

Ozzie's Girls (#4687). Adapted from the television series. Drawings by Gary Thomas. Copyright 1973, Filmways Television Corp. Published by The Saalfield Publishing Co. Captioned pictures.

The Partridge Family: A Coloring Book. Copyright 1970, Columbia Pictures Industries, Inc. ABC. Published by The Saalfield Publishing Co. Right: #3939; 1970, 1971. Both books contain the same pictures inside, although they have different covers.

The Patty Duke Show

Patty Duke became a child star on Broadway in the play *The Miracle Worker* in 1959. She was awarded an Oscar as best supporting actress in 1962 when she repeated her role as Helen Keller in the United Artists film version of the play. She secured more fame, however, with her television program "The Patty Duke Show," which was shown on ABC television from 1963-1966. Patty played a double role as cousins Cathy and Patty. Patty was American while Cathy was from England.

Peter Potomus

"Peter Potomus" was a Hanna-Barbera syndicated animated cartoon from 1964. Other characters besides Peter were a hippo and a monkey.

Planet of the Apes

The "Planet of the Apes" television series was adapted from the successful motion picture from 1968. It was first shown on television in September, 1974 and ended in December of the same year after only thirteen episodes. In the science fiction story, a U.S. space capsule passed the time barrier and emerged in the year 3085. The capsule landed in a place ruled by apes. The surviving astronauts were befriended by one of the intelligent apes (Roddy McDowall) as they tried to return to their home. Ron Harper and James Naughton were the astronauts.

The Quiz Kids

One of the best radio quiz shows of it era, "The Quiz Kids" featured Joe Kelly, the master of cermonies, asking a panel of youngsters very tough questions. The first broadcast of the program was June 28, 1940 when it was used as a summer replacement on NBC. That fall, the show got its own spot on the Blue Network and later was shifted to NBC on Sunday afternoons. Over fifty children under the age of sixteen were members of the panel during the time the show was aired.

Ramar of the Jungle

"Ramar of the Jungle" was a syndicated television series that took place in Nairobi, Africa. The show centered on the experiences of Dr. Thomas Reynolds, a research scientist, and his assistant professor, Ogden. Dr. Reynolds (Jon Hall) was called Ramar—White Witch Doctor. His assistant was played by Ray Montgomery. Fifty-two episodes of the program were syndicated in 1952.

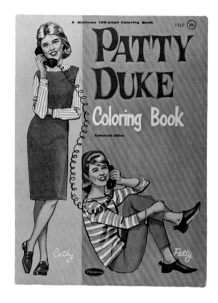

Patty Duke Coloring Book (#1122). Published by Whitman Publishing Co., 1964. Copyright by United Artists Television, Inc. Captioned pictures tell the story of Patty's television family's vacation. From "The Patty Duke Show."

Planet of the Apes Cut and Color Book (#2434). Copyright 1967, 1974 Apjac Prod., Inc. and Twentieth Century-Fox Film Corp. Published by Saalfield Publishing Co. Contains pictures of the cast to color plus many stand-up figures to color and cut out.

Ramar of the Jungle (#4529). Copyright MCMLVI, The Saalfield Publishing Co. Captioned pictures tell story.

Peter Potamus (#1139). Copyright 1964 by Hanna-Barbera Productions, Inc. Published by Whitman Publishing Co. Full of pictures of the cartoon characters.

The Quiz Kids Follow the Dots and Find the Answers (#270). Copyright MCMXLI, MCMXLII by Louis Cowan. Published by Saalfield Publishing Co. Book and photograph courtesy of Joseph Golembieski.

Rango

"Rango," a short-lived television series, was only on the air from January to June in 1967. Rango was played by comedy star Tim Conway. The show was a western comedy about an inept Texas ranger named Rango who comically could not function as well as his fellow officers.

Rat Patrol

"Rat Patrol" was another television series about World War II which ran on ABC from 1966 to 1968. The action took place in North Africa. Players included: Christopher George, Gary Raymond, Justin Tarr, and Larry Casey.

The Restless Gun

During the heyday of the television Western, film star John Payne joined the ranks of TV Western heroes in a show called "The Restless Gun." His part was that of Vint Bonner, an ex-gunfighter who aided people in distress during the period shortly after the Civil War. The program was broadcast over NBC from 1957-1959.

Sergeant Preston of the Yukon

"Sergeant Preston of the Yukon" was a television series syndicated in 1955. Richard Simmons played the leading role of Sergeant William Preston. Preston became a North west Mounted Policeman when he went to the Yukon to find his father's killer. His dog, Yukon King, also played a prominent part in the action.

Sesame Street

"Sesame Street," the wonderful, long-lasting educational television program for kids, premiered on the NET network on November 10, 1969. On November 9, 1970 it became affiliated with PBS and remains on that network today.

The show, which is geared towards very young children, consists of cartoons, stories, songs, and puzzles used in many ways to be educational. Jim Henson's Muppets have played a big part in the success of "Sesame Street."

Rango (#9575). Copyright 1967, Thomas/Timkel Productions. Based on the ABC TV Series. Published by The Saalfield Publishing Co. Contains captioned pictures to color.

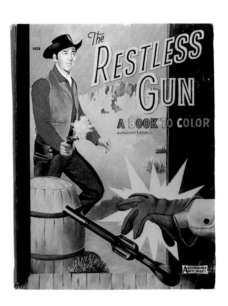

The Restless Gun A Book To Color (#4828). Copyright 1958, Window Glen Production Co. Published by The Saalfield Publishing Co. Captioned pictures of cast.

Sergeant Preston Coloring Book (#1329). Copyright Sergeant Preston of the Yukon, Inc. Published by Whitman Publishing Co., 1953. Action pictures of the show's characters. Another coloring book was published by Treasure Books, 1957.

The Rat Patrol; A Story Book To Color (#9559). Based on the ABC TV Series. Published by Saalfield Publishing Co. The captioned pictures tell a story of an adventure from the television series.

Sesame Street The Count's Coloring Book (#1131-2). Western Publishing Co. in conjunction with Children's Television Workshop, 1976. Copyright, Muppets, Inc. Illustrations by Joe Mathieu. *The Sesame Street Fire Department Coloring Book* (#1128-70). Pictures by Don Page. Copyright 1984, Western Publishing Co. in conjunction with Children's Television Workshop. Muppets, Inc.

The Shadow

"The Shadow" began as a radio character on a program for Street and Smith's *Detective Story*. At first, the announcer/narrator was "The Shadow." Later, the character turned into Lamont Cranston, a crime fighter who was the first to lead two lives, both as a regular man and as an invisible creature of the night.

By 1936, the radio program was on Mutual and the Cranston character had become the star of the show. Several famous actors played parts on the series through the years, including: Orson Welles, Agnes Moorehead, and Keenan Wynn.

Shari Lewis Show

The "Shari Lewis Show" was aired by NBC from 1960-1963. Shari Lewis was a famous ventriloquist, providing voices for her puppets Lambchop, Charlie Horse, and Hush Puppy. This show for children had music, stories, and various guests on the program.

Sigmund and the Sea Monsters

"Sigmund and the Sea Monsters" was a comedy program which aired on NBC from 1973 to 1975. The action concerned a sea monster named Sigmund (Billy Barty) who was rescued by brothers Johnny (Johnny Whitaker) and Scott (Scott Kolden). Sigmund's family had disowned him for not scaring people properly so the boys took him home to their club house and protected him from his sea monster family.

Six Million Dollar Man

The "Six Million Dollar Man" had its beginnings as a television movie in 1973 and with that success was made into a series for ABC that aired from 1974 to 1978.

In the story, Steve Austin (Lee Majors) was injured in an airplane crash and the Office of Strategic Operations spent six million dollars to repair his injuries. Nuclear power was used on his replacement parts. He turned out to be part human and part machine. His girlfriend, Jaime Somers (Lindsay Wagner), eventually had her own show called "Bionic Woman."

The Shadow coloring Book (#4636). Copyright 1974, The Condé Nast Publications, Inc. Published by The Saalfield Publishing Co. Art by Tony Tallarico with captioned pictures.

Sigmund and the Sea Monsters (#4634). Adapted from the TV series. Copyright 1974, Sid and Marty Krofft Prod., Inc. Published by The Saalfield Publishing Co. with captioned pictures from the series.

Shari Lewis and Her Puppets (#5335). Copyright 1961 by National Broadcasting Co. Published by Saalfield Publishing Co. Drawings by Jerry Robinson. Most of the captioned pictures are of Shari and her puppets.

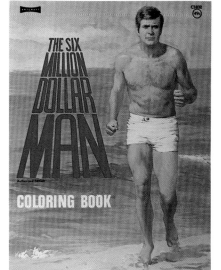

The Six Million Dollar Man (#c2471). Activity Book. Copyright 1977, Universal City Studios. Published by Rand McNally and Co. Includes captioned pictures, plus puzzles and stand-up figures to color and cut.

The Six Million Dollar Man (#c1832). Copyright 1974, Universal City Studios, Inc. Published by The Saalfield Publishing Co. with captioned pictures of an adventure.

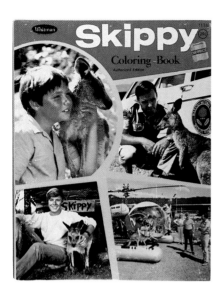

Skippy Coloring Book (#1116). Copyright 1970 by Norfolk International Films Limited. A Whitman Book, Western Publishing Co. Drawings by Sparky Moore with captioned pictures.

Soupy Sales (#8907). Fun and Activity Book. Illustrated by Tony Tallarico. Copyright 1965 by Soupy Sales—WMC. Published by Treasure Books. Includes pictures to color of Soupy, plus puzzles and things to make.

Skippy the Bush Kangaroo

"Skippy the Bush Kangaroo" was a syndicated thirty minute show made in 1969. The action took place in Waratah National Park in Australia, where the Chief Ranger (Ed Devereaux) and his son lived. Skippy was a kangaroo that was injured as a baby and the son (Garry Pankhurst) made a pet of him. The adventures centered around these characters.

Soupy Sales

"Soupy Sales" had several television shows for children over the years. He did local shows in Detroit beginning in 1953, in Los Angeles in 1959, and in New York in the mid-1960s. His network shows were "The Soupy Sales Show" on ABC from July 4, 1955 to August 26, 1955 and from October 3, 1959 to June 25, 1960. His New York show from WNEW—TV was syndicated from 1966 to 1968.

Space: 1999

"Space: 1999" was a syndicated English produced science fiction show that lasted from 1974 to 1976. Martin Landau played the Commander and Barbara Bain was Dr. Helena Russell. The crew was thrown into outer space by a nuclear explosion on the moon and had to cope with the situation.

Star Trek

"Star Trek," the animated version of the popular television series, aired on NBC from 1973-1975. This science fiction adventure took place in the 22nd century aboard the star ship U.S.S. Enterprise. Capt. Kirk, Officer Spock, Lieutenant Uhura and Dr. Leonard McCoy were leading characters.

Space: 1999 Coloring Book (c1881). Published by The Saalfield Publishing Co. ATV Corp. Captioned pictures of a space adventure to color.

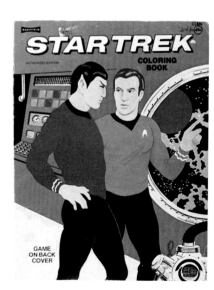

Star Trek Coloring Book (#c1856). Copyright 1975, Paramount Pictures Corp. Published by Saalfield Publishing Co. Drawings by Robert Doramus with captioned pictures of the story.

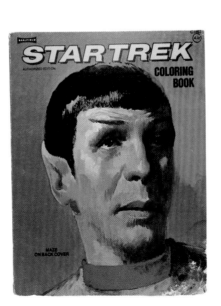

Star Trek Coloring Book (c1862). Copyright 1975, Paramount Pictures. Published by The Saalfield Publishing Co. with captioned pictures of the cast members.

Stingray

"Stingray" was a syndicated English produced puppet show from 1965. The marionation process was by Gerry and Sylvia Anderson. The World Aquanaut Security Patrol was based on the ocean floor and this organization played a big part in the action of the show along with the futuristic submarine, Stingray.

Tales of the Texas Rangers

The "Tales of the Texas Rangers" premiered on ABC in September, 1957 and after fifty-two episodes was discontinued in 1959. Stories for this western were based on early cases from the Texas Rangers, North America's oldest law enforcement organization. Willard Parker and Harry Lauter played the Rangers.

Tales of the Vikings

"Tales of the Vikings" was a syndicated program of thirty-nine episodes from 1960. It was an advernture series that took place in A.D. 1000. Leif Ericson (Jerome Courtland) and his sea raiders, the Vikings, were featured.

The Tales of Wells Fargo

"The Tales of Wells Fargo" began on NBC in 1957 as a thirty minute show. From September, 1961 through September, 1962 it was a sixty minute program. When the program first appeared it was set in the West in the 1860s and starred Dale Robertson as Jim Hardie, a Wells Fargo agent. Later, the show expanded to include Hardie's home life as a rancher.

Tarzan

The Tarzan character was created in stories by Edgar Rice Burroughs. Many successful motion pictures were made before NBC began the television series in 1966. The series lasted until September 13, 1968 and the fifty-seven episodes were put into syndication in 1969. Tarzan was raised by apes in Africa after his parents were killed. The television series involved Tarzan's efforts to protect his country from those who had set out to harm it. Tarzan was played by Ron Ely.

Stingray Coloring Book (#1133). Copyright 1966, A.P. Films Ltd. and ITC Ltd. Published by Whitman Publishing Co. Captioned pictures tell a story of the crew's adventures.

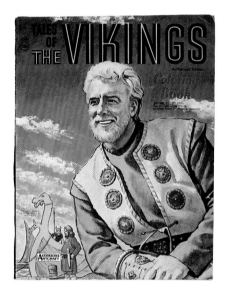

Tales of the Vikings (#4566). Published by Saalfield Publishing Co. Copyright by Bryna Prod. S.A. United Artists Tel. Presentation. Drawings by Norton Stewart. The captioned pictures tell a story.

Tales of the Texas Rangers Coloring Book (#2071). Published by Saalfield Publishing Co., 1958. Contains captioned pictures of cast members.

Tarzan Coloring Book (#1157). Copyright 1968, Edgar Rice Burroughs, Inc. Published by Whitman Publishing, Western Publishing Co.. Drawings by Arnie Kohn with captioned pictures to color.

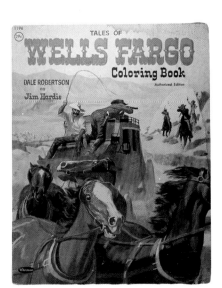

Tales of Wells Fargo Coloring Book. Copyright 1957, Overland Productions, Inc. Published by Whitman Publishing Co. Contains captioned pictures that tell several short sequences of events involving cast members.

That Girl

"That Girl" was broadcast over ABC from 1966 to 1971. The situation comedy was about a young woman leaving home, not to get married, but to pursue a career as an actress. This series provided a new role model for young women in that it was okay to be single and to seek a career. The would-be actress, Ann Marie, was played by Marlo Thomas. Ted Bessell was her boyfriend and Lew Parker and Rosemary DeCamp played her parents.

Thunderbirds

"Thunderbirds," an English-produced television show syndicated in 1966, was an adventure program about an International Rescue Organization. The program was a marionette series. Gerry and Sylvia Anderson did the marionation process.

Time For Beany

The "Time For Beany" program began in 1949 as a local show on KTLA in Los Angeles and became a syndicated show in 1950. Beany and Cecil were puppets. Beany was a boy whose trademark was a propellor topped hat. Cecil was a seasick sea serpent. The fifteen minute show won Emmy awards in 1949, 1950 and 1952. Bob Clampett was the creator of the program.

Trouble With Father

"Trouble With Father" was an early situation comedy which aired on ABC in 1950 and remained on the air until 1955. It was a typical family program with father Stu Irwin, a high school principal, trying to manage both his school and his family. Members of the family were June Collyer as his wife, Ann Todd as daughter Joyce, and Sheila James as daughter Jackie.

That Girl Coloring Book (#4513). Copyright 1967, Daisey Production, Inc. Published by The Saalfield Publishing Co. Based on the ABC television series starring Marlo Thomas. Contains captioned pictures that tell story.

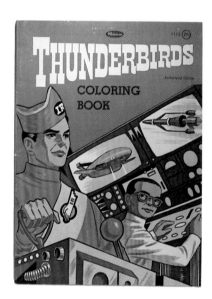

Thunderbirds Coloring Book (#1115). Published by Whitman Publishing Co. 1968. A.P. Films Ltd. Captioned pictures with adventures.

That Girl Coloring Book (#4510). "Based on the ABC TV Series Starring Marlo Thomas." Copyright MCMLXVII, MCMLXIX, Daust Production, Inc. Published by The Saalfield Publishing Co. Contains captioned pictures to color.

June and Stu Erwin "Trouble With Father" (#125810). Copyright 1954, Saalfield Publishing Co. with captioned pictures of the cast.

Bob Clampett Beany's Coloring Book. Copyright 1951, Whitman Publishing Co. From "Time for Beany" TV show. Contains assorted captioned pictures of Beany and friends.

Voyage to the Bottom of the Sea

The "Voyage to the Bottom of the Sea" program was supposed to take place in 1983, even though it aired from 1964-1968. The sixty minute show from ABC dealt with an atomic powered submarine and scientific research.

Admiral Harriman Nelson was played by Richard Basehart, David Hedison was Cdr. Lee Crane, and Henry Kulky was Chief Petty Officer Curley Jones.

The Waltons

The first glimpse television audiences had of the Walton family was in a television movie. Earl Hamner, Jr. was the creator of the series which was based on his childhood memories. The drama took place in Virginia in the 1930s. The stories revolved around a poor rural family as they tried to cope with the hard times of the Depression. Characters were: Father—Ralph Waite; Mother—Michael Learned; Grandpa—Will Geer; Grandma—Ellen Corby. The children included: John Boy—Richard Thomas; Mary Ellen—Judy Norton; Jim-Bob—David S. Harper; Elizabeth— Kami Cotler; Jason—Jon Walmsley; Erin—Mary Elizabeth McDonough; Ben—Eric Scott. The television series began on CBS in 1972 and ended its run in 1981.

Welcome Back Kotter

Although Gabriel Kaplan played the leading role of Gabe Kotter in the "Welcome Back Kotter" series, it was John Travolta who became the most popular actor in the show. The story took place at a Brooklyn high school where alumni Kotter returned to be a teacher. His pupils included Vinnie Barbarina played by Travolta, Frederick "Boom Boom" Washington, Arnold Horshack, Rosalie "Hotsie" Totzi and Vernajean Williams. These "sweat hogs" were especially appealing to junior and senior high school students of the era. The show aired on ABC from 1975 to 1979.

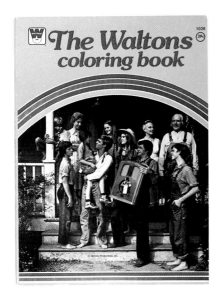

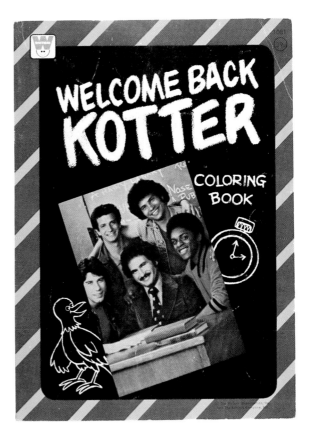

Voyage to the Bottom of the Sea (#1851-B). Copyright 1965 by Cambridge Productions, Inc. and Twentieth Century-Fox Television, Inc. Published by Western Publishing Co. Pictures by Jason Studios. The captioned pictures tell a story using the television characters.

The Waltons Coloring Book (#1028). Copyright MCMLXXV by Lorimar Prod., Inc. A Whitman Book by Western Publishing Co. Contains captioned pictures of cast.

The Waltons Color and Activity Book (#1254). MCMLXXV by Lorimar Prod., Inc. A Whitman Book by Western Publishing Co. Has pictures to color, puzzles, and activities.

Welcome Back Kotter Coloring Book (#1081). Copyright 1977 by The Wolper Organization and the Komack Co., Inc. Published by the Whitman Publishing Co. The captioned pictures tell stories from the show.

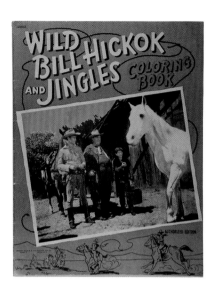

Wild Bill Hickok

The "Wild Bill Hickok" program first appeared as a syndicated show in 1952. In 1957 it was used on ABC and continued on that network until 1958, with a total of 113 episodes.

The program was a typical Western, based on the adventures of Wild Bill Hickok, a U.S. Marshall, and his partner, Jingles. Andy Devine made a memorable Jingles and former movie star, Guy Madison, made a handsome Hickok.

Wild Kingdom

Marlin Perkins was host of "Mutual of Omaha's Wild Kingdom." The program aired over NBC from 1963 to 1973 and then was continued in syndication. The shows documented the lives of wild animals from different parts of the world.

Wonderbug

"Wonderbug" was part of "The Krofft Super Show" shown on ABC in 1976. Wonderbug was a car that was a combination of several wrecked cars. Three teenagers, Susan (Anne Seflinger), Barry (David Levy), and C.C. (Anthony Bailey) used the car to fight against evil.

You'll Never Get Rich (Sgt. Bilko)

Phil Silvers created one of television's all-time great characters when he was cast as Sgt. Ernie Bilko in the series "You'll Never Get Rich." The program aired on CBS from 1955 to 1959. The 138 episodes were put into syndication and continued to be popular in this form as well. The show was a situation comedy about an army camp in Roseville, Kansas. Bilko was in charge of the motor pool and he spent every waking hour trying to make money the easy way—without working for it. Paul Ford played his commanding officer.

Wild Bill Hickok and Jingles Coloring Book (#120910). Copyright 1953, Saalfield Publishing Co. Illustrated by Henry Muheim. The captioned pictures tell a story.

Mutual of Omaha's Wild Kingdom Coloring Book. Copyright Don Meier Productions, 1976. A Whitman Book, Western Publishing Co. Contains captioned pcitures to color.

Wild Bill Hickok (#2907). Copyright 1961, Waldman Publishing Corp. Contains captioned pictures which tell story.

Sgt. Bilko Coloring Book (#330). Copyright 1959 Columbia Broadcasting Sys., Inc. Published by Treasure Books, Inc. contains captioned pictures of a cast adventure.

Wonderbug Rock-A-Bye Buggy Coloring Book (#1006). Copyright 1978 by Sid and Marty Krofft Productions, Inc. Published by Whitman, Western Publishing Co. with captioned pictures which tell a sotry.

Christmas Coloring Books

Although Christ was born in a stable nearly two thousand years ago, the customs that surround the celebration of his birth continue to evolve. Christmas coloring books from past years picture some of these innovations as the Christmas holiday changed from a quiet family gathering to the commercial extravaganza it is today.

Santa Claus Paint Book (#657). MCMXXXVI, Whitman Publishing Co. The book is almost completely full of pictures of toys.

Very early paint book with several Santa pictures to color, circa 1900. The Santa pictures are printed in both color and in black and white. The elves and the reindeer are also shown. There is no identifying marking on the book.

Merry Christmas Paint Book (#616). Copyright 1941, Whitman Publishing Co. The book, showing Santa on the cover in a red fuzzy suit, includes pictures of Santa, toys, and people making preparations for Christmas.

Santa's Toys to Color (#924). Published by the Saalfield Publishing Co., circa 1940s. The book contains pictures of toys from the era.

Christmas Coloring Book (#960). Published by The Saalfield Publishing Co., circa 1940s. The book includes pictures showing Christmas trees, toys, and Santa.

Santa's Book to Color (#925). Published by The Saalfield Publishing Co., circa 1940s shows pictures of toys and children.

Merry Christmas Coloring Book (#1164). Copyright 1954 by Whitman Publishing Co. The book contains old-fashioned pictures of Christmas preparations.

Fun! Fun! Fun! Christmas Activities (#1742). Copyright 1958, Whitman Publishing Co. Pictures by Clarence Biers. Captioned pictures of toys, trees, and Santas plus some follow-the-dot pictures, as well as various paper items to color and make. Several ornaments, to be cut-out and used, are featured on the back of the book.

Night Before Christmas (#1126). Whitman Publishing Co., 1963. Drawings by Dan and Norma Garris. The first part of the book is about what present day people are doing to get ready for Christmas. The last section is the story, "The Night Before Christmas."

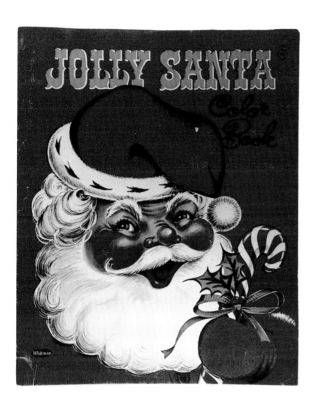

Jolly Santa Color Book (#1742). Copyright 1963 by Whitman Publishing Co. Drawings by Savy. Contains mostly pictures of Santa with a few toys.

Santa's Paint and Color Book (#1086). Copyright Whitman Publishing, 1969. Drawings by Hedwig Wylie. Includes things to make and color, plus regular pictures to color.

Jolly Santa Color Book (1073). Copyright 1965, Whitman, Western Publishing Co. Pictures of toys, Santa, and decorations.

The Santa Claus Coloring Book. Published by Treasure Books, copyright 1972 by Grosset and Dunlap. Most of the book contains Santa pictures to color.

Fictional Characters in Coloring Books

Billy Whiskers Painting and Drawing (No. 250). Published by The Saalfield Publishing Co. Copyright 1919. Pictures to copy and color of the "Adventures of Billy Whiskers" as written by Frances Trego Mongomery. Some of the pictures are printed in color.

Bobbsey Twins

The author of the series of Bobbsey Twins books was always listed as Laura Lee Hope. In reality, the stories were composed by the Stratemeyer Syndicate, formed by Edward Stratemeyer. He was responsible for most of the outlining and editing for several series of children's books, including the Bobbsey Twins. Stratemeyer then farmed out the actual writing to others. The Tom Swift and Bobbsey Twins series were the most popular syndicate books. Stratemeyer died in 1930 and his daughter, Harriet Adams, took over the operation of the syndicate. The business eventually produced over 1200 books during its years of operation.

The first Bobbsey Twins book was published in 1904. The characters included two sets of twins, Bert and Nan, who were eight years old, and Freddie and Flossie, who were four years old.

The Hardy Boys

The Hardy Boys series of books, published by Grosset, began in 1927. The mystery books featured brothers Frank and Joe Hardy who eventually solved a puzzle or crime. Although the books were credited to Franklin Dixon, the Dixon name was a collective pseudonym for several authors who wrote the books.

Harvey

The play *Harvey* opened on Broadway in 1944. It ran for 1,517 performances and won a Pulitzer Prize for its author, Mary Chase. The Broadway production starred Frank Fay as Elwood Dowd, and also starred Josephine Hull. A movie was made in 1951 with James Stewart playing the Dowd role.

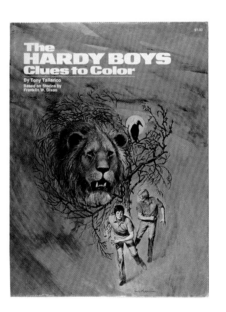

The Hardy Boys Clues to Color by Tony Tallarico. Based on stories by Franklin W. Dixon. Published by Treasure Books. Copyright 1978 by Stratemeyer Syndicate.

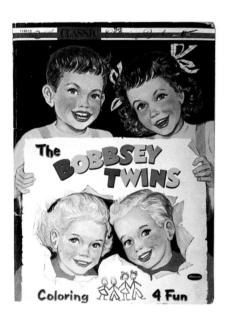

The Bobbsey Twins Coloring 4 Fun (#1130). Copyright 1954 by Whitman Publishing Co. Contains captioned pictures based on the books and stories by Laura Lee Hope.

Harvey the Invisible Rabbit's Own Coloring Book (#2533). Copyright 1944-1946, Brock Pemberton. Published by The Saalfield Publishing Co. "Harvey has come straight from New York City where he is the leading character in the Pulitzer Prize play written by Mary Chase." Includes pictures of Harvey and children he meets. No reference is made to other characters or the story of the play.

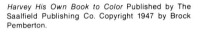

Harvey His Own Book to Color Published by The Saalfield Publishing Co. Copyright 1947 by Brock Pemberton.

A Story-Teller's Paint Book Little Black Sambo also Peter Rabbit (#402). Copyright 1941 by Reuben H. Lilja and Co., Inc. Contains pictures to color with long captions that tell both stories.

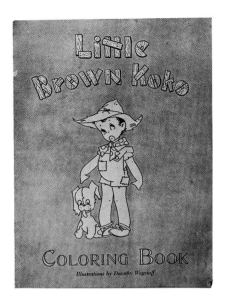

Little Brown Koko Coloring Book. Copyright 1941 by Capper Publications, Inc. Topeka, Kansas. Illustrated by Dorothy Wagstaff. Contains captioned (verse) pictures to color. The Koko character was a stereotype, black child featured in *The Household Magazine* by Capper Publications during the 1940s. The character was originated by Blanche Seale Hunt.

Painting and Drawing Book with Tale of Peter Rabbit by Beatrix Potter. Copyright 1915 by Hurst and Co. Pictures were printed in both color and black and white. Besides the illustrations for the Peter story, other pictures to color are included.

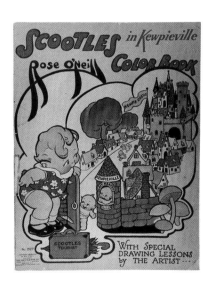

Scootles in Kewpieville Rose O'Neill Color Book (#2127). Copyright MCMXXXVI by Rose O'Neill. Published by Saalfield Publishing Co. The pictures include both the Scootles and Kewpie characters, and each picture is produced in both a finished colored product and in an uncolored version. The book also features drawing lessons by the artist. This coloring book is very collectible because each of the pictures printed in color would be suitable for framing.

Little Black Sambo
   Little Black Sambo was written and illustrated by a Scottish woman, Helen Bannerman, in 1899. Bannerman had married a surgeon in the Indian Medical Service of the British Army, and she lived with him in India for thirty years.
   Although the earlier books of *Little Black Sambo* are very popular with collectors, the story itself has come under fire in recent years because of accused racism.
The Tale of Peter Rabbit
   Beatrix Potter was born in 1866 and grew up in London. She first wrote the story of Peter Rabbit for a young friend, basing the character on her own pet rabbit. In 1901 she illustrated the story and had the small book published privately. A publishing firm called Warne agreed to publish the book commercially in 1902.
Scootles
   The famous illustrator, Rose O'Neill, received much of her fame because of her invention of the Kewpie character (see chapter on dolls). Besides Kewpie, O'Neill was also responsible for the popularity of another unusual character called "Scootles," developed in 1925. O'Neill designed a doll in this image and it has become a popular doll for collectors.
Sunbonnet Babies
   Bertha L. Corbett was a famous illustrator who was responsible for the design of the characters called the "Sunbonnet Babies." She was born on February 8, 1872 in Denver, Colorado. Corbett became an artist and soon published the books she illustrated about the Sunbonnet Babies. Later she added the "Overall Boys." None of the characters' faces were shown in any of the drawings. The girls' heads were covered with their sunbonnets, and the boys were shown from the back so that their straw hats were pictured.

Young American Painting Book. Published by the Ullman Mfg. Co., circa 1915. Small coloring book (5" x 7"). Among other pictures, it contains seven pictures based on the Sunbonnet Babies by Bertha Corbett.

Historical Coloring Books

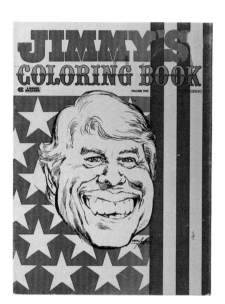

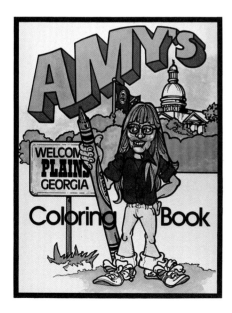

Jimmy Carter

Jimmy Carter was born on October 1, 1924 in Plains, Georgia. He graduated from the U.S. Naval Academy in Annapolis, Maryland in 1946 and was in the navy until 1953 when his father died of cancer. Jimmy Carter then returned to Plains to manage the family farm and peanut warehouse.

After serving two terms as a Georgia State Senator, Carter was elected Governor in 1970. After his term as Georgia Governor, Carter began working full time in a successful campaign to win the Democratic Party nomination for President.

After being elected in 1976 and serving one term as President, Carter was defeated by Ronald Reagan in 1980. Because of his large family and his tie to the peanut industry, cartoonists created lots of satire material during the Carter administration. Even Carter's daughter, Amy, was a center of attention as shown by the coloring book devoted to her life in the White House.

Queen Elizabeth

Queen Elizabeth II was born in London in 1926 to the Duke and Dutchess of York. Her father became King George VI in 1936 when Edward VII abdicated in order to marry "the woman he loved." Elizabeth became the heir to the throne at the age of ten. She also had one sister, Margaret, born in 1930.

In 1947 Elizabeth married Philip Mountbatten, formerly Prince Philip of Greece. Their first child, Charles, was born in 1948, followed by Ann in 1950, Andrew in 1960, and Edward in 1964.

Elizabeth became Queen of England in 1952 at the death of her father. She was twenty-five years old.

Jimmy's Coloring Book (#02840). "The Peanut Farmer's Own Coloring Book," copyrighted and published by Manor Books, Inc., 1976. Contains pictures of Jimmy Carter and other political figures during the time of his nomination and election to the presidency.

Coronation Coloring Book (#2415). Published by The Saalfield Publishing Co., 1953. Contains pictures of the Queen, or places, people, and vehicles involved in the Coronation.

Amy's Coloring Book. Copyright 1977 by Projection 21. Contains captioned pictures to color of Amy Carter from her life as a president's daughter.

National Flags 48 Full Pages to Color. Copyright by Whitman Publishing Co., 1938. contains flags of forty-eight different countries along with information about the color and what the flag represents.

New York World's Fair

New York has held a World's Fair twice in its history; once in 1939 when its theme was "The World of Tomorrow" and again in 1964-1965 with the theme "Peace Through Understanding."

The symbol of the 1964-1965 Fair was the Unisphere. Both fairs were held in Flushing Meadow Park in Queens. One of the highlights of the 1964-1965 Fair was the loan of Michelangelo's sculpture, Pietá from the Vatican. Fifty-one million people toured the Fair.

John F. Kennedy

John F. Kennedy was born May 29, 1917 in Brookline, Massachusetts to Joseph and Rose Kennedy. He was one of nine children.

John Kennedy graduated from Harvard in 1940. At the age of twenty-four he joined the navy, during World War II. After the war, Kennedy was elected as a Congressman from Massachusetts. He was returned for two more terms, and then ran for the Senate, defeating long-time Senator Henry Cabot Lodge.

Kennedy ran against Richard Nixon for the presidency in 1960 and was elected President of the United States.

Kennedy married Jacqueline Bouvier in 1953 and they had three children; Caroline, John, and a baby who died shortly after birth in 1963.

President Kennedy was assassinated on November 22, 1963 in Dallas, Texas. Lee Harvey Oswald was arrested for the murder but he was killed on November 24, 1963 before he could be brought to trial.

New York World's Fair The Official 1964-1965 New York World's Fair Coloring Book. Pictures by Ron Wing. Published by Spertus Publishing Co., 1963. Created and designed by Barry Martin Associates. Contains pictures of the fair to color.

All About the Seattle World's Fair! Official Century 21 Coloring Book. Century 21 Exposition Seattle 1962. Story and pictures by Ross Swift and Bob Godden. Published and distributed by Hays Distributing Inc. Copyright 1961. Contains pictures of the fair, including the Space Needle. The "Century 21 Exposition" was held in Seattle, Washington, in 1962 with the theme of "Man in the Space Age." A rapid monorail train was constructed to transport visitors to the fair. The symbol of the Exposition was a Space Needle that stands 606 feet tall.

JFK Coloring Book. Copyright 1962, Kanrom, Inc. Jackie Kannon. Drawings by Mort Drucker, copy by Paul Laikin, and cover by Beverly Clarke Roman. Contains pictures of President Kennedy, his associates, and his family with long captions heavy on satire.

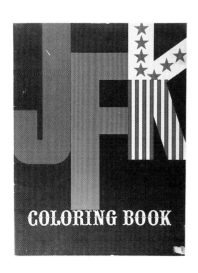

United States Map Including Alaska and Hawaii (#1157). Copyright 1960 by Whitman Publishing Co. Drawings by Sari. Includes maps, plus two to four pages of pictures to color for each state. This coloring book was published shortly after Alaska and Hawaii became states in 1959.

Williamsburg, Virginia

Williamsburg, Virginia was established by English colonists in 1633. Today, much of Williamsburg has been restored to look as it did in 1700. Over eighty of the original buildings have been restored, and fifty more structures have been built on the original sites.

The restoration process began in 1926 when John D. Rockefeller, Jr. provided money to establish the Colonial Williamsburg Foundation.

World War II

With the bombing of Pearl Harbor by the Japanese, on December 7, 1941, the United States was drawn into World War II. During the next few days, the United States declared war on Japan, Italy and Germany.

A major turning point in the war occurred on D-day, June 6, 1944. The Allied Forces used 5,000 ships, 4,000 smaller landing craft, and over 11,000 airplanes in the invasion of the Normandy coast.

By January, 1945, the Allies were nearing the Rhine River and before many months had passed, they were assured of a victory in Europe. On May 7, 1945 Germany officially surrendered.

The war with Japan ended after the Americans dropped atomic bombs on Hiroshima and Nagasaki. On August 19, 1945 Japan surrendered, and the war was over.

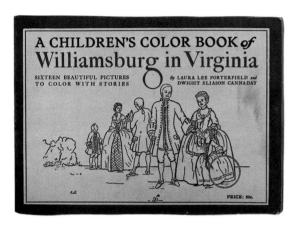

A Children's Color Book of Williamsburg in Virginia. Copyright 1942, Sixth Printing 1952. Published by The Dietz Press.
"Sixteen Beautiful Pictures to Color With Stories by Laura Lee Porterfield and Dwight Eliason Cannaday." Contains pictures of the buildings and people in early Williamsburg.

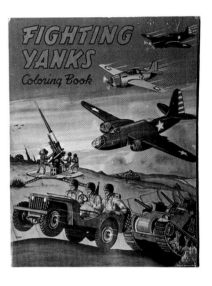

Fighting Yanks Coloring Book (#2469). Published by The Saalfield Publishing Co., from World War II era. Contains captioned pictures of activities from all branches of the service plus pictures of people doing jobs on the home front during the war.

America the Land of the Free Coloring Book (#306). Published by The Saalfield Publishing Co., 1942. Tells the history of the country in pictures to color.

America Our Land. Copyright MCMXLI, The Saalfield Publishing Co. Contains captioned pictures to color about the history of America.

Sky-Hy Coloring Book (#3437). Copyright 1942 Merrill Publishing Co. Although the cover of the book and a few of the inside pictures tie-in to World War II, most of the pictures are of children, animals, and the alphabet.

"Soldier Coloring Book (#1996). Copyright 1943 by Saalfield Publishing Co. These pictures are about training a soldier, but the soldiers are shown as children in uniforms.

Victory Coloring Book (#229). Published by The Saalfield Publishing Co., 1943. Contains captioned pictures which identify equipment. This is a large book with illustrations from the armed services and the home front during the war.

War Planes Tanks and Jeeps (#3469). Copyright 1942, Merrill Publishing Co. Contains captioned war pictures to color. Also has illustrations which show army and navy insignia, identification of planes (several countries), and decorations.

We Fly for the Navy (#3460). Copyright 1943, Merrill Publishing Co. Contains captioned pictures of all kinds of navy planes in action. Other coloring books published by Merrill about World War II include: *The U.S. Marines* (#3462); *Army and Navy Girls* (#3464); *Rangers and Commandos* (#3400); and *Flying Cadet* (#4808).

Young Americans Paint Book. Published by Whitman Publishing Co., 1942. Drawings by Emma Keto. contains captioned pictures of war time activity with children wearing the uniforms and doing the action.

Transportation Related Coloring Books

Railroad

Railroads with steam locomotives were used in England in the 1820s. It wasn't long until the invention was also being used in America. The first passenger trains between New York and Philadelphia were in operation by 1832. These first trains were made in England but soon companies in the United States began to manufacture them.

By 1840 there were 3,000 miles of track in the Eastern part of the United States. Congress approved the building of a transcontinental railroad in 1862. The Union Pacific and the Central Pacific began work on the line from opposite sides of the country. The two companies joined the railroad with a golden spike on May 10, 1869 and the United States was ready for its final expansion.

Apollo: Man on the Moon

On July 20, 1969, the Apollo 11 crew made history when they landed a space craft on the moon. Neil Armstrong and Edwin Aldrin were the first to walk on the moon later that same day. Armstrong's words as he stepped out on to the moon's surface, "That's one small step for man; one giant leap for mankind" are now a part of American folklore.

Fire Engines To Color—To Paint (#515). Published by Samuel Lowe Co., 1943. Contains captioned pictures of great fire engines from the era. During the early 1900s, steam pumpers pulled by horses were replaced by gasoline fire engines.

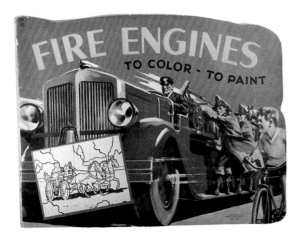

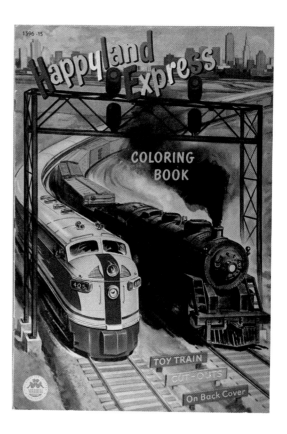

Trains To Color To Paint (#515). Published by Samuel Lowe Co., 1943. Excellent pictures to color of identified trains from the era plus historical trains from the past.

Happyland Express Coloring Book (#1569). Copyright 1951, Merrill Company Publishing. Includes toy train cut-outs on back cover. Contains illustrations of both the insides and outsides of trains but does not give identification.

Coloring Book of the Union Pacific West. Published by the Union Pacific Railroad (circa 1950s). Has color photographs with the same pictures in color book form. The photographs show places to see while on a trip on the Union Pacific West.

Union Pacific Centennial Coloring Book. Contains captioned pictures of the history of trains. The back cover has a colored picture of a modern train. The book was printed to celebrate the centennial anniversary of the driving of the golden spike in Promontory Point, Utah in 1869. This spike completed the transcontinental railroad and made it possible for the vast expansion of America.

Rocket Ships 'N' Jets to Color (#1519). Copyright 1951 by Merrill Company Publishing. Includes aircraft insignia and labeled pictures of planes and uniforms.

Apollo Man on the Moon Coloring Book. The Saalfield Publishing Co., MCMLXIX National Aeronautics and Space Ad. Program. Contains very good, detailed, captioned illustrations of space craft and astronauts.

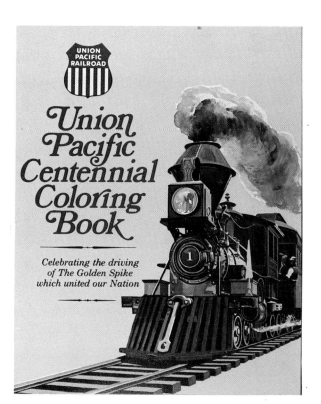

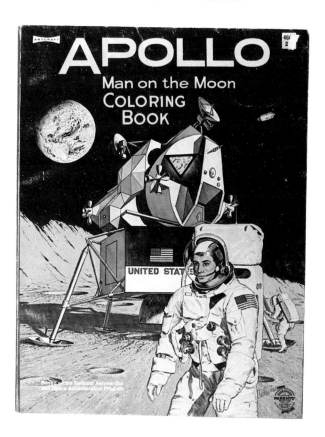

Bibliography

Block, Maxine. "Dinah Shore," *Current Biography 1942*. New York: H. W. Wilson Co., 1942.

Blum, Daniel. *A Pictorial History of the American Theater 1860-1980*. New York: Crown Publishers, Inc., 1981.

Brown, Les. *The New York Times Encyclopedia of Television*. New York: Times Books, 1977.

Buxton, Frank; Owen, Bill. *The Big Broadcast 1920—1950*. New York: Avon Books, 1973.

Campbell, Robert. *The Golden Years of Broadcasting*. New York: Charles Scribner's Sons, Rutledge Book, 1976.

Carpenter, Humphrey; Prichard, Mari. *The Oxford Companion to Children's Literature*. New York: University Press, 1984.

Dietrich, Fred; Reit, Seymour. *Wheels, Sails and Wings. New York: Golden Press, 1961.*

Ferguson, Barbara Chaney. The Paper Doll: A Collector's Guide With Prices. Des Moines, Iowa: Wallace-Homestead, 1982.

Finch, Christopher. *The Art of Walt Disney*. New York: Harry N. Abrams, Inc., 1975.

Fischer, Stuart. *Kids' TV The First 25 Years*. New York: Facts on File Publications, 1983.

Foulke, Jan. *9th Blue Book Dolls and Values*. Cumberland, Maryland: Hobby House Press, 1989.

Gaylesworth, Thomas G. *Television in America A Pictorial History*. New York: Exeter Books, 1986.

Gereau, Gerald. *The Capitol*. Washington, D.C.: U.S. Government Printing Office, 1981.

Gianakos, Larry James. *Television Drama Series A Comprehensive Chronical Programming 1980-1982*. Metuchen, N.J.: The Scarecrow Press, Inc., 1983.

Gianakos, Larry James. *Television Drama Series A Comprehensive Chronical Programming 1982-1984*. Metuchen, N.J.: The Scarecrow Press, Inc., 1987.

Gifford, Denis. *The International Book of Comics*. New York: Crescent Books, The Hamlyn Pub. Group Limited, 1984.

Hake, Ted. *Hake's Guide to TV Collectibles*. Radnor, PA: Wallace-Homestead, 1990.

Hambleton, Ronald. *The Branding of America*. Dublin, New Hampshire: Yankee Books, 1987.

Herbert, Ian, ed. *Who's Who in the Theater Vol. I Biographies*. Detroit, MI: Gale Research Co., 1981.

Hole, Christina. *Christmas and Its Customs*. New York: M. Barrows and Co., Inc. 1958.

Horn, Maurice, ed. *The World Encyclopedia of Comics*. New York: Chelsea House Publishers, 1976.

Kane, Joseph Nathan. *Facts About the Presidents*. New York: H. W. Wilson Co., 1974.

Lambert, Gavin. *The Making of Gone With The Wind*. New York: Bantam Books, 1976.

Lengyel, Cornel Adam. *Presidents of the United States*. New York: Golden Press, 1964.

Longest, David. *Character Toys and Collectibles Second Series*. Paducah, KY: Collector Books, 1987.

Maltin, Leonard, ed. *Leonard Maltin's TV Movies 1985-1986 Edition*. New York: New American Library, 1986.

Ragan, David. *Who's Who in Hollywood 1900-1976*. New Rochelle, New York: Arlington House Publishers, 1976.

Robinson, Jerry. *The Comics*. New York: G. P. Putnam's Sons, 1974.

Rothe, Anna, ed. "Walt Disney," *Current Biography 1952*. New York: H. W. Wilson Co., 1953.

Rothe, Anna, ed. "Faye Emerson," *Current Biography 1951*. New York: H. W. Wilson Co., 1951.

Shipman, David. *The Great Movie Stars: The Golden Years*. New York: Bonanza Books, 1970.

Shulman, Arthur, Youman, Roger. *How Sweet It Was*. New York: Bonanza Books, 1966.

Siedel, Frank and James. *Pioneers in Science*. Boston: Houghton Mifflin Co., 1968.

Smith, Patricia. *Doll Values: Antique to Modern Series Six*. Paducah, KY: Collector Books, 1990.

Terrace, Vincent. *The Complete Encyclopedia of Television Programs 1947-1979 Vol. I, Vol. II*. New York: A.S. Barnes and Co., 1979.

Welsh, Douglas. *History of American Wars*. Bison Books Corp., 1983.

Wlaschin, Ken. *The Illustrated Encyclopedia of the World's Great Movie Stars and Their Films*. New York: Harmony Books, 1979.

Woodcock, Jean. *Paper Dolls of Famous Faces*. Binghamton, New York: Printed by Niles and Phippe, 1974.

Young, Mary. *A Collector's Guide to Paper Dolls*. Paducah, KY: Collector Books, 1980.

Young, Mary. *A Collector's Guide to Paper Dolls Second Series*. Paducah, KY: Collector Books, 1984.

Zillner, Dian. *Hollywood Collectibles*. West Chester, PA: Schiffer Publishing, Ltd., 1991.

Index

Price Guide

The prices in this value guide should be used only as a guide and they should not be used to set prices for coloring books. Prices vary from one section of the country to another and also from dealer to dealer. The prices listed here are the best estimates the author can give at the time of publication, but prices can change quickly. Neither the author nor the publisher assumes responsibility for any losses that may incurr as a result of consulting this guide.

The first price listed is for the coloring book in used condition. The book may have been completely colored or have tears or marks on the cover. The second price is for a mint coloring book with no wear or colored pages. These books are hard to find. Most books fall somewhere in between and a value can be placed on a book by checking the number of pages that have been colored and the overall condition of the book. A mint condition book may bring over twice as much money as a used book, even if the coloring has been done nicely. The combination coloring and paper doll books may bring three times as much if the book is in mint condition and uncut, compared to a book that has cut, incomplete paper dolls.

TR= top right, TL= top left, MR= middle right, ML= middle left, BR= bottom right, BL= bottom right.

Page	Position	Price Range	Page	Position	Price Range	Page	Position	Price Range	Page	Position	Price Range
5	TR	20-50		BR	15-45		BR	50-100		BR	15-35
	BR	20-50	19	TR	25-60	33	TL	25-45	48	TL	15-30
6	TL	15-35		MR	25-60		TR	25-45		BL	15-30
	TR	10-30		BL	30-75		BL	25-45		BR	20-30
	ML	10-30	20	TL	20-40		M	25-45	49	TR	15-35
	MR	10-30		ML	15-40		BR	40-75		TL	15-35
7	TR	10-25		BL	20-45	34	TL	25-45		BL	10-20
	TL	8-20		BR	20-45		BL	25-60		BR	15-25
	BL	8-20	21	TL	20-45		BR	35-100	50	TL	20-45
	MR	15-35		TR	20-45	35	TR	15-40		BL	20-45
	BM	8-20		BL	35-75		BR	20-50		BR	8-15
8	TL	5-15	22	TL	20-60	36	TL	20-60	51	TR	20-50
	TR	10-30		BL	20-50		BR	15-40		BL	25-55
9	TL	8-20		M	15-30	37	TR	8-20		MR	25-50
	TR	5-15		BR	10-20		TL	20-50		BM	20-50
	BL	10-30	23	TR	15-40		M	5-15	52	TL	10-30
	BR	5-15		MR	30-75		BR	5-15		BL	30-60
10	TL	15-45		BL	20-50	38	TL	10-30		BM	30-60
	BL	15-45		BR	20-50		BL	10-30		BR	10-20
	BR	15-30	24	TL	35-80		BR	20-50	53	TR	5-15
11	TR	25-75		BL	20-60	39	TL	10-25		BL	10-25
	TL	25-50		BR	20-60		TR	10-25		MB	8-15
	M	25-50	25	TR	10-25		BL	20-50		BR	8-15
	BL	25-50		TL	40-90		BR	20-40	54	TL	5-10
	MR	20-35		M	15-40	40	TL	15-40		BL	5-10
	BR	25-50		MR	15-40		BL	25-50		BR	8-15
12	TL	15-30		BL	10-30		M	25-55	55	TR	8-15
	TR	15-35	26	TL	10-25		BR	30-60		TL	5-10
	BL	25-50		ML	15-40	41	TR	15-40		BR	5-10
13	TR	15-45		BR	15-40		TL	30-60	56	TL	5-10
	BL	10-20	27	TR	20-45		BR	30-60		TR	30-65
	BR	15-45		M	25-50	42	TL	20-45		BL	30-75
14	TL	35-75		BR	20-45		TR	10-20		BR	35-75+
	TR	50-100	28	TL	20-45		BL	15-35	57	TR	5-10
	ML	15-30		TM	20-45	43	TR	5-15		TL	30-55
	BL	20-40		TR	15-40		BL	5-10		M	10-20
15	TR	25-60		BL	20-50		BR	15-35		BL	35-65
	MR	15-40	29	TR	15-30	44	TL	20-50		BR	25-60
	BL	15-40		BL	25 65		ML	20-50	58	ML	35-75+
	BR	15-40		BR	10-25		TR	20-45		M	15-35
16	TL	40-100	30	TL	20-60		BL	15-30		TR	20-35
	ML	20-45		ML	20-60	45	TR	25-50		BR	20-35
	BL	25-60		TR	20-50		TL	30-60	59	TR	20-40
	BR	25-60		BL	20-50		BR	30-75		BL	10-25
17	TR	15-45	31	TR	35-60	46	TL	35-75		M	40-75+
	MR	10-25		MR	35-60		BL	15-35		BR	8-15
	BR	20-60		BL	40-75		M	20-50	60	TL	10-20
18	TL	20-55		BR	35-60		BR	20-45		TM	50-100+
	ML	20-50	32	TL	50-100	47	TR	35-75		TR	25-35
	M	20-50		TR	30-50		TL	50-100		BL	20-30
	TR	20-50		BL	50-100		BL	30-75		BM	25-40

#	Pos	Val	#	Pos	Val	#	Pos	Val	#	Pos	Val
61	TR	30-60		M	3-5		BL	15-25		BR	10-15
	TL	3-8		BR	20-35	94	TL	20-25		BM	10-15
	M	10-25	79	TL	3-5		ML	20-30	109	TR	15-20
	BL	35-75+		TM	20-30		M	25-35		TL	20-30
	BR	5-10		TR	3-5		BL	25-35		TM	20-30
62	TL	15-30		BL	20-30		BR	5-10		BR	15-20
	BL	8-15		BR	10-15	95	TR	5-10		BM	20-30
	MR	8-15		BM	3-5		TL	5-10	110	TL	20-25
63	TL	50-100+	80	TL	20-30		BR	10-15		TR	15-20
	TR	15-25		TR	3-5		BL	8-15		BL	20-25
	BR	50-100+		M	5-10	96	TL	35-55		BR	20-30
64	TL	20-40		MR	10-25		BL	35-55		BM	25-35
	BL	25-50		BL	15-30		TR	35-55	111	TR	15-20
	BR	35-75+		BR	5-10		BR	25-40		TL	10-15
65	TR	15-25	81	TL	3-5		BM	25-40		BL	10-15
	TL	10-20		TM	3-5	97	TR	35-50		BR	10-15
	MR	15-20		TR	8-15		BL	30-45	112	TL	25-35
	BL	5-10		ML	5-10		MR	30-45		TR	10-15
	BM	10-20		BM	5-10		M	10-15		BL	10-15
	BR	25-50		MR	5-10		BR	10-15		BR	25-35
66	TL	15-20		B	8-15	98	TL	15-20		BM	5-10
	TM	30-75	82	TL	5-10		BL	5-8	113	TR	20-30
	TR	5-10		TR	3-5		BM	20-25		TL	20-30
	BL	15-20		BL	5-10		BR	10-15		BR	15-20
	BM	20-35		BR	3-5	99	TR	15-20		BL	15-20
	BR	25-40	83	TR	3-5		TL	10-15	114	TL	15-20
67	TR	35-85		BL	3-5		TM	15-20		TM	15-20
	BL	15-20		BR	3-5		BL	10-15		TR	10-15
	BM	10-20	84	TL	20-35		BM	10-15		BL	10-15
	MR	25-40		TR	20-40		BR	10-15		BR	5-10
	BR	10-20		BL	15-25	100	TL	5-10	115	TL	5-10
68	TL	20-30	85	TR	5-10		BL	5-10		TR	3-5
	TR	35-85		BL	25-50		M	35-65		BL	5-10
	ML	5-10		BR	20-35		BR	30-50		BR	3-5
	MB	5-10	86	TL	20-35	101	TR	35-60	116	TL	35-50
	BR	8-15		TR	15-20		TL	25-40		BL	10-15
69	TR	10-20		BL	15-20		TM	20-30		M	5-8
	TL	10-15		BM	15-20		BR	8-15		BR	10-15
	M	10-15		BR	20-35		BL	20-30	117	TR	8-10
	BL	8-15	87	TR	15-20		BM	25-40		TM	35-50
	BR	10-15		BL	10-15	102	TL	5-10		TR	35-50
70	TR	35-85		BM	20-30		ML	20-30		BL	35-50
	L	25-35		BR	15-25		M	30-40		MR	50-100
	BR	20-45	88	TL	10-15		BL	20-30		BR	30-45
71	TR	35-85+		BL	10-15		BR	25-35	118	TL	10-20
	TL	10-20		M	15-20	103	TR	10-15		BL	10-20
	MR	35-50		BM	10-15		TL	20-30		M	20-30
	BM	10-20		BR	10-15		M	20-25		BR	10-15
72	TL	10-20	89	TR	10-15		BR	10-15	119	TR	10-15
	TM	35-85+		TL	20-40	104	TL	10-15		TL	10-15
	TR	35-75		BR	15-20		BL	10-15		BR	5-10
	ML	20-40		BL	10-15		M	20-30		BL	10-20
	BR	20-40	90	TL	15-25		MR	15-20	120	TL	8-15
73	TR	10-15		TR	10-15		BM	10-15		TR	20-35
	TL	10-15		BL	15-25	105	TR	10-15		M	10-15
	BR	20-35		BM	10-15		TM	10-15		BL	10-15
74	TL	5-10		BR	20-35		BL	8-12		BR	15-25
	BL	20-35	91	TR	8-15		BM	20-30	121	TL	15-25
	BR	20-35		TL	10-15		BR	15-20		TM	25-40
75	TR	10-15		TM	3-5	106	TL	15-20		TR	25-40
	TL	10-15		BM	3-5		ML	10-15		BL	25-40
	BL	5-10		BR	3-5		M	20-25		BR	20-25
	BR	10-15		BL	5-10		TR	20-25	122	TL	15-20
76	TL	40-100	92	TL	35-65		BR	3-5		BL	15-20
	BL	15-25		LM	10-20	107	TR	8-15		TR	20-25
	BM	5-10		M	8-15		TL	15-20	123	TL	15-20
	BR	5-10		BL	3-5		TM	8-15		TR	20-25
77	TR	20-35		BR	5-10		BR	10-15		BL	15-20
	BL	5-10	93	TL	8-15		BL	10-15		BR	15-20
	BR	35-75		TM	5-10	108	TL	8-15			
78	TL	25-50		TR	5-10		TR	20-25			
	BL	3-5		BR	15-20		BL	15-20			